CW01455694

"We are all in the same boat in a stormy sea, and we owe each other a terrible loyalty."

G. K. CHESTERTON

CONTENTS

PREFACE

The events surrounding the disappearance of the Hull trawler Gaul are factual and documented in the Public Inquiry reports and in various newspaper articles and the Channel 4 Documentary Series "Dispatches: The Secrets of the Gaul." The series won a Royal Television Society Award in 1997 for best current affairs programme. This can be found on YouTube.

This documentary proved once and for all that the British Government did use British trawlers to spy on Soviet ship and submarine movements during the Cold War.

Having spent the first year of my working life at the age of 17 working on Hull's Fish Dock, I have always had a fascination with the fishing industry and with the events surrounding the Gaul and other lost trawlers.

The rest of the events and characters in this story are entirely fictional and purely the product of my imagination.
I hope you enjoy the story.

Dave Rogers

FOREWORD

What do you do when you have a case written off as death by natural causes and 36 years later you suspect it may have been a case of murder? The records are virtually non-existent and any potential witnesses are long gone. There is one hope. Call in the original detective who investigated the case.

Meet Frank Fogg - retired Police Officer and shortly to become a cold case investigator who turns up a few little surprises along the way.

CHAPTER 1

Thursday 26th March 2009

T he call had come totally out of the blue. He had been in the garden tending to his vegetables, doing a bit of planting, when his wife called to him to say that there was a Detective Chief Superintendent Brooks from Humberside Police on the phone. His curiosity piqued, he had gone to find out what the Police wanted with him, ten years after his retirement from the force, with the rank of Assistant Chief Constable.

"I'm very sorry to disturb you, sir" said Brooks, the deference to a senior officer still there even though he was long retired. "I wondered if I could come round and see you and pick your brains about one of your old cases from the 1970s. We think it may have some relevance to a current murder investigation." So reluctantly former detective and ACC Frank Fogg had agreed. He didn't really want to get involved. He was quite happy, living in his little bungalow just outside Hull with his second wife Janice. He divided his time between growing vegetables in his back garden; walking the dog; his latest project restoring a disused railway line on the Yorkshire Wolds; and being churchwarden at his local Church of England.

However, when Brooks had mentioned the name Billy Bielby, he had instantly got Frank's attention. The case of the murder of Billy Bielby had haunted him all his career. No detective likes an unsolved case, especially a murder case. And Frank had been convinced at the time, and still was, that there had been some kind of cover up and he had been deliberately ordered to stop the investigation. Granted, it had been going nowhere. But no unsolved murder case is ever closed. This one, however, had been put very firmly on the back burner, and Frank did not like that. In fact at the time he had thought it stank.

Now here he was being reminded of that name, Billy Bielby, coming back to haunt him. After making an appointment with Brooks and putting the phone down Frank returned thoughtfully to his garden. He remembered Billy Bielby. Billy had been a superannuated trawlerman. He had worked on the trawlers from leaving school at 14. It was a precarious existence. Not only was it very dangerous, physically demanding, work – you never knew if you would come back from a fishing trip in one piece, or at all. It was also financially precarious. As a trawlerman you were in effect casual labour. You signed up for a trip, in the old days normally about three weeks, up to Iceland or the Barents Sea. You got paid a very basic wage for the hours you worked, and a share of whatever the catch fetched when it was brought to market. If you had a good skipper who knew where to find the fish, and you arrived back at market at the right time when the price was high, you could do quite well out of it. Of course most trawlermen blew their earnings within a few days of being home. There was no sick pay, no pension, nothing like that.

Frank knew all about this because his Dad had been a trawler skipper, a very good one by all accounts. His Dad (and to a lesser extent his Mam) had always expected him to follow in Dad's footsteps. He'd done all the right things. He'd gone to the Nautical College in Hull (Trinity House School) and done his exams. But when Frank was just 13 his Dad had been lost at sea. Nobody really knew what had happened. Dad had been on deck when a freak wave hit and that was the last anyone saw of him. When Frank left school at 16 he'd signed on for a trip on the trawlers as a "deckie learner", as the apprentices were called. But he'd decided it wasn't for him. The biting cold, the grindingly hard work, the long hours, the danger, and the seasickness, all put him off. Some of his mates had laughed at him and said he wasn't hard enough. They'd soon thought twice about that when he became a copper. Although they didn't like him for doing it (who likes a copper?) they respected the Police.

All this passed through his mind on hearing the name Billy Bielby. He supposed Billy had been one of the lucky ones in an ironic sort of way. In his 50s he had contracted emphysema, which meant he was no longer able bodied enough to work. For most trawlermen that would have been the end. But sometimes the shipowners took pity on them and offered them shore jobs. Billy had got a job as a watchman. It wasn't much. Casual labour. But it was easy money. All you had to do was sit on the bridge of a trawler that was in dock, keep an eye out for intruders, do an occasional round to make sure nobody had got on board to pilfer anything. It was well known that the watchmen often invited their mates on board for a beer or two, maybe a game of cards, or to look at Scandinavian porn.

Like lots of his mates, Billy had been known to the Police, but not for anything serious. The occasional drunken brawl, some petty pilfering, some suspicions of importing illegal booze, fags and porn, but nothing that would bring him major attention.

Frank had taken the call at 6.30am. He remembered it to this day. He was rudely woken from his slumbers by the phone ringing by his bedside (before the days of mobiles). He'd sat up with a start, grabbed the phone to stop it ringing and turned around to make sure it hadn't woken Sandra – and realised with a sudden sinking feeling that she wasn't there. She'd left him about a month before and gone back to her mother's. Looking back now he thought their marriage had been a mistake. They had both been too young. He was 22, and an ambitious young PC wanting to get into CID. That meant working long hours and showing willing with any job they threw at you. She was only 19 and her ambition was to be a housewife and a mother, like her mother before her. She could not understand his driving ambition, and she found it really hard tolerating the long hours he had to work. So in the end she had left. And no amount of pleading and cajoling on his part had brought her back.

All this had flashed through his mind as he picked up the phone on that cold, frosty, foggy November morning. He wasn't supposed to be on duty until 8.00 so he knew something serious must be up. The uniformed Inspector, Colin Faraday, who was on night shift, informed him that they'd had a call from the British Transport Police, who policed the docks. Somebody had reported seeing a body floating in the Fish Dock. They had hauled the body out and it was confirmed dead, but they suspected foul play, so were calling in the local Police. His colleague, Jim Hendricks, who was the night duty DI that week, was busy attending another serious incident involving a stabbing. It was touch and go whether the victim would survive so that might well turn into a murder case. Hence they were ringing Frank to see if he could attend the Fish Dock, and do the preliminaries on the investigation into a suspicious death.

Dragging himself from his bed, he felt the effects of that last single malt from last night. Lagavulin, his favourite. He loved malt whiskey from the Scottish islands, and nowhere, in his opinion, did they make a finer single malt than Islay. But since Sandra left he had been imbibing too much of the stuff, drowning his sorrows, and he reminded himself that he had a job to do and he needed to be compos mentis to do it.

There was no chance of a cup of coffee, he didn't have time. But popping an Alka-Seltzer in a glass of freezing cold water from the tap, he stood and watched it fizz and froth as he wondered what he would be walking into. He had only been a DI for a few months. Although he had assisted with murder enquiries, he had never been the lead officer. He wondered if his suspicious death was going to very quickly turn into a murder investigation. If so, would the Chief let him run with it, or would the Chief take it on himself or put someone else in charge. Naturally Frank was keen to head up a murder investigation himself, if that is what it turned out to be.

CHAPTER 2

Thursday 8th November 1973

Frank Fogg stumbled out of his house and into his somewhat ancient, and very messy, Ford Cortina. He mumbled a short prayer of thanks when she started first time in this cold and very damp weather. Then he cursed as he realised he had forgotten to get any more de-icer and would have to clear the windscreen by hand and rely on the dodgy interior heater to keep the inside clear. As for getting his 12-track cassette player to work in this weather, not a prayer.

So he drove in silence along the icy roads from his West Hull suburb down to the fish dock, praying that none of his colleagues in Traffic would choose this morning to decide to stop him and breathalyse him. That was the last thing he needed.

Driving down West Dock Street he turned right into the subway and pulled up to the main dock entrance where a uniformed British Transport Police Constable was on duty as usual. Flashing his identification he was quickly let through. He drove past familiar landmarks, the Lord Line building to his right, and the Sea Fish Industry Authority building on his left, sitting at the back of the bull nose, the end of the lock pit where people would greet incoming trawlers. As he passed over the lock pit onto the southern side of the dock he could quickly see where all the action was. Several Police vehicles were drawn up on the side of the dock and a gaggle of Police officers and civilians were gathered around a tent-like structure.

Frank remembered that, when they first came into port the fishing vessels would tie up on the north side, the "wet side" where the fish market was, to unload their catch. There was great competition amongst the skippers about who would get in first, winds and tides permitting of course. Fish from the earliest vessel to get in was auctioned off first and often fetched the best prices. The fish market began very early in the morning, sometimes as early as 5.00am selling fish brought overland from other ports. The Hull fish was always auctioned at 7.30am.

So across the dock unloading was just winding up. The "bobbers" would have been in at 2.00am to start unloading the fish from the holds, loading up baskets of fish which were winched out, swung across and tipped into "kits" for the market. After the trawler had been emptied and the hold cleaned out, she would be towed by tug over to the "dry side" on the south of the dock, for any urgent repairs and reprovisioning ready for the next trip. All this had to be done in 36 hours – the ultimate "just in time" industry, before the management consultants even thought of the term.

Pulling up as close as he could to the scene of the action, Frank took out his ID card and approached the small knot of people. He was stopped by a uniformed BT Police Constable, who, on seeing who he was, said "Come on through, Sir, Sergeant Barraclough over there is in charge." Frank was delighted to see his old mucker, Tom Barraclough, was in charge. He had worked with Tom on a number of cases over the years, both during his time in uniform and in CID.

Going over to shake his hand he said: "What have we got, Tom?" "Hiya Frank" was the reply. "Well, a body was spotted in the dock about 4.30 this morning by this young rigger here, Andy, who was working on the rigging of the Dane" he said, pointing to the trawler nearest to them. Frank knew that sometimes the riggers, and fitters, and other trades worked overnight on the trawlers to get urgent repairs done so they would be ready to meet their 36 hours turn around time.

"We fished the body out of the dock, with some difficulty I might add, and laid him out here and called the Police Surgeon. Doc arrived about 6.00 and pronounced him dead, but was suspicious because there are what appear to be some suspicious marks around the neck, but they're not very clear. So I called it in to my guv'nor and he said to call you lot. Oh, here's the Doc now."

Dr. Charlie Robinson was a gregarious, sociable character, always up for a laugh and joke, fond of his pipe, his vintage sports cars, and a nice drop of whiskey. Frank had thought it must be his British Racing Green MGA that he had parked in front of when he arrived. "Now then, Doc," Frank said, "what have you got for me today?" Robinson, unusually for him, frowned and said: "I'm not sure Frank. Body's been in the water a couple of days at least, you can see from the skin colour, and the way the marine life has been nibbling. I'll know better when I get him on the slab. Initial assessment is that his neck's been broken. That could have been caused by a fall into the water but there are some suspicious bruise marks around his neck that I'm not happy about. I think they must have been caused peri-mortem. It's unlikely that he died from drowning, but again I'll know for certain when I open up his lungs. Is that enough for you for now? It had bloody well better be 'cos there's not a lot else I can tell you right now and I'm freezing my cobs off here."

"OK Doc," said Frank "thanks for that, and you will let me know when the PM is going to be won't you?"

"You'll know as soon as I do my old chuck," said Robinson "but until I get back I don't know how many other stiffs I've got stacked up waiting for me."

Then to both Robinson and Barraclough he said: "I don't suppose we've got any ID on him yet have we?" Both shook their heads. "He's not got anything on him," said the Doc "I've been through his pockets. Although looking at his hands, and especially that missing finger on his right hand that's been gone for a few years, I'd hazard a shrewd guess that he's a working man, possibly even a trawlerman."

"Right you are. Thanks Doc. See you soon." Then turning to Barraclough Frank said: "You're going to have to work this one with me, Tom, for the time being at least, until I can get some more of our team down here."

"No problem, Sir," said Barraclough. "I spoke to my Super in York when I called it in and he gave me permission to offer you whatever co-operation you needed with this one. So we shouldn't get into any turf wars here."

"That's great, Tom. Thanks. And less of the Sir. It's Frank to you. We've known each other long enough. And anyway, even though we may be working this together, I'm technically not your senior officer am I?"

"OK then, Frank it is, Frank."

"Right, now, first things first, where's that young rigger of yours, Andy did you say his name was?" Frank had it drummed into him as a Detective Constable and then a Sergeant, to always be suspicious of the finder of a body until you could clear them of any suspicion. His boss, Detective Chief Inspector Dunhill, repeated this message ad nauseam, so Frank wanted to make sure he covered this base first.

"I take it you've done an initial interview with him, Tom?" said Frank.

"I have," Tom said. "Claims he was on a rush job to get the wireless equipment on the Dane all shipshape and seaworthy. She's due to sail on the next tide and that's why he was working overnight. He happened to look over the side and see something in the dock. At first he thought it was a seal or something that must have got through the lock gates so he came down from the rigging to have a look. Claims he's a bit of a wildlife freak.

Anyhow when he got down on deck and looked over he could see it had clothes on so he thought it must be a person. Went over to the Ship's Husband's office to get them to ring us lot."

"OK. Well it won't do any harm to see if his story checks out when he tells it to us again, will it?" said Frank. "By the way, have you called in forensics?"

"No I haven't" said Tom. "I didn't see the point as we haven't got a crime scene yet. We don't know where he was killed. Could have been anywhere around the dock and that's a lot of space to search. Or he could even have been killed somewhere else and dumped in the dock."

"Good call, Tom," said Frank. "There's no point in wasting their time searching for a needle in a haystack. If we can get an ID on him we might get a better idea of where he might have been killed, if indeed he was killed and it wasn't just an accident. For the time being, until the Doc gives us a more definite answer, we're going to have to treat it as suspicious. Although I'm not sure why somebody would choose to dump a body in the dock. It was bound to be found sooner rather than later. The river would be a much better bet if you wanted a body to disappear, or at least reappear well away from the crime scene. The currents in there would carry a body for miles either way, depending on the state of the tide, and you'd have no means of knowing where it went in."

With that, they went off to interview young Andy the rigger again. This did not produce anything new. Frank pressed him on the point of why he had been working there at that time of night. But he stuck to his story that he had been doing a last minute job on the wireless equipment because the Dane needed to catch the next tide. He got quite agitated about not having the work completed and how he would be in trouble with the Ship's Husband if they missed the tide. In the end they let him get back to work. There seemed no point in keeping him any longer. They could easily check out his story later and they had taken his name and address so that someone could take a formal statement from him later.

As they were finishing with Andy a uniformed Constable came up and said: "Sorry to disturb you Sir, but the Coroner's Officer is here. He wants to know if you are ready to release the body to the morgue yet." "OK. I'll come and have a word with him" said Frank.

"I don't think there's anything more to be learned here, Tom, do you? If there's any evidence on the body, Doc will find it at the morgue. I'm going to call in the divers to have a search around the bottom of the dock where his body was pulled out just to check we're not missing anything. But to be honest I don't hold out much hope of them finding anything. It's too murky down there, and the water gets churned up every time the lock opens. We don't know how long he's been in there, or where he went in. So we don't know where to look. Doc said he could have been in there a couple of days at least, so the lock gates will have been open quite a few times with the amount of traffic in and out at each tide. Let's go and tell them they can remove him. But we need an ID on this man and we need it quickly so we can begin to track his movements prior to his death. Can you get some of your lads to start doing enquiries along the dry side, see if anybody knows who he might be? See if they know of anybody that might have gone missing the last few days."

"I'll get onto it right away, Sir, er Frank I mean" said Tom.

"I'll be back at the office if you get any leads. Ring me."

CHAPTER 3

Friday 27th March 2009

It was the next day after Frank had received the phone call from Detective Chief Superintendent Brooks. Frank had arranged for Brooks to call at his house the following afternoon, intrigued by the little information Brooks had given him over the phone. All Brooks would say is that they were involved in a current murder investigation that might have some links to his original investigation of the murder of Billy Bielby. He was very reluctant to disclose any further details over the phone so Frank had been left on tenterhooks until the next day. Brooks arrived at the door promptly at 2.00pm as arranged. Showing his warrant card to Frank, he asked if he could come in. Frank showed him into the sitting room of their bungalow and Janice put her head around the door to ask if they would like some tea. Both said yes, and she went away and busied herself with a tea tray, including biscuits.

"So what's this all about? I thought maybe the call was an April Fool joke." asked Frank, beside himself with curiosity.

"No, no, Sir, far from it" began Brooks. But before he could go any further Frank interrupted him. "For a start, you don't need to call me Sir. I'm no longer a serving Police officer. I'm retired. So Frank will do very nicely. And what's your first name?"

"Jim" said Brooks. "I'm the Senior Investigating Officer on a current potential murder enquiry. We have a victim who has died in suspicious circumstances. We are not yet clear about the cause of death. However this victim's name is Tommy Bielby. It would appear that he is related to a Billy Bielby who was killed in suspicious circumstances in 1973, and whose death you investigated. That murder was never solved. No one has ever been brought to justice for it. Now I have read the files on that original murder investigation but there appear to be significant gaps and I wondered if you might be able to shed some light on some of those gaps."

At that moment Janice knocked on the door and appeared with a tray containing a tea pot, cups and saucers, milk jug, sugar bowl, and a plate of biscuits. "Thanks love" said Frank. As she left the room he said to Brooks: "She likes to do things properly. Me, I'd be happy with a mug of builder's tea. But there you go. Anyhow Jim, I hope you're not suggesting that there were gaps in my investigation of Billy's murder?"

"No, no. That wasn't what I meant at all. I'm sorry if it came across that way. It's just that it's a bit puzzling because some of the evidence that I would have expected to see in the original investigation file is missing. I've been told that this could be down to the fact that the files have been moved from their original storage at Queen's Gardens Police Station to the Force HQ at Priory Road. But I don't entirely buy it myself. It looks to me like some evidence has been deliberately removed from what is left in store."

"Jim, I like your style" said Frank. "You've got a suspicious mind. Like every good detective should have. So where do you want to start?"

"My victim's name is Tommy Bielby. He was aged 58. He was killed in a Road Traffic Accident on Hessle Road on 3rd April this year. Nothing particularly suspicious about that you might think. He was crossing the road on a Pelican crossing. Witnesses say the lights were just changing from red to amber as he started to cross. But the car that hit him, according to the witnesses, accelerated towards him instead of slowing down. The number plates on the vehicle were so smeared with mud that they were unreadable, either by the witnesses or any CCTV in the area. The vehicle drove off without stopping. Have I got your interest now, Frank?"

"You certainly have" said Frank. "And now you've unearthed that Tommy Bielby was the son of Billy Bielby who also died in suspicious circumstances back in 1973, and whose death I investigated. Oh yes, you've got my interest now alright. I never did get to the bottom of Billy's death, and I thought I never would. There seemed to be so many obstacles placed in my way, I was never going to get to the truth of what happened to Billy. And that rankles. I don't like people not getting the justice they deserve."

"Right. Well we might be able to help each other here then. You might be able to fill me in on some of the gaps in the investigation into Billy's death, or should I say murder."

"Well, I always believed it was murder" said Frank. "So tell me more about Tommy. I knew there were sons, but they never really featured in my investigation other than to rule them out as having any part in his death."

"OK. Well Tommy was the eldest son. He was 15 when his Dad died. That's an impressionable age, and he didn't take it well. His Mam and Dad had been separated for a couple of years. The usual story, when Billy was fishing he was away for most of the time, and then he'd come home with money to burn in his pocket, go out and get roaring drunk, and then come home and twat his missus. Of course in those days nobody reported domestic violence to the Police. It was just accepted as what happened, especially in the fishing community. If it got too bad they dealt with it themselves in their own way. But they never reported it to the Police."

"Hah! You don't need to tell me. I was there. I lived it all. I was a beat constable on Hessle Road in the 1960's. I dealt with all the pub brawls between trawlermen, the domestics occasionally reported by neighbours 'cos they thought it was getting out of hand and she might be taking too much of a beating. Mind you, a lot of the wives gave as good as they got. All that sort of thing. The petty pilfering of fish from the dock. The theft of coal from the railways. The illegally imported booze and fags before we were part of the EU. The trade in Scandinavian porn. We dealt with it all."

"Right. Well apparently Gill Bielby eventually got fed up of Billy's violence and chucked him out. We found all this because Tommy was writing his memoirs and kept them all on his laptop at home. Apparently he'd joined some local history group at the College and they'd encouraged him to write down what he remembered about his Dad and the fishing industry. So Gill chucked Billy out, and he had nowhere to go. He ended up dossing at a mate's house. At the same time he was diagnosed with emphysema, probably from his days as a stoker on the old steam trawlers. That meant he couldn't work at sea any more. He wouldn't have been safe. Because he'd been really well behaved with the trawler owners they offered him occasional work as a watchman on board trawlers in dock."

"This much I know," said Frank "from the investigation. And as you probably know there were no pensions for fishermen, no ill-health retirement, nothing like that. If you were out of work you signed on the dole, or in Billy's case sickness benefit. He got paid cash in hand for his watchman job and never declared it to Social. We checked. But I don't think that's what got him killed. So go on. What else did you learn from Tommy's memoirs?"

"Well now, here's a strange thing," said Brooks. "We thought at first that he couldn't have got very far with writing them. But when we turned the laptop over to our techie guys they told us that there had been a lot more. They said there had been some recent changes to the file on his computer, just before he died. Apparently it had been much bigger but somebody had deleted a big chunk of it. Now it's possible Tommy could have done that himself. But the interesting thing is, if he'd simply deleted it, they would have been able to recover it from the hard drive. But this was a very professional job. Apparently all the code was scrambled so there was no way they could restore it. Now either Tommy did that himself, although as far as we have been able to find out he wasn't that tech savvy. Or somebody else did it, somebody who knew what they were doing and didn't want anybody else to know what had been on that file. Now I'm asking myself, why would you do that? They could have just stolen the whole laptop and trashed it or dumped it. They could have deleted the whole file. So why go to all that trouble to make it look like Tommy had not got even half way through his story? That's a lot of trouble to go to to cover your tracks. So what was on there that was so important?"

"You're right Jim," said Frank. "I'm beginning to smell a very large rat here. I've never liked coincidences. They always made me suspicious as a detective. And there are just too many coincidences about your Tommy's death. There's the coincidence of him and his Dad both having been probably murdered in circumstances that make it look like an accident. There's evidence missing from the file on Billy's death. And now you tell me there's evidence missing from Tommy's laptop and somebody's tried very hard to hide that fact. My antennae are twitching with curiosity here."

"Good" said Brooks, "because I've got a proposition for you. I've spoken to my ACC and she has OK'ed this. I want to officially reopen enquiries into the death of Billy Bielby. However we're very shorthanded in CID with a lot of work on, and it is a very cold case. So the only way the ACC would agree to do it is if I brought someone in from outside to help. She was delighted when I suggested your name and you are the obvious choice because you know more about the original investigation than anyone else. I will officially be the Senior Investigating Officer on the deaths of both Billy and Tommy. I've got one of my best DCIs working on Tommy's death, and I want you to come and join us to focus on Billy's case. What do you think?"

"Well Jim, I'm a bit rusty. It's a lot of years since I did any frontline detective work. The old brainbox isn't as quick as it once was. But if you think I can help, I would love the challenge."

CHAPTER 4

Thursday 8th November 1973

Tom Barraclough struck lucky with his fourth interview of the morning. He and a young PC were doing the rounds of premises on the dry side. It was still early, only 8.00am, although much of the Fish Dock had been busy for hours. They'd called in Stanton's Café for a bacon butty, and to ask around, see if the staff or customers had seen anything odd. There was nothing doing there. They drew a blank. It was too early for the main offices to be open – the bosses and office staff didn't get in til 9.00. So they pitched up at the Ship's Husband's Office for British Allied Trawlers.

The Ship's Husband's job was to take care of everything that needed to be done on the trawlers while they were in dock on their 36 hour turn around. This included reprovisioning with everything from fuel to food and drink for the crew, ice for packing fish, spares for the ship – everything you can think of that might be needed at sea. They also had to make sure that any necessary repairs and maintenance were done in time for the next sailing. And they had to make sure that a crew turned up in time to make the tide – which sometimes involved sending someone to drag them out of their beds or the nearest pub.

Harry Beadle, the BAT Ship's Husband was the ideal man for the job. He'd been a mate on the trawlers until an unfortunate accident at sea, all too common sadly, had left him with a disabled and useless arm. But he knew his job, knew everything that a ship would need while in the hostile waters of the Arctic. Harry was a big bluff fellow, six foot two in his stockinged feet, and built like the proverbial brick toilet. Few people messed with Harry. He dressed in the classic trawlerman's off duty uniform, a sharp double-breasted chalk-striped suit, with wide bottom trousers with turn-ups. After introducing themselves, although Tom knew Harry from of old, they asked him if he had noticed anything unusual in the last few days. Harry scratched his head, and after a moment's thought said, "only that little shit Billy Bielby".

"What about him?" asked Tom.

"He was doing night watchman duty on the Newby Wyke, let's see, when was it? What's today? Thursday. So it must have been Monday night. Vessel was all provisioned and ready for the early tide on Tuesday. All he had to do was sit on the bridge all night and keep watch. Clocked on all right didn't he, but come morning there was no sign of him where he should be. Probably got pissed and had a date with some floozie. Wait til I get hold of him. He won't be doing night watchman for me ever again."

"I suspect you're right there" said Tom. "If that's who we pulled out of the dock this morning, he certainly won't be doing any more night duties, 'cos he's stone cold dead."

"Oh shit," said Harry, "what happened to him then?"

"Don't know as yet" said Tom. "Too early to say. We're still trying to identify the body. I don't suppose you happen to know if he was missing a finger on his right hand, do you?"

"As a matter of fact, yeh, he was. Lost it in an accident with a net years back."

"Do you know who his next of kin is, Harry?"

"His missus, Gill, I think she's called. They haven't been together for a couple of years but they're still married as far as I know. I've got an address for her here somewhere, if you give me a minute."

Harry began rifling through a rolodex on his desk looking for the information.

"And where would the Newby Wyke be now?" asked Tom.

"All being well, 48 hours steaming, she'll be about 60 miles north of the Faroe Islands heading for Iceland."

It was Tom's turn to say: "Oh shit." "There goes our possible crime scene. The boss will not be pleased. I need to borrow your phone Harry."

Frank had made it, frozen, damp and hungry, as far as his desk at Queen's Gardens Police Station. He was just catching up on what had been left on his desk from the outgoing night shift when his phone rang. Picking it up he snapped: "DI Fogg."

"Boss, it's Tom. I'm ringing from the BAT Office. We've got a possible ID on the body – one Billy Bielby. I've got a name and address for the next of kin. That's the good news. The bad news is that he was last seen working a shift as night watchman on the Newby Wyke, and she is now well on her way to Iceland to start fishing."

"Right Tom, can you follow up on the next of kin, see if you can get someone to the morgue to get a positive ID on the body. I will get on to the trawler company and see if we can get that boat turned round. If there was a crime committed there probably won't be much evidence after two days at sea, but if there is, there'll be even less by the time she comes back after fishing. Are you in Harry Beadle's office, by any chance? If so can you put him on?"

"Hi Harry. It's Frank Fogg here. How're you doing? I hope the missus is well, and those sprogs of yours are keeping out of mischief?"

"Good. Listen Harry, I need to get the Newby Wyke turned around and back to port as soon as. Who do I need to speak to?"

"Wow," said Harry, "that's way above my pay grade. You probably need to speak to the Managing Director, Mr. Fellows, Mr. Graham Fellows that is. But he's not going to like it cos it means losing money, and you're going to have one very unhappy skipper and crew."

"Harry, I don't give a monkey's fart about the company losing money, or the skipper and crew for that matter. That's my crime scene up there and I want it back. Can you put me through to this Fellows fella?"

"I doubt it" said Harry. "I haven't seen his Bentley arrive yet."

"Well, when it does, tell him he needs to ring me at Queen's Gardens nick, straight away. Alright?"

"Aye. OK Frank. Whatever you say but I ain't looking forward to the earful I'll get telling him what to do."

"Just tell him this is a potential murder investigation and I need his full co-operation" said Frank and put the phone down.

A few minutes after 9 o'clock Frank's phone rang again. Picking it up he grunted: "Frank Fogg."

A cultured voice came on the phone. "I believe I'm speaking to Detective Inspector Fogg? Is that correct?"

"It is" said Frank. "And who are you?"

"My name is Graham Fellows. I'm the Managing Director of British Allied Trawlers. I believe you wanted to speak to me."

"I did and I do," said Frank. "One of your trawlers on its way to Iceland is a potential crime scene and I want it back here as soon as possible."

"And on what grounds do you believe it is a potential crime scene? Or am I just supposed to take it on your say so, Detective Inspector?" said Fellows.

"Look, sir," said Frank, getting somewhat exasperated, "I am not at liberty to discuss that with you. Suffice it to say that I am dealing with a possible murder enquiry here, and it is vital that we secure any evidence as soon as possible if we are going to track down the perpetrator."

"Well I am afraid that is not good enough, Detective Inspector. Do you know how much it costs to send a trawler out on a fishing trip?"

No, but I'm sure you're going to tell me, thought Frank to himself, but didn't say it.

"There's the cost of the boat itself," went on Fellows, "the fuel, provisions for the crew, their wages and so on. If I order the boat to turn around all of that is lost. Wasted expenditure. I can't do it. I'm not prepared to do it. Not on your say so. I shall speak to the Chief Constable about this."

"Don't tell me, sir," said Frank, "you know him from the Rotary Club? Or are you golfing buddies?" He nearly said 'are you in the Masons together?' but thought better of it, knowing he would not get an answer.

"Look here, Detective Inspector," said Fellows "I don't think I like your attitude. I shall be mentioning that to the Chief Constable too."

"Please yourself, sir," said Frank, putting a bit too much emphasis on the sir. "I have a job to do and that is to bring criminals to justice. And I don't like people who get in my way" and he put the phone down.

"Jumped up effing public school boys who think they were born to rule the world and look down on us mere mortals" he muttered to himself, just as his Detective Sergeant, Tony Muldowney walked in.

"Morning boss," he said. "Somebody's not a happy bunny this morning."

"No I am not Tony. I don't like being dragged out of my bed at half past six with no breakfast or coffee. And I especially don't like people who try to get in the way of my murder investigation. Sit down and I'll bring you up to speed. But first you can get someone to make us a coffee. Mine's black, no sugar."

CHAPTER 5

Monday 30th March 2009

Frank walked into Queen's Gardens Police Station on that March morning, and remembered his first day in CID spent in this very same nick. Of course back then it had been the City of Hull Police. That had all changed with the Local Government Act in 1972 that created, amidst a lot of local opposition, the new County of Humberside, with a Police Force to match. These days, although Humberside had not survived as a county, the Police Force had, and there was even talk of merging with neighbouring forces into something much bigger. But Queen's Gardens nick was still the headquarters of the Hull Division of the Humberside Force. It was showing its age a bit now, the old building, he thought. Built in the 1960's, in spite of several refurbishments, it now looked cramped and old and tired.

As he was shown into the CID room by a plod from the front desk, the main thing that had changed from his day was that every desk had a computer and the whole thing looked much more high-tech. Although he had been forced to change with the times, and use the technology when he was still a serving officer, he'd never been entirely comfortable with the damn things. He freely admitted to being a techno-phobe.

As he was shown into Jim Brooks' office, where Brooks was sitting at the desk, he noticed a tall well-dressed young woman in her mid-30s standing to one side. Brooks stood up and said: "Frank, let me introduce you to DCI Mary Fowler. She is leading the investigation into the death of Tommy Bielby, which we are now officially treating as murder."

Mary walked up and shook his hand in a firm and confident handshake. "Pleased to meet you, sir" she said in what sounded like a London accent.

"Pleased to meet you too, Mary" said Frank "but can we dispense with the sir. Plain Frank will do nicely thanks."

"Right, to business" said Brooks. "Mary here is going to brief you on where we've got to so far in the Tommy Bielby investigation. We've dug all the information we can out of the old files about Billy. But as I said to you when we met, some of it has gone missing. That's where we need you to fill in some of the blanks from your memory. We're a bit in the dark about some of it and are hoping you can enlighten us. When I spoke to you, you seemed to think there was something a bit off about the Billy Bielby case. I'm thinking the same thing about this investigation into Tommy's death. So I just want to emphasise that confidentiality is of paramount importance here. For the time being the three of us in this room are the only people who need to know all the details of the investigations. I want regular briefings from both of you, as the SIO on both cases. The ACC is obviously aware of your involvement, Frank, and has OK'ed that. But she is not in on the details of the investigations and doesn't want or need to be at this stage. It's especially important that the press don't get wind that there might be any linkage between the two deaths, or they'll have a field day with conspiracy theories and goodness knows what. Are we clear?"

"Yes, sir" said Mary. "Of course" from Frank.

"Right then. I'll leave you two to get on with it" Brooks said with a dismissive wave of his hand.

"So Mary," said Frank, when they got to her office, "why don't you tell me where you're up to with your investigation into Tommy's death. Then I will have a read through the files on Billy, see what's there, and see what other bits I can remember to fill in the gaps. How's that?"

"Sounds good to me Frank. Well, where we're up to with Tommy is not very far. As you know it was reported as a Road Traffic Accident. It appeared that Tommy tried to cross the road just as the lights were changing and was struck by a vehicle. This was on the crossing just outside Boyes on Hessle Road. The vehicle drove off without stopping. An ambulance was called but he was pronounced dead at the scene. So as with any fatality Traffic were called in and did their investigation of the scene. They couldn't find any skid marks, or any sign of the vehicle trying to stop, either before or after the impact."

"Any luck in tracing the vehicle?"

Mary shook her head. "Witnesses said it was a 4x4 of some kind. A big thing with those bull bars on the front. But it was so bladdered up with mud they couldn't see a make and model or a registration plate. I've had the Traffic boys look at some of the CCTV footage and they've identified it as a Land Rover Discovery. We picked it up on CCTV on Hessle Road heading east but then it appears to have turned right at Daltry St. under the flyover and probably headed off up the A63 westwards. Because it's a trunk road, not a motorway, Highways Agency don't have any CCTV on there. So we've got no means of finding it after that. Eyewitness statements said it appeared to speed up as it approached the crossing, as if it was deliberately trying to run him down."

"I suppose there's no means of identifying the driver from the CCTV or witness statements?" asked Frank.

"Not a prayer" said Mary. "The windows were way too filthy to have any chance of seeing who was driving."

"Any help from the body?"

"It was pretty messed up as you can imagine. Traffic estimate the vehicle was doing 50 to 60mph when it hit him. He didn't stand a chance. Usual injuries you'd expect from that sort of high speed impact. His legs were broken. He was thrown up in the air over the vehicle. Broke his neck on landing. Substantial internal injuries. SOCOs found a tiny fleck of British Racing Green paint on the body, presumably from the vehicle. But they reckon it's probably too small to match with any damage on the vehicle if we do find it. Of course there will have been damage to the vehicle. The bonnet took quite an impact from his body bouncing off it. But so far we have had not a sniff of this vehicle. If we could find it we might get some forensics off it that would help to identify the perpetrator if we ever do catch him."

"You're assuming it's a him then?" said Frank.

"I'm not assuming anything at this stage Frank. That was just a slip of the tongue. I should have said him or her. Although the MO feels more like a man's way of killing than a woman's, don't you think? But no. I'm keeping all possibilities open at this stage until I can rule them out."

"Good. That's good detective work" said Frank. "Have we any idea of any possible motive yet? I take it you've been through the usual – money, sex, drugs and so on. "

"So far we have not been able to dig up anything on Tommy. He's clean as a whistle. Nothing on the PNC. No cautions. Not even a speeding ticket. He was 58. Never married. No kids. Worked for the Council and took early retirement at 55 during one of their rounds of workforce cuts. We've talked to his ex-work colleagues, and the neighbours. Nobody's got a bad word to say about him. Thoroughly nice bloke, straight as a die by all accounts. And I know what you're going to say. That doesn't mean there wasn't anything dodgy about him. It just means we haven't found it yet. But until we do, I've got no leads to go on."

"So, the only odd thing we 've got so far," said Frank, "is this unexplained gap in the files on his computer. Have you talked to anybody at the College about his interest in local history? Somebody might have some idea of what he was working on."

"I talked to the Local History tutor at the College. He knew Tommy reasonably well. Said he was an interesting and very articulate guy, who had lots of memories of the fishing industry and Hessle Road, and stories his Dad had told him about life at sea. He'd encouraged Tommy to start writing some of them down because he thought they might be of interest to other people. He'd also put him in touch with Adrian Hill, the local historian, who has written several books about Hessle Road and the fishing industry. I've spoken to Adrian myself, and he said he had met with Tommy. Adrian confirmed that he was an interesting guy, but according to Adrian he'd got a bit obsessed with some story about a trawler that was lost at sea in 1974, called the Gaul, I think. According to Adrian, Tommy had been doing lots of research about this ship, talking to relatives of the ship's crew, who were all lost in the accident. Apparently it's the subject of lots of conspiracy theories about spying on the Russians, and Adrian seemed to think Tommy had bought into this."

"I remember the Gaul going down," said Frank. "It was only about three months after Billy Bielby's death, if I remember rightly. Somewhere round about February 1974, I think. My Dad was a trawler skipper, so I always took an interest in what was happening with the fishing. As I remember it the official line was that she must have sunk whilst fishing in very stormy weather, and got capsized by a freak wave. But I remember some of the old fishing hands were a bit sceptical about that because they said no skipper would actually be fishing in weather like that. There's always been a bit of a mystery around the Gaul, and of course that generates conspiracy theories."

"That's as may be," said Mary, "but I don't see any connection between Tommy's interest in something that happened over 30 years ago, and the cause of his death."

"I agree with you," said Frank. "I can't see a connection. But that doesn't mean there isn't one."

CHAPTER 6

Thursday 8th November 1973

Half an hour later, after he'd brought Tony up to speed on their new case, the phone on Frank's desk rang again. This time he ignored it. His team were in now. They could deal with it. A couple of minutes later Tony came up to his desk and said: "The Super wants to see you right away, guv."
"The Super?" said Frank. "What does he want?" Normally he dealt with DCI Dunhill, his immediate boss. "I don't know," said Tony, "but it sounded urgent. I think his exact words were 'Tell Fogg to get himself in my office, now.'"

"Better go see what he wants then," said Frank. He made his way up the stairs to the top of the building where the upper echelons of management lived. As he climbed the stairs, he thought to himself, sounds like I've put my foot in it with Mr. High and Mighty Fellows.

The Super's secretary was sitting at her desk outside his office and told Frank to go straight in. He was expected. Frank knocked on the door and walked in, standing to attention in front of the Super's desk. "Sit down Frank," said Supt. Walker indicating one of the chairs in front of his desk. Supt. Walker was an old school copper, who had come up through the ranks. He was close to retirement. This was his last job. He had risen as high in the ranks as he was going to, and he was tired. He just wanted everything to go smoothly until the date of his retirement.

"Do you want some coffee?"

"No thanks, Sir. Am I in trouble, Sir?"

"Why Frank? Do you think you should be?"

"No Sir, it's just it's unusual for you to ask to see me without the DCI."

"Look Frank, I've had the Chief Constable on the phone. Apparently you've been pressuring British Allied Trawlers to return a trawler to port."

"Yes Sir, I have. It's my crime scene and I want it back so we can do forensics on it."

"OK. Look Frank, first of all, do you have any proof that it is a crime scene? Do you have any proof that a crime has been committed? My understanding is it could have been an accident."

"Sir, I'm waiting for the Post Mortem report to confirm the cause of death but the doctor at the scene thought that the marks around the victim's neck looked suspicious. So until I know for sure otherwise, I am treating this as a suspicious death. You know as well as I do that in those circumstances my first priority has to be to secure the scene in case it turns out to be criminal."

"OK. I'm following your logic so far. But how do you know this trawler was the crime scene?"

"Sir, it's the last known place the victim was seen before he ended up in the Fish Dock. So I think it is highly likely."

"Well Frank, that's a lot of ifs and buts and maybes on which to base a request to return a trawler to port. If it is a crime scene, what sort of evidence do you think there will be after three days at sea heading up to the Arctic?"

"I don't know, Sir. That's what I want to find out. But I know there will be a lot less evidence when she comes back after fishing."

"Frank, I appreciate that you are keen to do things by the book. You're still new to this role of DI. This'll be your first murder case isn't it?" Frank nodded. "You're keen to make an impression by solving it quickly. I understand that. I was where you are once. But you have to understand that we police by consent. The trawler owners are powerful people in this city. We need their help and co-operation with all sorts of other crime – illegal booze and cigarettes, theft, all sorts of things. If I order BAT to bring this trawler back, it's going to cost them a lot of money and our name as a Police Force will be mud with the trawler owners for years to come. I just can't do it based on the evidence we have in front of us."

"So that's it then is it, Sir? My crime scene is gone? Are you ordering me to back off on this, Sir?"

"Yes, Frank, I am. That is an order. You can have your crime scene, if that's what it is, when she comes back to port in the normal course of things, not before." (By which time there'll be bugger all left thought Frank to himself but didn't say it.). "In the meantime I want to be kept up to date on every aspect of your investigation as it progresses. I will be keeping a close eye on this one."

"In that case, Sir," he said, "I am formally requesting that you put that order in writing, making clear that is your decision, and that you copy it to the DCI. Will that be all, Sir?"

"Yes, it will Inspector Fogg. Dismissed."

"Bugger, bugger, bugger" said Frank as he walked into the office.

"Oh dear, boss," said Tony, "sounds like your bad day just got worse.

"It has," said Frank. "We now have no crime scene to work on, and I have been well and truly warned off making a fuss about it. I've now got the Super breathing down my neck, wanting to know the far end of a monkey's fart about this investigation. Which is absolutely nothing so far. We know who the deceased is now. We've got no cause of death, no witnesses, no crime scene. How the hell are we supposed to proceed from here?"

"Can I make a suggestion boss? Let's go and see Billy's widow and see what more background we can find out about him. That might give us some leads about what he was into, and whether there might have been anybody who had a grudge against him bad enough to want to kill him."

"Good idea, Tony. I'm not thinking straight, am I? I don't like being pressured by the Super. There's something a bit odd about it. When does he ever take an interest in ongoing murder investigations?"

At that moment the phone on Frank's desk rang yet again. Picking it up he grunted: "Fogg. This better be good news with the day I'm having."

"Frank, it's Tom." Tom Barraclough and his team had been continuing their questioning of people around the dock side to see if they could find anyone who knew anything about Billy Bielby. "I think I might have some good news for you. We went back to Stanton's Café, cos you know how the clientele changes during the day. By now the gossip is all over the dockside that it's Billy Bielby was fished out of the dock this morning. Anyway we might have a lead. A guy in Stanton's, Tom Thorne, said he was drinking in Rayners on Monday night with Alan Wilson. He is an old shipmate of Billy's. When they left the pub about 11.00pm Tom asked Alan if he was going home, and Alan said no, he was going to have a beer with Billy who was on night watchman duty on the Newby Wyke. So it's quite possible this Alan Wilson might have been the last person to see Billy alive."

"That's great work, Tom," said Frank. "Do we have an address for this Alan Wilson?"

"Sorry, no we don't" said Tom. "According to Tom Thorne this Alan Wilson was in the same position as Billy. His missus had chucked him out and he was sleeping on mates' sofas, whoever would have him. Tom assumed that's why he was going to see

Billy. It was somewhere to go for the night."

"Alright. Thanks Tom. You've done a great job finding that much. We'll take it from here. I'll get the team on doing some enquiries to see if we can track down Wilson. He could be a key witness. Thanks again. Speak to you soon."

After he'd put the phone down Frank said to Tony, "Tony, I want you to take Mark and Steve, go down to Rayners, and make some enquiries. See if a guy called Alan Wilson is in there. If not, see if anybody knows where we can find him. And when you find him haul him in here. He could have been the last person to see Billy alive."

"Got it boss. I'm on my way."

An hour later Tony stood in front of his desk again. "We found him boss. He's in Interview Room 2 downstairs. He was in Rayners. Fortunately he's not too half cut yet. He's not very happy about being hauled in here and he swore blind on the way that he knew nothing about Billy."

"Alright Tony. You and I will go and interview him in a minute - see what he's got to say for himself."

CHAPTER 7

Thursday 8th November 1973

Frank was aware of his own limitations as a copper. He sometimes lacked imagination, so found it difficult to think his way into other people's shoes, especially the villains. But one thing he knew he was good at was interviewing. He was a keen observer of people. He read their body language very well; and he had a nose for a lie. Some people called it copper's instinct, but he liked to think there was more to it than that. It was about asking the right questions and watching and listening very closely to someone as they answered them, looking for little telltale signs of nervousness and discomfort. He had a good Sergeant in Tony Travers. They made a good team. Tony seemed to know instinctively when to step in and take over the questioning, to give Frank some thinking space, or time to observe.

As they walked into Interview Room 2 that evening, neither of them quite knew what they would get out of Alan Wilson. He was their best lead so far. Probably the last person to see Billy alive. As always, that made him a potential suspect in the death, or at the very least a witness to it. So they were optimistic as they went into the interview.

"Good evening sir," said Frank. "Thank you for coming in. I am Detective Inspector Fogg. This is Detective Sergeant Travers, who you have already met. You are Mr. Alan Wilson, I understand – currently of no fixed address."

Wilson was another trawlerman in the Harry Beadle mould, a huge man, six foot four, and broad across the shoulders. He was going to seed slightly now – too much weight around the middle, probably from supping too much ale thought Frank. He was glad Wilson had decided to come in quietly, and not forced them to bring him in. He dreaded to think the damage Wilson could have done to the lads sent to bring him in if he'd decided to cut up rough.

"That's not a bloody crime now, is it, being of no fixed address?" Wilson responded belligerently.

"No sir, it is not" said Frank. "I thank you for being willing to come in and answer a few questions in respect of an ongoing enquiry."

"I didn't say I was willing. Didn't have a lot of bloody choice, did I? Never do wi' you lot."

"Alright, Wilson, settle down" said Frank, thinking I need to take control of this interview before he starts kicking off. "First of all can you tell us where you were on Monday night, sir, between the hours of around 7.00pm and 2.00am?"

"I were in Rayners, like I am most nights. Ask anyone there. They all know me. Why, what's this all about?"

"I'll ask the questions Mr. Wilson, if you don't mind. We'll get to what it's all about in good time. Now, were you in Rayners all night?"

"I were 'avin a drink wi' my mate, Tom Thorne. We go back a long way, me and Tom. We were int' Navy together years ago, afore we went on fishing. We were 'avin a crack about old times. That were while about eleven o'clock. They'd just called last orders. I got a few Brown Ales and walked down to Dock."

"And which Dock would that be?" asked Tony.

"Why, Fish Dock, young 'un. There's only one Dock to us lads."

"And why did you go to the Fish Dock, Mr. Wilson?" asked Frank, hoping he would corroborate what Tom Thorne had told them about going to see Billy.

"Look, I know I weren't supposed to be there nor nought, I weren't working – but it's 'ardly crime o't century is it, sneakin' onto Dock at night. I don't know why a bloody Detective Inspector wants to question me about that."

"Mr. Wilson, just answer the question please," said Tony, "why did you go to the Fish Dock?"

"Look, I don't want to get 'im in no trouble, see, the bloke I went to see. 'E were on night watchman duty, an' they're not supposed to 'ave visitors. An' I know what they're like, them ruddy trawler owners. Sack you for the least little thing. Don't need much of an excuse. That job's important to Billy."

"Billy who, Mr. Wilson?" asked Frank. "You went to see a guy called Billy on night watchman duty. What's his second name and which ship was he on?"

"Alright. 'Is name's Billy Bielby an' 'e were on't Newby Wyke. It were 'er last night in port. She were all ready to sail in't mornin'. Billy 'ad night watchman duty. I said I'd go an' keep 'im company. Nought better to do wi' my time. I just took 'im a few beers to 'elp pass the night. There's nought wrong wi' that, is there?"

Frank decided to ignore the minor issue of trespassing on the Dock. That was the preserve of the Transport Police anyway.

"So what time did you get to the Newby Wyke, Mr. Wilson?"

"It were about five and twenty past eleven, I reckon."

"And were you there all night, drinking with Billy?"

"Bloody 'ell, no. I'd 'ad quite a few in Rayners afore I got there. An' when I did get there, Billy 'ad a half bottle of whisky. Well if I'd started on that I would have been there all night and they'd have found me in mornin' when she sailed wi't tide. I didn't want to get Billy in no trouble. I stayed while about two and then made me way 'ome."

"So, how was Billy when you left him, Mr. Wilson?"

"Billy were fine and dandy. He'd 'ad a couple o' Pale Ales an' 'e were set for t'night. When I left 'e were just goin' to do his rounds, make sure everything were secure. Look, 'as summat 'appened to Billy? Why you asking me all these questions?"

"Did anybody see you leave?" asked Tony.

"Well I don't bloody know, do I? You'd 'ave to ask them. I didn't see nobody on my way off Dock. There were some riggers pullin' an all night shift on't next boat, but I doubt they saw me. Last thing I wanted was to be seen by anybody. Didn't want to get Billy in any trouble like I keep tellin' yer. Now are yer goin' to tell me what this is all about?"

"I take it you haven't heard yet, then, Mr. Wilson. I'm sorry to tell you that Billy is dead. His body was found in the water in the Fish Dock this morning. We think he died sometime on Monday night. You were probably the last person to see him alive."

"But why? What 'appened? 'Ow did he die? Billy dead? I can't believe it. I saw 'im large as life o' Monday an' 'e were fine. 'As 'e 'ad an 'eart attack or summat?"

"We don't know how he died yet, Mr. Wilson. That's what we're trying to find out" said Frank. "Is there anything else you can tell us about that night? Was Billy acting normal? Did he seem ill at all? Was there anything unusual going on?"

"Nah! Billy were just 'is normal miserable self. Cheerful soul is our Billy. Allus' expect the worst in life, an' you'll never be disappointed, is 'is motto. But 'e were in good health. A bit short 'o breath, but that were 'is emphysemia – bad lungs you know. But no, apart from that there were nought wrong wi' 'im. 'e'd done 'is rounds earlier on an' it were all quiet. Nought to report 'e said. An' 'e were 'opin it were goin' to stay that way all night. 'e just wanted a quiet life."

"All right, Mr. Wilson. I think that'll be all for tonight," said Frank bringing the interview to an end. "But we might want to ask you some more questions later. On your way out, please give Tony here an address where we can get in touch with you if we need to. Thanks very much for your help. And I'm sorry that your friend has died."

After Alan Wilson had left, Frank and Tony returned to their office. "Well Tony, what did you make of him?" asked Frank. "Is he telling the truth."

"I believed him boss, yes."

"So how did you arrive at that judgement?" asked Frank.

"Well, boss, for a start he seemed genuinely shocked when you told him Billy was dead. Either he is a bloody good actor, or he genuinely didn't know. Secondly, he didn't show any signs of nervousness. He was trying to protect Billy by not telling us everything at the beginning. He wouldn't do that if he knew Billy was dead. Why bother? He seemed like he was telling the truth. Thirdly, he spoke about Billy in the present tense. Billy is a cheerful soul, he said, not was. You've got to be pretty shrewd to avoid slipping into that trap when you know someone is dead. And he didn't strike me as the sharpest card in the deck. He wasn't going to give us a name and then he said 'Billy needs that job'. So all in all I thought we got the truth out of him. I don't think he knows what happened to Billy."

"Well, as it happens Tony, I totally agree with you. So did we learn anything from him then?"

"We know a little bit more about what Billy was doing just before he died. But it doesn't get us any nearer finding out how or why, does it?"

"There is one little detail I want you to follow up on Tony. Wilson mentioned some riggers working an all night shift on another boat. I want you to ask the Transport Police to see if they can find out which boat it was and what they were doing. We need to talk to those riggers, to find out if they saw anything. But it's getting late now. It'll keep til the morning. You get off home now Tony."

"OK. Thanks boss. Will do."

CHAPTER 8

Monday 30th March 2009

Frank and Mary had taken a break for coffee. Frank had decided to try to find out a bit more about Mary's background. He liked to know who he was working with. "So Mary, judging by that accent I assume you are from the Met originally. What brought you to Hull?"

"I came up here to get married," said Mary. "My partner works up here, and when we decided to get married it was a case of one of us had to move. Comparing the house prices up here with London, it was a no-brainer really."

"So what does your husband do? Don't tell me he's a copper too."

"No she's not," said Mary "*she* is a teacher. Now you're going to tell me I'm very young to be a DCI and that I must know people in high places. Well for your information, I don't. I'm a woman. I'm gay. And I've had to fight every inch to get to where I am on my own merits, thank you very much."

"Whoa" said Frank, taken aback by the vehemence of her reaction. "Let me just tell you something Mary. I was not making any assumptions about you, first off, so please do not assume that because I'm retired I'm some sort of dinosaur who doesn't understand the need for the Police service to move with the times. One of my responsibilities as ACC before I retired was personnel issues. I oversaw the adoption of a new equality policy. I had to push very hard against some of the old guard to get LGBT rights included in there. I was also responsible for a major new recruitment drive because we were lagging way behind other parts of the country in recruiting women, people from ethnic minorities and LGBT people. And we were reasonably successful with that. Now enough of blowing my own trumpet. I just want you to know that I try not to be prejudiced. I am the product of my gender and generation so I don't always get it right. But I expect people to tell me when I don't and I'll try not to do it again. OK. Are we good? Because we have to work this case together so we need to be on the same wavelength."

"Yes, Sir. Sorry about that. I get a bit defensive sometimes because of all the shit I've had to put up with in the Police. Sometimes I wonder how I've stuck it out this far. And I'd heard on the grapevine that you were a bit of a Bible-basher so I assumed you would be anti-gay."

"You see, we all have our prejudices and make assumptions about other people, Mary. I know some Christians come across as vehemently anti-gay. But please don't tar us all with the same brush. I am not one of them. I don't want to get into a philosophical and theological debate about why just now. We've got work to do. But I'll explain it to you over a drink sometime, if you're up for that." Mary nodded.

"Right, so you need to tell me about the file on Billy Bielby. Jim said there was stuff missing from it that he expected to see there. Can you tell me what? Have you looked at it? And can I get hold of a copy myself to refresh my memory?"

"That's a lot of questions all at once Frank. Yes, I have seen it. Yes, you can have a copy, for what it's worth. But there's not much in there. What's missing? Well there's no forensics. The Post-Mortem report has gone missing. And most of your notes as Investigating Officer are not there either. There are one or two witness statements, but we suspect that there must have been others. In fact there's very little that you would expect to see after an investigation, however inconclusive it turned out to be. The official line is that they must have got lost. The original file was stored here at Queen's Gardens and then eventually it was moved to Priory Road. So what I've been told is that some of the file must have gone missing, either when it was in store here, or during the move, or possibly some of it was water damaged at Priory Road during the 2007 floods. I don't really buy that one because there's no evidence of water damage to the rest of the file, and I don't see how only part of it would be damaged. So my guess is either accidentally or deliberately lost."

"OK. Well I can fill you in on some bits of that. We never found any forensics. There was nothing on the body. Hardly surprising since he'd been in the water for a couple of days before he was found, and there was plenty of marine life in the fish dock, eels and crabs and so on, that had taken bits out of him, aside from the water damage. The Post Mortem concluded that he died of natural causes, specifically a heart attack brought on by his emphysema and an unhealthy diet and lifestyle. I never believed that for a moment. It could have been an accident. He might have fallen in the water, but he definitely didn't die by drowning. There was no evidence of water in the lungs. No sign of any blunt force trauma so he didn't fall and hit his head on something on the way into the water. Then there was some strange bruising around his neck which the Pathologist noted. It could have been consistent with manual strangulation, but it was difficult to tell because of the deterioration of the body. The hyoid bone was not broken, which it usually is with strangulation, and there was no petechial haemorrhaging. According to the Pathologist this bruising was down to swelling of the body after the heart attack whilst he was wearing a shirt a collar size too small. So the long and short of it is that the Post Mortem was a cover up. When it went to the Inquest the Coroner returned a verdict of death by natural causes. You'll be able to read it all in the record of the Inquest of course."

"I've already done that thanks," said Mary. "But I wanted to hear it from you just to confirm that I wasn't missing anything. So what's your best guess, Frank? You pursued this for long enough as a murder enquiry. I'm surprised the bosses let you get away with it for so long when it was producing no result."

"Oh, they tried very hard to shut it down, Mary, believe me. I was pressured from on high right from the off. The Super took a personal interest in this one, which he never did normally. Even my DCI thought that was a bit odd. After a few weeks, when the investigation was going nowhere, I kept getting told that there was no evidence of any crime having taken place. So it was a waste of Police time and resources to keep investigating. I was very firmly told to stop, and prioritise other things, unless and until any new evidence came in. Well, I didn't drop it. I couldn't. I'd got the bit between my teeth by then. I was sure there was something not right about Billy's death, and I wanted to prove it. But I had to do it a bit clandestinely, in my own time. My DCI knew what I was doing and I kept him fully informed, but we didn't want the Super getting wind of it."

"So come on then, Frank, what was your guess at the time about what happened?"

"I hate guessing, Mary. I like to find evidence to prove things beyond a reasonable doubt, so they stand up in court and people get brought to justice for their crimes."

"But you must have had some sort of hunch you were working on, surely?"

"I did and although the Pathologist pooh-poohed it, the Police Surgeon thought it was a realistic scenario. I think somebody put a plastic bag over poor Billy's head and suffocated him. There wasn't any petechial haemorrhaging, which you expect to find with suffocation, but the Pathologist was very clear that just because it's not there doesn't rule that out as a cause of death. Apparently it's not always there in cases of asphyxiation. So that was the theory I was working on, although, as I say, there was insufficient evidence to prove it. That is until a witness came forward and confirmed it."

"So what about the crime scene? Was there no evidence from there?"

"Ah! The crime scene. I nearly lost my job over that. The last place Billy was seen alive was on board the Newby Wyke, an old steam trawler. He was doing night watchman duty. A friend went to visit him and they had a couple of beers, sitting on the bridge. We ruled the friend out of our enquiries fairly early on. I can't remember his name now. But he swore blind Billy was still alive and kicking when he left him. The Newby Wyke sailed the next day and was half way to Iceland by the time we picked Billy out of the dock. I tried to get her turned round so we could find whatever evidence there might be. I even spoke to the Managing Director myself and asked him to authorise her coming home. He had connections with the Chief Constable apparently, and a humble lowly Detective Inspector is not supposed to speak to such exalted beings. So I got blown out and told in no uncertain terms I was not getting my crime scene until she returned to port 10 days later. We got forensics to crawl all over her when she finally got back, but of course any evidence had been destroyed by then. So that's why there's no crime scene forensics in the file."

CHAPTER 9

Friday 9th November 1973

It was Friday night. They had made absolutely no progress with the investigation into Billy's death that day. They'd interviewed Gill Bielby, who said she knew nothing about Billy's whereabouts that night. She had a cast iron alibi, having been at her mother's all night. Tom Barraclough had rung round all the trawler companies to find out which ones had had their riggers working all night on Monday, and drawn a total blank. Nobody knew anything about any riggers doing night shift. Frank was tired, and very frustrated. He knew how crucial the first 48 hours are in any murder investigation. Billy had now been dead since Monday night (as far as they knew). He felt like they were getting nowhere fast.

Frank had clocked off for the day, although his mind was still working overtime on the riddle of Billy. He was sitting drinking Lagavulin with his best mate, Tim. They had grown up together as childhood friends, living close to one another in Hawthorne Avenue, playing out together, going to school together at Wheeler Street Primary School. Tim had won a scholarship to the local grammar school, Hymers College, at the age of 11, whilst Frank had gone off to Trinity House School. But they had kept in touch.

In some ways they had gone in very different directions. Tim was very academic. After Grammar School, he had spent a year working on the Fish Dock as an Office Junior, but his long term goal was academia. While he was having his gap year on the Fish Dock Tim's world had been turned upside down. His Dad was a mate on a trawler, the Kingston Aquamarine. She had set off on a trip to Iceland, reported in that the weather was rough and she had some build-up of ice on the rigging, and then was never heard from again. It took 10 days for the owners to finally confirm that she was missing, presumed sunk with all hands. She was never found, and the assumption was that she must have turned turtle with the build up of ice, as sometimes happened. In spite of this Tim had gone off to Cambridge, but maybe because of it he suddenly changed his plans from studying history to reading Divinity. Frank had fully expected him to end up as a Cambridge don, teaching other students. Frank, meanwhile, after school, had drifted a bit. He'd tried his hand at being a Deckie Learner, but he'd hated that. He'd only done it out of respect for his Dad, because he knew that was what his Dad would have wanted. After that he'd drifted from one job to another. It was the sixties and you could walk out of one job and find another easily enough. But he wasn't happy doing any of them. Then, much to everyone's surprise, his own included, he had signed on to the Police Training College, ended up passing out with honours, and started as a rookie beat Bobby on Hessle Road.

During this time when they were going their separate ways, Frank and Tim had always kept in touch. When Tim was in town visiting his mother they would always go out for a pint somewhere – usually in town, because Frank didn't like drinking on his own patch.

Then, to Frank's surprise though no one else's, Tim had announced that he had a call from God and was going to train to be a Church of England priest. So Tim had gone off to Oxford, to St. Stephen's House, an Anglican Theological College, or as Tim liked to call it seminary, to do his three years training. Then he had returned to Hull, and served a Curacy in the Parish of St. Mary, Sculcoates. When Tim returned to Hull, he and Frank had slipped back easily into their old friendship. Every couple of weeks, when their busy schedules permitted, they would go out for a pint and put the world to rights, or they would meet at one of their houses and have a good yarn over a glass or two of single malt.

Eventually, Tim had landed his dream job, being the Vicar of the Church of St. John Newington, just off Hessle Road. This was the fishermen's church, or at least in Church of England terms. The Fishermen's Bethel on Hessle Road, where the Mission to Seamen was based, didn't count as a "proper" church in Tim's world.

Although they were close friends, Tim was a bit of an enigma to Frank. Frank had always believed in God. He didn't know where it came from. His parents were not really religious, although his Dad, like most of the fishing community, was very superstitious. They had had him christened as a baby but that was more about family tradition than any active faith on their part. But from as early as he could remember Frank had always been convinced that God was there and that he could talk to God. He'd been encouraged by Miss Martin, who taught RI at Wheeler Street School. When he got to Trinity House he would go to the church services in the Chapel, as the boys were required to do. But he wasn't particularly religious, in a churchy kind of way. He didn't attend church regularly. He had learned a lot more about the Christian faith from Tim, who was always pressing him to be confirmed. But Frank didn't see the point. He was happy with things as they were.

He didn't quite understand how Tim had become so religious in a very Catholic kind of way. He was one of those Anglo-Catholics who were more Catholic than the Catholics. He liked to be called Father, although in the modern way it was always "Father Tim", never Father Baker. He always wore a soutane, a cassock with a cape, and his clerical collar wherever he was going. He said Mass every day in church, and on Sundays and Holy Days it was always High Mass with loads of acolytes, candles, incense, lots of crossing, the full works.

Fussy religion, Frank called it. He always joked with Tim that it didn't do much for him. Nevertheless, they remained the best of friends. When they got together their conversation was always interesting, and sometimes Tim had a sparkling wit which made Frank go home chuckling to himself. Their topics of conversation ranged over politics, religion, football, cricket, the fishing industry, modern policing, current affairs, and history, for which they both shared a passion.

Frank was not in the habit of discussing his current cases with Tim. That would have been a breach of professional standards, for which Frank was a stickler. However this evening their conversation had got round to the fishing industry. Having both lost their fathers to the industry, they both took a keen interest in safety. Tim was a frequent writer of letters to the Board of Trade, as he still liked to call it, and the newspapers, about this issue. He felt both a personal and professional interest, as many of his parishioners worked in the industry. It was just over five years since the infamous "Triple Trawler Tragedy" as it was called, when three Hull trawlers had been lost in the same month, January 1968. This had sparked an outcry from the community, and what came to be an organised campaign by many of the women of Hull's fishing community, for improvements in safety standards. The Headscarf Revolutionaries, they had come to be called. Of course, like all campaigns, the heat which was sparked by the immediacy of the tragedy, had gone out of it. As is the way of these things, improvements in safety regulations took a very long time to work their way through the system of consultation and legislation. But Frank and Tim liked to keep an eye on their progress.

This is what they had been discussing, when Tim suddenly said: "I don't suppose you have anything to do with investigating Billy Bielby's death, do you Frank? I know you're not supposed to talk about these things, but I have a personal interest because I knew Billy. He was one of my regulars here at St. John's."

"Well, you do surprise me," said Frank. "I didn't have Billy down as a churchgoer, but it takes all sorts. As a matter of fact, I picked up the case on Thursday morning, almost by chance, but now I'm the investigating officer. I suppose you've read about it in the Hull Daily Mail."

"Well, I did of course, but Billy's widow, Gill, was on the phone to me as soon as she heard. She wanted help arranging a funeral, whenever the Coroner releases the body, and she wanted it to be in church. I knew they were not together of course – a sad symptom of modern life – but I tried to support them both through the break up of their marriage and I continued to see both of them on a regular basis."

Frank decided to break his rule, and tell Tim where they had got up to with the case. After all, if you couldn't trust a priest to keep a confidence, who could you trust? And besides, Tim knew Billy. He might be able to shed some more light on what kind of person he was, and why someone might want him dead. So, after briefly describing his progress so far, which didn't take long, Frank asked Tim, "So any ideas about who might have had a grudge against Billy? Bad enough to want him dead?"

"Frank, I have not got a clue," said Tim. "I know Gill said once or twice she wished he was dead. I know you will look into the next of kin as a matter of course. But really, that was just heat of the moment stuff. She does not have it in her. She was just pissed off about his philandering and drinking. Normal stuff. She would never have done anything like that."

"Well, that ties in with what I thought about her. But it doesn't get us any further. There's got to be some reason why somebody wanted Billy dead."

"Could it just have been an accident?" asked Tim.

"I don't think so. I have a feeling in my water about this case.

There's something very wrong. I just can't put my finger on it at the moment. Of course I can't even prove at the moment that it was a murder. I might know more when the Post Mortem result comes in".

"Well, my friend, I'm sure if anyone can crack it, you will in the end" said Tim. "I don't suppose Billy saw something he shouldn't have did he? I hear rumours about nefarious things that go on around the Fish Dock."

"Yeah, but that's mostly pilfering and a bit of smuggling. The worst we've ever come across on the Fish Dock is a bit of minor drug smuggling. Even that's not major, because the big boys in the drug world tend to use the cargo port and smuggle in on containers or roll-on roll-off lorries. There's nothing going on there that would warrant killing somebody to keep it quiet – not that I know of anyway. Unless you know any different, Tim?"

"No, I don't know!" said Tim. "I've just got this feeling that something big was happening there that was upsetting people but either nobody really knew, or they didn't want to talk about it."

Their conversation moved on to other matters then, and eventually they called it a night, and Frank took himself off home.

CHAPTER 10

Saturday 10th November 1973

Frank had had a fitful night's sleep, tossing and turning and waking every half hour or so. At about 6.00am he decided he'd had enough of trying to sleep with everything that was going round in his mind. Although he was not due in over the weekend, he decided to go into the office and, if nothing else, get on top of some of the paperwork which increasingly went with his job. After downing a strong cup of black coffee he went out to start clearing the ice from the car. He still hadn't remembered to get any de-icer.

It was another morning of freezing fog, as he eased the car towards the city centre. Something was niggling at the back of his mind. He thought it was something Tim had said last night. At the time he had thought it of no consequence, but now it was niggling away at him and he couldn't for the life of him recall what it was. On a whim he decided not to go into the office straight away. He was not expected after all. He turned southwards to head towards the Fish Dock. He wanted to breathe in some of the atmosphere again – get a better feel for the place. And maybe what was bothering him would come back while he was there. Passing through the Transport Police check point, he parked up close to where he had been on Thursday. Getting out of the car he decided to go for a walk. Passing between the buildings near the lock pit, he walked through to the river side of the dock and started walking westwards towards Hessle.

It was a still morning with no wind. It was still dark, and the fog was even thicker down here by the Humber. With very little light, it was like walking in a dream world. You could hardly see your own hand in front of your face. He could hear the river on his left, but could not see it – just the sound of small waves lapping against the wooden piers. He had no idea of the state of the tide, but it must be fairly high to be making those noises. There was that familiar smell hanging in the air. The smell of the river; the smell of fish; and especially the smell of the fish meal factory, where all the leftovers, fish heads, bones and so on, were processed to make fertiliser and glue. On a bad day, if the wind was in the west, the smell would permeate the whole city. Frank started to shiver. He didn't know if it was the freezing fog cutting through even his winter coat, or if it was the eerie atmosphere created by the fog. Not normally one to have a vivid imagination, he began to think he could hear the cries of generations of lost mariners. But perhaps it was just the gulls beginning to wake up with the dawn.

Having had enough he decided to make his way back to the car. When he got there he noticed that Stanton's Café was open. In need of a hot drink and a warm up, he went in. There weren't very many customers at that time of the morning on a Saturday. Two men were in an animated conversation in one corner, full English breakfasts in front of them; and at another table three people sat, not speaking, staring glumly into their drinks. As Frank entered all eyes turned to look at the newcomer, and the conversation immediately dried up. Frank was used to this, as a copper. Nevertheless, his nosey mind couldn't help wondering what they had been talking about that shouldn't be said in front of a policeman.

He ordered his coffee and a bacon sandwich and sat down at a table on his own. He was still mulling over what it was that had been niggling at the back of his mind all night, but still it would not come to him. As his bacon sandwich arrived, he was surprised to see one of the two men who had been in animated conversation approach his table.

"Mind if I sit here?" he asked.

"Go ahead. It's a free country," said Frank.

"You the copper that's investigatin' our Billy's accident?"

"If you mean Billy Bielby, then the answer's yes. And you are?"

"Tom Bielby. Billy were my kid brother," said Tom reaching over to shake Frank's hand.

"So, have you got something on your mind Tom?" asked Frank.

"Yeah. Only that it weren't no accident. He were killed see. And I want to see the bastard caught what did it."

"And if you don't mind my asking, how do you know this, Tom?"

"I hear things see. I hear people talking. And the talk is it weren't no accident. The talk is that he seen somethin' what he shouldn't a seen and that's what got him done in."

"Tom, I'm not sure this is the best place to have this conversation. Why don't we go down to the Station and you can tell me more about what you've heard?"

"Oh no. I ain't goin' near no cop shop, me. I've heard what you lot are like. You're not getting' me in a cell and beatin' me up."

"I'm not going to put you in a cell, Tom. You haven't done anything wrong. Look, why don't we go and sit in my car and talk about this?"

"Promise you're not goin' to get me in that car and drive me off to't station."

"Tom, I promise. I just want to chat with you somewhere a bit more private. That's all."

"A'right then" said Tom.

They left the café and made their way to Frank's car.

When they were seated in the car, Frank turned on the engine to get the heater going. Tom made to get out of the car again.

"What you doin' mister? I thought you said we weren't goin' nowhere."

"We're not Tom. I just turned the engine on so we can have some heat going to try and stay warm. Now tell me. What have you heard, and where did you hear it from?"

"Don't know, mister. I ain't heard nowt."

"But Tom, you said in there that you heard people saying it wasn't an accident. You came over to talk to me so it's obviously on your mind. So where did you hear this from?"

"Don't know, mister. Can't remember. But I know it weren't no accident. An' it's not fair – our Billy gettin' killed like that. He never did no 'arm to nobody."

"Tom, do you remember anything about where you heard this? Where you got this information from?"

"Don't know, mister. It were just people talking, in the café like. I don't know who. But I listen, see. People think I'm stupid and I don't know anything. But I listen an' I 'ear things. I'm not in trouble am I?"

"No Tom, you're not in any trouble. But I need to know where I can find you if I need to talk to you again." Frank had decided by this time that he wasn't going to get anything more out of him just now. He needed to get him to come in to the station without frightening the life out of the poor man. "Where do you live?"

"I live wi' my sister off Spring Bank."

"Do you know which house Tom? Maybe I could give you a ride home."

"Don't wanna go 'ome now mister. Five o'clock is goin' 'ome time."

"Alright Tom. You go back to the café then. Here, take this and buy yourself a cup of tea" said Frank, giving him one of the new

50p coins which had replaced the ten shilling note.

He could easily find out where Tom's sister lived, and he decided he might be better off questioning Tom with his sister present. In the meantime he needed to get some people asking around, see if they could find out what the rumour and gossip was. He decided that might well be a job for the Transport Police, so he headed back to the station to put in a call to Tom Barraclough.

CHAPTER 11

Monday 30th March 2009

As Mary and Frank were just about to wrap things up, having got as far as they could in sharing information, the phone rang on Mary's desk. "DCI Fowler" she answered. After a moment she said: "Just hold on a moment. I'm going to put you on speaker phone. I've got someone here who needs to hear this."

"This is the control room. We've had a report in from Traffic of a burnt out 4x4 vehicle, probably a Land Rover Discovery, matching the description of the one involved in your hit and run on Hessle Road. They thought you might want to go and have a look."

"Thanks," said Mary. "Make sure they have the vehicle cordoned off. I don't want any sightseers gathering round. I'll ring SOCO and get a team out there as soon as we can. Can you give me the location of the vehicle."

The Control Room Operator gave some map co-ordinates and hung up. "Right Frank," said Mary, "I'm going to Google Map these co-ordinates while you get your coat on. I think you need to come with me on this one."

"At your service," said Frank.

It turned out the abandoned vehicle had been left on a disused railway line at the end of a farm track close to the village of Barmby on the Marsh. If Frank remembered his local history correctly, this particular piece of railway was part of the ill-fated white elephant which was once called the Hull & Barnsley Railway, or to give it its more grandiose title The Hull, Barnsley and West Riding Junction Railway and Dock Company, although it never quite made it all the way to Barnsley. It had been funded by the merchants of Hull in an attempt to break the monopoly stranglehold of the North Eastern Railway on traffic into and out of Hull. It was one of the last railways to be built in the 19th century. Unfortunately, its construction was prohibitively expensive because the North Eastern already had the flat route in and out of Hull along the banks of the Humber. So the H&BR engineers had to tunnel and cut their way through the chalk of the Yorkshire Wolds, and then they had to get the railway across the River Ouse, which was navigable and very busy at least up to York. This entailed building a very expensive swing bridge across the Ouse. And by this time the good burghers of Kingston upon Hull had had quite enough of railways crossing roads on the flat on level crossings, so the H&BR had to make its way around Hull to its new dock on the east side via an elevated railway with lots of bridges. All of this made it a bit of a white elephant which never turned a profit and was fairly quickly taken over by the North Eastern Railway. It was one of the first lines to close in the post war era, losing most of its passenger service even before the days of Dr. Beeching.

Barmby on the Marsh was a village at the end of the road to nowhere, in the old Boothferry district of Humberside, and in the shadow of the mighty Drax Power Station just across the river. Making their way there as quickly as possible through heavy traffic coming from the Docks, they arrived to find the Traffic Officers had the area cordoned off. There was no sign of the SOCO Team as yet. They got out of the car and went to speak to the Traffic Officers. Mary showed her Warrant Card and said to them: "So what do we know so far?"

"Well Ma'am, the farmer who owns the land found the vehicle and called it in. He doesn't know how long it's been there. He'd come down this way to spray the vegetables growing in this field. He says the last time he was down here was last Monday and it wasn't here then so it could have been dumped any time between then and now."

"H'm" said Mary, "well that ties in. The hit and run took place last Monday so it's possible it was dumped here and torched last Monday evening. I'm going to need this farmer's name and address so we can interview him, find out if he knows anything else. I don't suppose he saw anything?"

"No Ma'am. He lives about two miles west towards the village, and as you can see this area is screened by this belt of trees to the west, so it's unlikely he would have seen anything."

"OK. I'll need to get some uniforms doing house to house to find out if anyone else saw or heard anything." This was more of a note to herself than anything else.

"OK" she said to the Traffic Officers, "what can you tell me about the vehicle?"

"Not a lot so far Ma'am. We didn't want to touch it in case you wanted SOCO to go over it for evidence. So we haven't done a detailed examination. As you can see it's been torched, so there probably is not a lot of evidence left. But we can tell from the shape that it's a Land Rover Discovery. And as you can see, if you walk round this way Ma'am, there is a dent in the bonnet. That has not been caused by warping from the fire. It's been caused by an impact. And it's consistent with a body hitting the bonnet and bouncing off. I've seen it before at RTAs. We'll be able to tell more when SOCO have finished with it here and we can get it back to the garage and get our Forensics boys to take it apart. There are no plates on it. Whether they've been lost in the fire or deliberately taken off, I can't say. But we might still be able to get a VIN number off it to find out who owned it. Although in my experience Ma'am, if someone's going to use a vehicle in a hit and run, it's usually stolen."

"I agree" said Mary "but we still need to know where it came from. If it's been stolen somebody might have witnessed who did the theft. So we need to track down the owner. Can you check back with Control and get them to dig out any reports of Land Rover Discoveries being stolen in the last couple of weeks. Get them to send the information, to my Sergeant, John Townsend, at Queens Gardens."

"Will do, Ma'am" was the reply.

"Now where's that bloody SOCO Team got to. It's none too warm standing out here. Why is it always so windy and freezing cold up north?"

"You'll get used to it," said Frank, who had been watching proceedings with interest. "Can I ask a question?"

"By all means, that's what you're here for" said Mary.

"Do we know if there are any bus services in the area that operate on a Monday afternoon or evening. Because if not whoever was driving this vehicle must have had an accomplice to get away. It's a very long walk to anywhere from here."

"Good thinking, Frank. I'll ask the Traffic boys. They might know."

When Mary asked the question, it got a derisive laugh from the Traffic Officers. "Bus services out here. You've got to be kidding. I'm not sure they've seen a bus in Barmby for years now. And probably never will again."

"OK. That answers that question. So we could be looking for another strange vehicle in the area at the same time this one was dumped. It's a dead end isn't it, at Barmby? So there can't be that much traffic in and out. We might just get lucky and find somebody who saw something or someone unusual. We need a break in this case, the sooner the better."

"Right, I'm going to get on to John and get him to organise a team out here to do house to house. Somebody must have seen or heard something. Then we'll go and pay a visit to Farmer Giles, see what he knows. Are you with me, Frank?"

"I am indeed," said Frank, loving being back in the hunt, enjoying the thrill of the chase.

Mary put in her call and they jumped in her car and sped off westwards towards the village, to the address they had been given by the Traffic Officers. Unfortunately when they got there, there was nobody home. "He's probably out working somewhere in the area," said Frank. "Why don't we have a drive around and see if we can track down a tractor at work somewhere in the area?"

After about half an hour of fruitless searching, they were about to give up when Frank spotted from the corner of his eye a tractor at the far end of a field they were passing. Stopping the car, Mary said, "What now? How are we going to get his attention above the noise of the tractor?"

"Leave it with me," said Frank and climbed over the gate into the field and started waving his arms wildly to get the driver's attention. Eventually the tractor pulled up, the engine shut down, and a shout of "Oi" rang across the field. "What you doin' in 'ere. It's private property."

"Police" shouted Frank back across the field. "Need a word with you." The man jumped back in the tractor, the engine started up and it sped around the side of the field towards them. Pulling up the man jumped out and said: "What do you lot want then? I ain't done nothing dodgy."

Mary walked up to him, showing her Warrant Card, and checked that he was indeed the man they were looking for, whose name they had been given by the Traffic Police.

"We're looking into the vehicle found on your property. It may well have been stolen and used in a crime."

"'s a bit over the top, in't it, a Detective Chief Inspector investigatin' a stolen car?"

"We think it may have been involved in a serious crime," said Mary, not wishing to get drawn into the reasons for their visit. "We just need to know if you saw or heard anything unusual on or around last Monday when we think it was probably abandoned on your land and torched."

"Not that I can remember, no."

"When where you last in the field where you found the car, Mr. Giles?"

"Well, it were last Monday afternoon. I were spraying in there. It were't last job o't day so I must have finished about half seven 'cos it were getting' dark, I remember. I went 'ome, put tractor to bed, made my supper, and sat and watched telly for a bit. There were nought unusual I saw."

"And you didn't see the fire at all, when the car went up in flames?"

"Well no, I wouldn't if it were Monday night. Like I said I were in't kitchen getting' my supper and in't sitting room. They both face west. So I wouldn't 'ave been looking in't direction o'that field."

"Alright. Thanks, Mr. Giles. We'll leave it there for now. But I might want to come back and ask you some more questions at some point."

"Aye. If you must. Oh, there were one thing, now I think on it. I were down't pub Tuesday. I were talking to Harry, my neighbour, and he were askin' me if I'd seen a black Range Rover around the place Monday night. 'E's a stock farmer, see. Me, I'm strictly arable. Don't 'ave nought to do wi' animals. But Harry's always vigilant 'cos they have a problem wi' rustlers on stock farms see. People nickin' their animals in't night. So 'e keeps an eye out for strange vehicles 'cos they might be casing the joint, lookin' for their next haul, see. 'E said it were a black Range Rover, top o'the range model, wi' them tinted windows. It passed 'im in a hurry 'eadin' back towards motorway as 'e were comin' back to't village."

"OK. Mr. Giles. That's really helpful. Just tell me where we can find Harry, and we'll let you get back to your work. Thanks for your time."

"What did you make of that then, Frank?" said Mary as they headed off towards the village to try and track down Harry.

"I think he's hiding something" said Frank. "He doesn't want us nosing around too much, especially at his property, I think. But I also think he was telling the truth about not having seen anything when the vehicle was dumped. Why would he leave it so long to report it otherwise? And if he had something to do with it and knew it was there, why report it at all? He could have left it there and we'd be none the wiser."

"I think you're right" said Mary. "Let's go and see what Harry has to say about it." Which they did, but Harry was not able to tell them any more. He just confirmed what they had already been told, that a black Range Rover with tinted windows had been seen in the area around 10.30pm the previous Monday evening. Armed with that information they decided to head back to Hull and call it a day.

CHAPTER 12

Sunday 11th November 1973

Frank was in the office early again on Sunday morning. He'd decided to go through all the witness statements they had so far. He knew there must be something somewhere that would give them a lead on Billy's killer. He was more and more convinced that this was a case of murder, although he was not sure the Super would see it that way. About 11 o'clock he received a call from Tom Barraclough to say that their enquiries about the source of any rumours about Billy's death had so far drawn a blank. That reminded Frank of his conversation with Billy's brother Tom the previous day. He decided to get in touch with Tom's sister Mary and to see if they could interview Tom with her present. They arranged to meet that afternoon.

Frank had summoned Tony and said he would pick him up on the way to Mary's house which was in the relatively new Council Estate just off Spring Bank. As they were on the way, Tony expressed his doubts about the value of interviewing Tom. "Sounds to me, from what you told me about him boss, that he's a sandwich short of a picnic. Are we really going to get anything useful out of him."

Tony was taken aback by the vehemence of Frank's response. "He is not, as you so delicately put it, 'a sandwich short of a picnic'

Tony. From my observation of him I would say that he's probably autistic."

"What's that then, boss?" asked Tony.

"Look Tony, I know a bit about this because I grew up with someone who's autistic – my kid brother. I don't broadcast it about the force because like you, most people don't understand. My brother Dave is not an idiot – in fact I would say he's highly intelligent. His observation skills are much better than mine. He's got brilliant memory recall. If he was sitting where you are he could observe a string of cars going past you on the other side of the road and recall every registration number. I bet you couldn't do that. He's just different. He hasn't got the social skills that most people have. He doesn't know how to interact with other people."

"But what makes them like that then, boss?" asked Tony.

"Oh, don't get me started on that one. They used to say that autism was a kind of schizophrenia – a mental illness. But that idea's been well and truly debunked. I think the answer is the doctors don't know, although they never like to admit that. The latest idea coming out of the States is that it's down to parenting. Some American headshrinker has come up with the theory that autism is caused by what he calls "refrigerator mothers" that don't love their children enough. A load of rubbish if you ask me. My mother loved me and Dave just the same, but he turned out very different from me. I think he was just born that way, end of story."

"Anyway Tony, just leave the questioning to me. My guess is we will get something useful out of him, but it will take some patience."

Frank had already asked Mary on the phone if she would sit in on the interview with Tom and she had agreed. He knew that any witness statement they got from Tom would not be admissible in court, but he was still convinced that Tom had some useful information to give them that might get them further forward in the investigation. It was a cold bleak overcast afternoon, already beginning to get dark at 3 o'clock, with the clouds threatening rain or sleet. They gratefully accepted Mary's offer of a cup of tea.

When they were settled, Mary began: "Now, Tom, these two gentlemen are policemen. You've met Mr. Fogg before. He's the Inspector. You two met yesterday in Stanton's didn't you?"

"Yes. I know. I remember Mr. Fogg. He bought me a cup of tea." said Tom.

"Well this is his Sergeant, Mr. Travers," continued Mary. "Now Tom, you're not in any kind of trouble. They just want to know what you've seen and heard down on the Dock because it might help them find out what happened to Billy. You want to help find out what happened to our Billy don't you?"

"I do," said Tom, "and I know stuff 'cos I hear and see lots and people don't notice me. I'm good at not being noticed."

"I bet you are Tom" said Frank. "So what can you tell us about what happened to Billy?"

"Oh, nothing. I wasn't there. I never saw nothing. I can't tell nothing."

"OK, Tom. I didn't say you were there. But yesterday you told me you had heard things about what happened to Billy. What did you hear, Tom?"

"I can't tell, Mr. Fogg. I shouldn't have said that. It's secret."

"What's secret, Tom?"

"It's all secret. I can't tell. Billy said never to tell."

"What didn't Billy want you to tell anybody, Tom?"

"Well I can't tell you that, silly. It wouldn't be secret then would it?"

"Billy", said Mary sharply, "don't you be so rude to Mr. Fogg. Now you just tell him what he wants to know. If something bad was happening on the Dock it might be what got Billy killed. You want to know why Billy was killed don't you?"

"Yes. Sorry Mary. Sorry Mr. Fogg. Billy seen things on the Dock when he was on nights and he told me but he said never to tell anyone."

"Tom, I don't think he meant you can't tell the Police," said Mary.

"But Billy said it could be dangerous and he didn't want me getting into trouble."

"Now Tom," said Frank, "if Billy knew something, that could be what got him into a whole lot of trouble, and made somebody want to kill him. We need to know what that was. If we know about it we can protect you from any danger can't we?"

"Yes Mr. Fogg. All I know is Billy said someone were spyin'. And 'e weren't 'appy about it 'cos 'e said if they found out the trawler could be in real trouble and the crew wouldn't be safe. But 'e said nobody would do ought about if 'e did tell so there were no point."

"Billy, this is really important. Did he say which trawler he was talking about?" asked Frank.

"No, Mr. Fogg. God's honest truth, 'e never told me that. He never said if it were one trawler or more than one."

"And do you know what he meant by spying, Billy?"

"Mr. Fogg, I swear on my sister's life, that is all I know. He just said 'e'd seen stuff an' it were dangerous. That's all I know."

"Alright Billy. Thanks for your help. And thank you Mary for seeing us. If either of you remember anything else, please get in touch with me or Tony at Queen's Gardens Station. We'll be happy to talk on the phone or come and see you again."

As they made their way back to the station Frank asked Tony: "What did you make of that Tony? Do you think he was telling the truth? Do you think he's told us everything he knows?"

"I do boss" said Tony. "I don't think you were going to get

anything more out of him because I don't think he knows anything. But what do you think he meant by spying?"

"I don't know Tony. My best bet would be industrial espionage. I know there's a lot of competition between the trawler companies, not just here in Hull, but around the country, and with other countries. They're always trying to improve the technology. The sidewinder trawlers, that bring the catch home packed in ice, are on the way out now. Freezer trawlers were the next leap forward. And then they got the factory ships where they process the fish at sea, gut it and fillet it before freezing, and bring it home ready to be sent to the shops. Then they're always trying to improve the sonar so they can detect where the fish are. Gone are the days of skippers like my Dad who relied on experience and instinct to know where and when to fish. It's all technology these days. Who knows? Maybe they're spying on each other. It seems a bit over the top to go to the lengths of killing somebody to protect a trade secret, but who knows? There's big money involved. And where there's big money there's always a potential motive for murder."

CHAPTER 13

Monday 12th November 1973

As he had expected, first thing Monday morning Frank was called into the DCI's office. Jim Dunhill was a good boss. Frank had found him good to work with. He was very fair. He supported and encouraged his officers, and didn't try to take credit himself for their successes. Frank thought he could have had a lot worse bosses, from his experience in the Police force. As he sat down in Jim's office he was asked for an update on the progress of his investigation. When Frank told him he was still waiting for the result of the Post Mortem, he was concerned. "I'll try and put some pressure on the Coroner," he said. "Now you're aware that the Super is taking a personal interest in this case. I have no idea why. He is not letting on to me. I get the impression he is under pressure from on high. And I know he will do anything for a quiet life. So he has made it very clear that he thinks this is a case of accidental death and we should not be wasting our time on it. He's putting me under pressure to focus on all the other stuff that's on our desks, the burglaries and assaults in particular. He thinks this is a wild goose chase. So Frank, be very careful how you tread, and what you say about this case. It seems there are some powerful people who want this incident brushed under the carpet. I am not saying, by the way, that I want you to stop investigating. Until we get a conclusive verdict from the Coroner we treat this as a suspicious death. Understood?"

"Loud and clear, boss," said Frank.

"Then get on with it. Dismissed."

Frank was on his second cup of coffee of the morning when he decided to go out for a smoke. Although everybody still smoked in offices back then, Frank liked to go outside for his cigarette. And he liked to go alone. It was his thinking space, he said. So, as he walked round the perimeter of Queen's Gardens, his mind started working on what the DCI had told him that morning – "it seems there are some powerful people who want this incident brushed under the carpet." What did that mean? Obviously somebody was leaning on people higher up the food chain than he was. But who? Was it the Chief Constable's golfing buddy, Mr. High and Mighty Graham Fellows? In policing, sometimes there was doing a favour for a friend. Most police officers had done that. Caught a colleague speeding and let him off with a caution, for instance. But trying to cover up a murder, if that's what it was? That was stretching credulity, and he found it hard to believe of the CC. Fellows would have to have some real dirt on the CC and be blackmailing him to think he could pull that one off.

Then his mind went back to his conversation with Tony yesterday, following their interview with Tom Bielby. They had talked about industrial espionage. What had sparked that off? Oh yes. Tom's comment about "Billy said someone was spying and he wasn't happy about it."

Just then he remembered that something had been niggling at the back of his mind since Saturday morning, before he bumped into Tom Bielby in Stanton's. Now what was it that had been bothering him. Something Tim had said on Friday night that at the time he thought was not significant, but with hindsight maybe it was. Think Frank, think. What did Tim say? "I hear rumours about nefarious things that go on around the Fish Dock." That was it. And when Frank had asked him what nefarious things Tim had said: "I don't know! I've just got this feeling that something big was happening there that was upsetting people but either nobody really knew, or they didn't want to talk about it."

Right, said Frank to himself, his head starting to hurt with trying to unravel the puzzle, I need another brain on this one. Going back into the office he looked for Tony, his DS. Finding him he said: "Tony, I need to borrow you for a few minutes. Come in my office, and shut the door behind you."

"Oh dear, guv. That sounds serious. Am I in for a bollocking?"

"No, no, Tony. Nothing like that. I just need to bounce some ideas off you. My head is spinning with this Billy Bielby case. I need someone with a sharp brain to help me sort some things out."

With that he told Tony what the DCI had said to him that morning and warned him that whatever they said between them must be kept in strictest confidence. Then he outlined his thoughts, following their conversation about industrial espionage, about somebody leaning on someone high up the food chain.

"There is another possibility, guv," said Tony. "Have you thought that it might be someone from the government leaning on the CC?"

Although the Police were operationally independent, so that in theory they could investigate crime by anyone without fear or favour including politicians, in practice every copper knew that there was a murky world where considerations of "national security" took precedence over the independence of the police.

This was 1973, and the IRA had begun a campaign of bombing on the mainland the previous year, and every police officer was on high alert for threats. So Frank supposed it could be a possibility that there was some national security connection to this somewhere. Although he could not, for the life of him, think what connection there might possibly be between the IRA and a trawlerman from Hull. But life was full of strange coincidences, and his motto as a detective was never rule out anything, even the strangest of possibilities.

"Right Tony," said Frank, "I hadn't thought of that, but of course it is a possibility. So now we've got two possible lines of inquiry here. It's becoming more and more clear that someone somewhere would like Billy Bielby's death to be treated as an unfortunate accident. That makes me suspicious. It makes me think that perhaps it wasn't an accident. So who might want to cover it up if it was something more than an accident? Now we've come up with two possible answers to that question. Number one – it might be the trawler owners because there was some sort of industrial espionage going on, and Billy found out something he shouldn't have. Number two – it might be the government, which would suggest it has something to do with national security. Either of those would fit with the information we have from Tom that Billy thought somebody was spying and he wasn't happy about it. If it's the second one, the government, it makes it all the more important that we keep this between ourselves. Don't talk about it with the team and don't write anything down just yet. Because we could both be in danger of losing our jobs here, or worse, and I don't want to put you in that position."

"Right guv. There's one thing that's bothering me here. It's a little loose end that we haven't tied off yet."

"OK. Go on," said Frank.

"Well, do you remember when we interviewed Alan Wilson, the last person to see Billy alive we think? He said that as he was leaving Billy he saw some riggers on the next boat working a night shift."

"I do remember. And I think we asked the Transport Police to follow it up and see if they could find out which company had riggers working that night. They drew a blank. They couldn't find anybody who had any riggers working that night."

"Well, guv, what if they weren't riggers? Or at least not official company riggers? What if they were somebody else up to no good, spying as Tom said, and Billy saw them. Maybe he went snooping around to see what they were up to and saw more than was good for him. Tom said that it was upsetting him, this business about spying. Billy said it was putting people in danger, according to Tom. And Tom also said that Billy said it was no use reporting it to anyone. So maybe he decided to do a bit of private sleuthing and find out more about what was happening."

"Yeah, good thinking Tony. You might be on to something there. So nobody has any knowledge of these "riggers", at least not officially. So what we need to find out now is which boat they were working on. See if you can find out which boat it was tied up next to the Newby Wyke that night. But do it on the quiet. Don't let on to anybody why you need the information. In fact, rather than go through official channels, why don't you pop down to Rayners and see if Alan Wilson is in there. See if he can remember which boat it was he saw the riggers on. You never know, while you're in there you might pick up some useful gossip about spying. Tim said something big was going down and it was upsetting people. Maybe somebody will talk about it."

"OK. I'm on it guv."

"And Tony...thanks. I think we might be getting somewhere. I don't know where but it sort of feels like progress. Now go see what you can find."

CHAPTER 14

Tuesday 31st March 2009

O n her way back to the office the previous day Mary had rung in and asked her team to check any CCTV cameras in the area for a black Range Rover around 10.30pm the previous Monday. She didn't hold out much hope because the only CCTV cameras in the area were likely to be on the motorway and in the town of Goole. And indeed that proved to be the case. When she got into the station the next day, the officer assigned to the task had drawn a total blank.

Turning to Frank who was by her side she said: "Well that's no great surprise, is it?"

"It does tell us one thing though," Frank said, "whoever did this is professional. They knew where the cameras were and they knew they needed to avoid them."

"Why do you say that? Professional? Do you think this was a deliberate hit job?" said Mary.

"Well, look at the facts Mary. You've got what looks like a deliberate hit and run contrived to look like a Road Traffic Accident. The vehicle is totally unidentifiable and it avoids any CCTV just in case. When we find the vehicle it's totally burnt out destroying any potential evidence. I'll bet you forensics will find absolutely nothing on it. The pickup vehicle also avoids any

CCTV. Then you've got Tommy's computer. It seems, from what the Tech boys say, that somebody did a very professional job trying to hide the fact that anything had been wiped from it. Somebody is going to great lengths to be very careful here."

"OK. I buy that. But who? And why? Is there something you haven't told me yet about Billy's case, something that was missing from the files?"

"Oh no," Frank replied, "you would have never found this in the files, even if they were complete – although the fact that they are not adds to my suspicion of a very thorough cover up job. Now who would have the clout to do that? I mean, the fact that a murder is done professionally could mean a contract killing. But who would want to put out a contract on Tommy Bielby? A mild mannered bloke, never in trouble with the law, worked for the Council until he retired, and was doing a bit of local history research. There's nothing in there to suggest that he might have upset somebody who would be willing to pay to have him killed, or that he might have something somebody wanted badly enough to kill him for it."

"OK then. So what are you driving at Frank? You think there's some kind of link between Tommy's death, and his Dad's death over thirty years ago in somewhat suspicious circumstances that was never even proven to be murder. I wouldn't have found anything in the files even if they were complete. So you obviously have some theory about Billy's death that you never put down in writing. It's just a suspicion, a hunch, but what you've seen about Tommy's death is confirming your hunch. So spill the beans. What is it?"

"Well think about it Mary. Billy thought there was something suspicious going on, something to do with spying his brother said. I was leaned on from a great height to stop investigating it as a murder. Who has the power to do that? Then somebody made sure that the crime scene was at sea for long enough that any potential evidence was washed away. Somebody has apparently made official police files disappear. Somebody has the means to do a very professional hit on Tommy Bielby and is tech savvy enough to make what he was looking into disappear and look like it was never there. So I'm thinking somebody in the government, more specifically the security services."

"Whaaat?" said Mary. "You think this is a spook job. You think British security services are running around killing British citizens on their own soil? For what purpose?"

"I don't know Mary. If I knew that I might have cracked the case long ago. I do know that somebody with an awful lot of power and influence is behind all this. I also know from the facts that these are very ruthless people who will stop at nothing to prevent the truth from coming out. So I would advise you to be very careful and watch your back. If the truth is worth killing for twice, then it will be worth killing for again. They will stop at nothing."

"Oh, come on Frank. Don't you think you are being just a little bit paranoid and melodramatic here?"

"Mary I really don't. Think about it. Who else would be able to pull off all of the above? And another thing. What did you say was the name of the boat that Tommy was taking such an interest in? You said he'd bought into conspiracy theories about it."

"Oh yes. The Gaul. What about it?"

"Can you get online with that machine on your desk?" asked Frank pointing to Mary's computer.

"Yes, of course. Why?"

"Just have a look at some of the archive stuff about the Gaul. She went down with all hands in early February 1974 as I recall. She was fishing in the Barents Sea in stormy weather."

"The Barents Sea? I've never heard of it. No idea where it is," said Mary.

"Ah, the benefit of local knowledge. It's off the north coast of Norway. I only know that because my Dad was a skipper and fished those waters. The weather was and is notoriously treacherous there. But, as everybody said at the time, no skipper in his right mind would actually be trying to fish in those conditions. The waves were reported to be up to 9 metres high as I remember. So what else does the marvel of the World Wide Web tell you about her?"

"Well," said Mary skim reading, "she sent in a report by radio to the owners at 9.30am on 8th February that she was "laid and dodging off the North Cape Bank." What does that mean?"

"Laid and dodging would mean that she had laid off fishing and was simply dodging the heaviest waves. So that was somewhere off the North Cape. That's the very top of Norway. What else have we got?"

"She was due to report in at 16.30 that day and failed to report. When she still hadn't reported and nobody had heard anything from her by 10th February a full scale search was launched. It involved a Royal Navy frigate HMS Mohawk, the aircraft carrier HMS Hermes, four other British ships, three Norwegian ships and nineteen trawlers that were in the area, plus maritime patrol aircraft and Sea King helicopters. But they found nothing, no survivors, no wreckage, no trace of anything."

"I believe they called off the search after five days if memory serves. I remember some of the families were quite upset about that. They thought it should have gone on longer until something was found."

"Right, let's see what else this tells us. So she was a state of the art trawler, 18 months old. She was a factory ship, built for catching fish, processing them at sea and then freezing the processed fish. When she disappeared the government said they had done a thorough search of 177,000 square miles and found nothing. The official theory was that she sank after being hit broadside on by a succession of huge waves that caused her to take on so much water she lost buoyancy and sank. One strange thing though is that there was no distress call from her. A MayDay call was never picked up. I mean I know virtually nothing about ships but I do know it's normal in those circumstances where a ship is in distress to issue a MayDay call asking for help from any other vessels in the area. And I believe maritime law says they have to respond to it. Surely she can't have sunk so quickly she didn't have time to send out a MayDay call. I mean doesn't it take some time to take on that much sea water that you sink?"

"It does Mary. You're right. Look I know you are the Senior Investigating Officer on this. But I would like to make a suggestion. I think we may be onto a lead here which is worth following up. I'm also aware that you have other cases requiring your attention. I do know that after much reluctance on the part of the British Government there was finally a proper Inquiry into the loss of the Gaul. I think it was about five years ago. I remember John Prescott was Deputy Prime Minister at the time. He was a former official of the National Union of Seamen and was quite sympathetic to the families of the crew. He helped them to finally get an official inquiry. Why don't I go away and read up on that and see what conclusions they came to and then we can meet up again? And while I'm at it I might also phone a friend who keeps up on these matters. How does that sound?"

"That's great, Frank. Just keep me posted with what you find. And Frank, I'm still not entirely convinced that this has anything to do with the Security Services. But if it does, the same warning applies to you. Be careful and watch your back."

"Oh, I will, Mary, I will."

CHAPTER 15

Tuesday 31st March 2009

J anice was out for the evening at a WI meeting. Frank had sent off for a copy of the Public Inquiry Report when he arrived home. Then he had rung his old friend Tim to ask if he had time to meet up. Tim had suggested they go to one of their old haunts, one of the pubs in the Old Town. However Frank wanted to keep their conversation from listening ears, so they had agreed to meet at Tim's new home. It had been a while since they had seen each other.

Tim had recently been appointed Master of the Hull Charterhouse. The Charterhouse was a very ancient institution dating back to the Middle Ages. There were a number of Charterhouses around the country, Carthusian monasteries, named after the place of origin of the Carthusian order, Chartreuse in France. They all disappeared at the Dissolution of the Monasteries in the 16th century. However the part of the Charterhouse that survived was a separate foundation, an almshouse endowed to provide a home for 13 poor men and 13 poor women, with a priest to provide divine services. And so it continues to this day. The existing buildings date back to the 17th century. The original ones, being outside the city walls, were deliberately blown up during the Civil War to prevent them falling into the hands of the Royalists, and the residents moved inside the city. So after the Civil War the Charterhouse got brand new buildings, and it was in one of these, The Master's House, dating from 1650, that Tim now lived.

Arriving at the door Frank rang the bell and was ushered in by Tim.

"Nice gaffe you've got here" said Frank, eyeing the high ceilings with beautiful ornate coving.

"Come in. Come in," said Tim ushering him into a very comfortably appointed sitting room. "Let me take your coat. It's still quite cold and these old buildings can get a bit draughty so I've lit the fire. Have a seat," he said pointing Frank to one of two deep armchairs sitting either side of a fire blazing in a huge ornate fireplace.

"Now, what will you have? Tea, coffee, beer, a drop of whiskey perhaps?"

"Whiskey sounds good to me, Tim. Thanks."

"I've got some of your favourite, Lagavulin, I hope that's OK. I presume you still take it with just a drop of water, no ice."

"Absolutely. Don't ruin a good single malt with anything else in it."

"Now then," said Tim when they were settled with their drinks in front of the fire, "what's this all about? It sounded a bit mysterious on the phone, a bit cloak and dagger – you not wanting to meet in a public place in case there were listening ears."

"OK. Well, can you remember 35 years back?"

"Hey, I might be getting on a bit but there's nothing wrong with my memory yet. Of course I can. What, in particular are you asking me to remember?"

"Not what so much as who. A trawlerman called Billy Bielby."

"Billy. There's a blast from the past. Was a trawlerman, worked on the old sidewinders. Then he contracted emphysema and had to give up going to sea. But the owners took pity on him and gave him occasional night watchman jobs for a bit of cash in hand. He died in suspicious circumstances. Last seen doing night watchman on the Newby Wyke. You were the investigating officer who picked up the suspicious death case. If I remember rightly it was your first murder case, although it was never officially proven to be a murder."

"Hey, that's not bad, Tim. Maybe you're right. Maybe you haven't got dementia yet. OK. I'm going to tell you something now and it's got to remain strictly between us, partly because it's ongoing Police business, and more importantly for your own safety. Did you know that Billy's son Tommy died recently in a Road Traffic Accident on Hessle Road?"

"Yeah. I saw it reported in the Hull Daily Mail. I thought how sad for Gill. She's still alive you know. She's in her nineties now. Lives in Pickering and Ferens Homes. Losing her husband and then her son in accidents must be devastating. Don't tell me the Police don't think it was an accident?"

"Well, that's the thing," said Frank, "they don't." He went on to outline to Tim everything they had found out so far about Tommy's death, and the fact he appeared to have been working on writing some memoirs which had subsequently disappeared. Then he told Tim about his suspicions about the involvement of British Security.

"Ah, that wouldn't surprise me at all," said Tim, "but go on. Finish your story and then tell me how I can help."

"So, it would appear that Tommy had become a bit obsessed with the disappearance of the Gaul. Apparently he was doing a lot of research about some of the conspiracy theories surrounding her. Now the name of the Gaul came up in our original investigation. She was the boat moored next to the Newby Wyke the night Billy had his 'accident'. We had a report of some riggers working all night on her superstructure, but we were never able to pin down who they were. The owners swore blind they didn't have any staff working that night and we were never able to prove otherwise. The name of the Gaul comes up coincidentally in two murders which are made to appear accidents. I don't buy that. I don't like coincidences. So, to save me a bit of time doing loads and loads of reading, can you tell me everything you know about the Gaul."

"Of course. What do you want to know? She was a state of the art trawler, built to withstand conditions like those in the Barents Sea. She goes down with all hands without even a distress call. The official explanation given at the original Public Inquiry was that she must have taken on too much water and been overwhelmed by the waves hitting her broadside. Nobody who has anything to do with the industry buys that one. The British Government refuses to launch another search for her. The MOD says it would be too expensive and a waste of resources, even though Norwegian trawlers are reporting snagging their nets on an underwater obstruction in the area where she probably went down."

"Remember, this was the height of the Cold War," continued Tim. "These British trawlers were fishing in the area where Soviet warships and submarines were passing through regularly. The Soviets had just launched their new Delta class nuclear subs that could launch ballistic missiles which could hit the US from the seas around the Arctic. There was a lot of paranoia and fear about.

Do you remember me saying to you at the time of Billy's death that something big was going on around the Fish Dock, people were not happy about it and nobody wanted to talk about it? Well it came out eventually that what people were concerned about was rumours about British trawlers being used to spy on the Russians. Of course the Government denied it. Do you remember Bill Rodgers, one of the notorious Gang of Four who defected from the Labour Party to set up the Social Democrats? He was Secretary of State for Transport in the late 1970s. He was asked a question in Parliament about whether the British fishing fleet was being used for "intelligence gathering" about the Russians. He categorically denied it. Said it was totally untrue. It was his words that turned out to be totally untrue. Have you never seen the Channel 4 Dispatches programme they made in 1997?"

Frank shakes his head.

"Frank, where have you been? On another planet?"

"I think I was a bit busy with other police work at the time. I didn't have time to keep up with the fishing industry gossip."

"Oh, this was more than gossip and rumour and innuendo. They interviewed people who worked in the industry. Do you remember Mason Redfearn and Walter Lewis, both skippers? They were interviewed and they gave chapter and verse about the Naval Officer who recruited them, Commander Hardcastle, and even showed some of the equipment he gave them like cameras and ship recognition charts. And of course the bosses, the trawler owners, were in on it. One of them, Tom Boyd, even admitted it on camera.

Anyhow, as I said the Government was very reluctant to launch another search for the Gaul. Apart from being too expensive and a waste of money, they said, there were lots of wrecks of Second World War shipping in the area which would make one wreck very difficult to find.

Unfortunately for the Government their own National Maritime Institute did detailed tests and proved that the Gaul could not have sunk purely due to the size of the waves hitting her, even if they were broadside on. They concluded that something catastrophic must have happened, like the bridge getting damaged by a freak wave and so letting water in.

All of that made the families more determined to find out what really happened to her. They were sure the government was covering something up and really did not want her found. There were all sorts of theories. Some people thought she might have been spying and got caught by the Russians, and the boat was either sunk by a warship or impounded and the crew all put in a jail in Siberia, or even worse shot.

Some people said she could have snagged her nets on a submarine and got dragged under. The subs used to hide under commercial vessels, you know, to avoid detection. Of course the Government said that wasn't possible. But then the MoD had to admit in 1990 that a Royal Navy sub had sunk the Scottish trawler Antares. Mind you, I always thought that theory was a bit far-fetched. The Antares was only a small wooden boat whereas the Gaul was 1100 tons. It would have to be a pretty powerful sub to drag that under. You see the lack of information, of hard facts, spawned all sorts of theories, some of them wilder than others.

Then Channel 4 did their Dispatches documentary in 1997. That totally blew the lid off the Government's claims that she was too difficult to find. The Channel 4 team found the wreck. Now they did have more sophisticated sonar equipment than was available in the 1970s to the original search teams. But guess where they found her? Exactly where the Norwegian fishermen said they would, where they had been reporting snagging their nets on an underwater obstruction. And the nearest World War 2 wreck.... was about 40 miles away."

"I do vaguely remember seeing the news reports that they had actually found the Gaul," said Frank. "So did they learn any more from the wreck?"

"Well there was no sign of catastrophic damage to the bridge, as the National Maritime Institute had suggested. When they found her on the ocean floor she was positioned head in to the wind direction on the day she went down. So that suggests the broadside waves theory is not a runner. The second public inquiry concluded that her position on the sea floor meant nothing as she could have turned during sinking. Make of that what you will.

The documentary makers also interviewed a sailor from HMS Hermes. He said he'd spoken to one of the sailors from HMS Mohawk, the Frigate that was first on the scene, who swore blind that they knew within hours exactly where the Gaul had gone down. They reported it but nobody ever did anything. You can see why people think the Government has something to hide here can't you?"

"I surely can," said Frank. "So from what you just said I take it there was another Public Inquiry eventually?"

"Yeah. There was. Do you want another drink before I carry on with the story? Me, I can ramble on all night on this topic."

"Yes please," said Frank, "and then do carry on. This is all really useful background information for me. It really helps."

When Tim came back with their topped up drinks he continued: "So, you are right. There was public pressure building on the Government now that the wreck had been located. So eventually John Prescott, who was then in charge of Environment and Transport and also Deputy PM, commissioned a Government survey of the wreckage and another Public Inquiry, since it was obvious by this time that the first one had come to an erroneous conclusion.

So they sent down a submersible with cameras and did a thorough survey of the wreck. The Marine Accident Investigation Branch produced a very thorough report looking at all the possible explanations for Gaul sinking. They couldn't find any evidence of substantial damage such as if she'd been in collision with another ship or a sub. It didn't appear that she was fishing at the time so that ruled out getting dragged under by a sub. They even considered the possibility she'd been scuttled but couldn't find any evidence. In the end they came to the conclusion that for some reason she'd got turned abeam to the sea just at the wrong moment and was hit by a series of massive waves on her port side. The first one was what they called a knock-down. It tilted her over to starboard 90 degrees.

That started the flooding. It also shifted the cargo, fish and meal, and all the stowed trawl gear came loose. She would have lost all power because of water flooding the engine room, which explains the lack of a MayDay call. She would normally have righted herself eventually but the loose cargo gave her a list to starboard and then the following waves just overwhelmed her. There were some hatches and a door open which shouldn't have been and that didn't help. So basically they came to much the same conclusion as the previous Inquiry. Naturally the families weren't happy. They didn't think they'd got the whole truth but there was nothing much else anybody could do. I think they resigned themselves then to the fact they were never going to get to the truth."

Just at that moment Frank's mobile rang. Looking at the screen he said: "I'd better take this. It's Janice." Answering the phone he listened with a look of growing concern on his face. "Have you called the Police?" he asked. "Alright love, I'll be home as soon as I can. 10, 15 minutes tops."

"I'm really sorry, Tim. Janice has got in from her WI meeting and the house has been burgled and the dog's gone missing. She's really upset. I'm going to have to go." "Of course, of course," said Tim. "I'll call you a taxi." Five minutes later the cab was there and they bid their farewells.

CHAPTER 16

Tuesday 31st March 2009

Arriving home Frank noticed a Police patrol car with blue lights flashing standing outside the house. Rushing in he ran to Janice and took her in his arms. "Tell me what's happened, love," he said.

"Well you can see for yourself. Just look around. Somebody has been in and made a right mess of the place. They've had everything out of every drawer and cupboard."

"Is anything missing?" asked Frank.

"I don't know. I haven't had chance to look. The only thing I know and care about is that Toby is missing. I swear if somebody's done something to that dog I don't know what I'll do," replied Janice.

"He's probably just run off scared. I can't imagine anybody wanting to steal him. I know he means everything to us but he's hardly a valuable pure breed, is he? Poor mutt."

A uniformed constable arrived in the room at that point and introduced himself. "PC Bennett, sir. I've done a thorough check of the property. There are no intruders still present. It looks like they came in through the back door. There's a pane of glass been removed. We'll check the neighbours to see if anybody saw or heard anything, but being a detached bungalow it's unlikely."

His colleague WPC Saunders came through the front door. "I've done a thorough check around outside. No sign of anyone around. Sorry, my name's PC Saunders. Can I get you a cup of tea or anything?"

"Yes please. That would be really welcome," said Janice.

"And for me too," added Frank. "Thank you."

"Mr. and Mrs. Fogg," said Bennett, "we are going to need statements from both of you describing the events of this evening. We can either do that now if you are feeling up to it, or you can arrange to come into the station and do it. I've reported the burglary to control and it's been logged. They will try to get a Scenes of Crime Officer here tomorrow. But that all depends on what else they have on their plate."

"Yeah, yeah. I know how this goes officer. I am ex-job so I know the pressures on SOCOs. You might have another crime on your hands if we can't find the dog. My knowledge of the law is a bit rusty but I'm pretty sure that's theft."

"It is sir, you're right. That is noted. If you do find the dog please let us know as soon as possible."

"Of course we will, constable."

At that moment there was a knock on the door. Janice rushed to answer it, thinking it might be one of the neighbours who had found Toby. When she answered the door a woman stood there and asked for Frank.

"Frank," she called, "it's for you. Someone called Mary."

Frank came to the door. "Mary? What on earth are you doing here? Do DCIs always respond so quickly to a report of a burglary these days?"

"I heard it on the Police radio, Frank, and I recognised the address as yours. I thought I'd pop round and see what's happened. It might be related to the case and I didn't want some plod brushing it off and just offering to give you advice about beefing up your security. Although maybe you need to do that anyway."

"Come on in, Mary. This is my wife, Janice. Janice, this is Mary, the officer I told you about who's in charge of that case I've been working on."

Mary showed her warrant card to the uniformed officers, which received a "Ma'am" from both of them.

"I'm pleased to meet you Mary," from Janice. "Frank has told me good things about you. Sorry it's not the best of circumstances to be meeting in."

Then Mary said to the uniforms who were looking on in slight bemusement at the sight of a DCI attending a burglary, "Mr. Fogg has been assisting me with another enquiry. I heard about the break in and thought I would pop round and make sure everything was OK. Please don't let me stop you doing whatever you need to do."

"Thanks, Ma'am, I think we are about finished here," said PC Bennett. "Would you like me to lean on the SOCOs to make sure they prioritise coming round as soon as possible. There's a chance they might find fingerprints, or even footprints outside in the light of day."

"Yes please, constable. You can tell them the request comes from me."

"OK. We'll be off then Ma'am. We've just had another shout come in. It's a busy night. Mr. Fogg, please let us know if you find anything is missing so we can add that to the crime report. Do you need a number for an emergency glazier to board up that window?"

"We will let you know if anything is missing Constable Bennett, and I will do a temporary job boarding the window and we'll get a glazier tomorrow. Thanks for your help, both of you," replied Frank.

"Now Frank, Janice, please sit down," said Mary. "There are things we need to talk about."

They sat in the wreckage of what had once been their lovely sitting room, Janice almost in tears as she looked around her.

"First of all," said Mary, "before I leave I would like you to have a good look around and see if anything is missing. On the face of it this looks like a burglary, but as you know Frank, burglars usually take whatever is easy to take and whatever is easy to sell on – cash, jewellery, phones, IT equipment like laptops, TVs if they're not too big. A quick in and out is usually their MO. The quicker they are the less chance of getting caught. So we need to check and find out what is missing, if anything."

"Secondly, Janice, I'm sorry I can't tell you much about the case that Frank and I are working on. But I have a suspicion this break in may be related to it. I need to ask you Frank, did you have anything in the house relating to the case – any old files, notes on a laptop, that sort of thing?"

"No, not that I can think of," said Frank, "and Janice love, I'm so sorry if what I'm working on is the cause of all this. I've been telling everybody else to be careful and watch their backs but I didn't think they would target me."

"Nigh on forty years you were in the Police weren't you. And nothing like this has ever happened before," said Janice. "Why would you have reason to think it might?"

"Well, let's just say, we are up against some very powerful people who have done some very bad things. And it appears that they will stop at nothing to make sure they cover their tracks and nobody gets to the truth of what has been going on."

"In which case," said Janice, "all the more reason why you should go after them and bring them to justice. That's who you are Frank. That's what you've always done."

"I admire your spirit, Janice," chipped in Mary, "but you need to be aware that we seem to be dealing with some very dangerous people and I do not want either of you putting yourselves in harm's way. What if you had come home tonight while they were still here? I dread to think what might have happened. I want you both to think seriously about going to stay somewhere else until this business is over. Do you have any friends or relatives you could go and stay with?"

"Absolutely not," replied Janice. "Over my dead body. I am not moving out of my home. They've taken my lovely dog. They are not going to take my home away from me. Anyway I need to be here in case Toby comes back."

"Well, I think you need to talk it over between you and come to a decision. There's a limit to what protection the Police can offer you, as Frank will know. I can get a patrol car to come round and check on the property regularly. But I cannot offer you round the clock protection or take you into protective custody. So you need to be very aware of the risks. These are dangerous people."

"Now," continued Mary, "can you have a look around the house and see if anything is missing please."

They did so but after a thorough search they could find no trace amongst the chaos of anything actually having been taken, apart from the dog.

"Right," said Mary, "I'm going to go now. I think you will be safe for the rest of the night. I don't think they will come back tonight. Whatever they were looking for, they don't seem to have found it. Try to get some rest, and I will see you in the morning Frank."

"OK boss," said Frank with a mock salute. Mary just grinned at him.

After she had left Frank and Janice took a walk around their garden and then the local neighbourhood, calling for Toby, but could find no sign of him.

When they eventually gave up and came back indoors Janice said she was exhausted and was going to bed. Frank said he would board up the broken window. He also needed a bit of thinking time, and he needed something stronger than tea to drink.

CHAPTER 17

Monday 12th November 1973

Tony arrived back from Rayners looking despondent. "No joy, boss," he said. "Alan Wilson's gone missing. Hasn't been seen since we pulled him in for questioning on Thursday. Nobody has seen hide nor hair of him since then."

"Well, that's a bit odd," said Frank. "It didn't seem like he had anything to hide from us. So he can't be running scared of us. So maybe somebody else has scared him off and made him go to ground. Have a word with Uniform and get the beat bobbies to keep an eye out for him. He's got no fixed address at the moment so it's no good trying to go to his house. But I bet you he won't be far. Somebody will spot him sooner or later. See if you can find out if he's got any family around who he might be staying with."

"Right, Tony, let's try a different approach then. Get on to the Harbourmaster's Office at the Fish Dock and see if they have a record of which vessel was tied up next to the Newby Wyke last Monday night, will you? Meanwhile, I will try Harry Beadle, the Ship's Husband, and see if he can tell me anything. Alright, let's get to it."

Just as Frank was about to pick up his phone to call Beadle it rang. "DI Frank Fogg, how can I help you?"

"Frank, it's Jim Dunhill. Can you come through to my office

please."

"Sure thing, boss. I'm on my way."

When he got there Jim said: "Come in. Sit down Frank. Right, first the good news is there's going to be a Post Mortem tomorrow morning at 9.00am."

"In that case I'd like to be there, sir" interrupted Frank.

"Um, that's a bit of an unusual request. Is there any particular reason why you think you need to be there?"

"Because sir," said Frank, "when I attended the body as it came out of the dock Doc Robinson said there were some suspicious marks around the neck that he wasn't happy about and wanted to take a closer look. I'm anxious to find out what that means, and the sooner I do so the better."

"OK," said Jim, "I will ask the Coroner's Office if it is possible for you to attend. I don't see why not myself. Now the bad news, if you want to call it that, is that Doc Robinson will not be doing the PM. They have assigned a Home Office Pathologist to the task. Don't ask me why, because I don't know. But obviously this case is meriting attention from somewhere."

"And doesn't that make you a bit suspicious, sir? I mean, call me paranoid if you like, but there's something very odd about all this. If this is just a straightforward accidental death, why do we need to bring in the big guns and have a Home Office Pathologist doing the PM? And if it's not a straightforward accidental death, how on earth does anybody with the authority to call in a Home Office Pathologist know that before the PM? Do you see what I'm getting at?"

"I do, Frank, I do. I'm with you on this. Something stinks like rotting fish. But at the moment my hands are tied. The Super has been very clear that he does not want me committing resources to investigating this as a possible murder until after the Coroner has issued a verdict. If it is ruled an Accidental Death, then that's it, case closed as far as he's concerned. And unless and until the Coroner says otherwise, that it is suspicious, I am not to investigate any further."

"But sir, isn't that arse about face? Shouldn't we be treating it as a suspicious death unless and until proven otherwise by a Coroner's verdict?"

"Yes, Frank, of course that would be normal procedure and if the circumstances were different I would be giving you a bollocking if you were not investigating it at this stage. However, as I said, my hands are tied. The Super has given me a very clear order that that is how it has to be. So of course I am obeying that order, like a good DCI does. So I have to tell you Frank that you are to stop investigating Billy Bielby's death, on Police time, until we have the verdict of the Coroner and we have sufficient grounds for believing it is suspicious. Don't let me *catch* you doing anything different or it will be grounds for disciplinary action. Do we understand each other Frank?"

"Yes, sir. Message received loud and clear. You will not catch me investigating Billy Bielby's death on Police time sir. With one exception. I would still like, with your permission, to attend the Post Mortem, sir."

"And like I said, Frank, I will see if I can arrange that. I will let you know. Now I'm sure you've got plenty of other crime to be getting on with investigating, haven't you?"

"Yes, sir."

"Then, get out of here, Frank, and get on with it."

Going back to his own office Frank called in Tony and relayed to him the gist of his conversation with Jim Dunhill.

"Well, that's just great, boss. So what do we do now? Just drop the investigation?" asked Tony.

"Well, you and the rest of the team do, that's for sure. I'm not having any of you get into trouble and having a disciplinary on your record for disobeying orders. As for me, I'm going to do as I was told and not get caught investigating Billy's death on Police time."

"Hold on a minute, boss," replied Tony, "I totally agree with you about not involving the team. But you can't do this on your own, especially in your own time. I'm happy to join you and keep the whole thing under the radar."

"I can't put you in that position, Tony," said Frank. "You've got a job and a career to think of, not to mention your family."

"I appreciate the sentiment, boss, but I think I just volunteered to be put in that position and, without wanting to sound cheeky I think that is my decision to make, don't you?"

"Well, alright then. I do appreciate your loyalty and support Tony. And since you put it like that, your offer is gratefully received, as long as you know what you're letting yourself in for. But if this all goes tits up and the shit should hit the fan, you know nothing about it right. You had no idea what I was up to and I didn't tell you anything. Are we clear?"

"As crystal, boss."

"Now, did you learn anything from the Harbourmaster's Office, while I was being put in my place and told to keep my nose out?"

"As a matter of fact, boss, yes I did. The boat immediately ahead of the Newby Wyke was the Gaul. She's one of the new factory ship stern trawlers. She's only recently transferred to Hull. She was previously registered in North Shields, and belonged to Ranger Fishing, but was transferred to Hull and renamed Gaul when they were taken over by British United Trawlers."

"Oh yeah. I heard about that. So she's one of these what they're calling supertrawlers, that catch the fish, process it at sea and then pack and freeze it, so it's all ready for transport to final destination when it's landed. Right Tony, we'd better drop this for now. I'm sure you've got lots of other crime to solve. I'm going to make a phone call and then try to shift some of this paperwork off my desk, since I'm officially off my murder investigation. Do you fancy a pint after work?"

"Yeah, boss, I'm up for that. See you later."

As Tony left his office Frank put in a call to Dr. Robinson. He was greeted by the receptionist who asked him to hold, and then after a moment the Doc came on the phone. "Now then lad, what can I do for thee?" he asked, betraying his West Yorkshire roots.

"Hi Doc, I was wondering if you fancied a pint after work this evening. There's something I'd like to talk over with you and ideally I'd like to do it before tomorrow morning."

"I can do that lad. This'll be to do with that body we pulled out of the Dock no doubt. Post Mortem scheduled for tomorrow I hear and my services not required. I'll see thee in the Old Black Boy at seven, alright."

"That suits me. Thanks Doc. See you later."

If there was one thing Frank was not good at it was waiting. However, on this occasion there was no alternative. So, in order to try to distract himself, he pulled out a pile of paperwork from his in-tray and tried to concentrate on the various reports of which he needed to be aware, and the forms he needed to authorise. But his mind was not on the job. It kept coming back to Billy Bielby. What did you see Billy? And where did you see it? And why is somebody so anxious to shut down this investigation before it begins. He began running through in his mind and making a list of the things that had made him suspicious about this death.

Number one – Doc Robinson had said at the scene that there were some suspicious marks on the neck which warranted further investigation.

Two – the reluctance of the owners to bring back the Newby Wyke, which was a potential scene of a crime. Of course that could be explained on financial grounds, but he would have expected to get more backing from his bosses to insist upon it.

Three – he had been warned off conducting this investigation several times now and it seemed someone high up was determined to shut it down.

Four – the length of time it had taken to arrange a Post-Mortem and the fact that a Home Office pathologist had been brought in to do it. Whilst this was not unusual in the case of a murder where evidence from the PM could be crucial at a trial, and the Pathologist might be called as an expert witness, the high-ups were insisting this was an accidental death unless it could be proved otherwise. Had they brought in the pathologist to prove otherwise, or just the opposite, to prove that it was an accidental death and hush up any evidence to the contrary?

Five – the feeling that something "big" was going on at the Fish Dock and people were not happy about it. Tom Bielby had mentioned that someone was spying and Billy knew something about it. His friend Tim had mentioned the gossip and rumour about something happening but nobody being willing to talk about it.

Six – now Alan Wilson had disappeared. He had not been seen since talking to them last Thursday.

All of which did not add up to any proof of anything. But it did add up, as Jim had put it, to a stink of rotting fish. Something was not right somewhere, and he could not get the stink out of his nostrils. He was going to have to find out what was causing it.

CHAPTER 18

Wednesday 1st April 2009

The next morning Frank awoke after a fitful sleep in which he had dreamed of his house being burgled in the middle of the night and him getting up and chasing the burglars down the street semi-naked. When he got up and went to make coffee for himself and Janice, he noticed what a beautiful spring morning it was, and thought to himself, walking the dog will be a pleasure this morning. And then it hit him. There was no Toby there to greet him this morning because he had either been scared away, kidnapped, or worse killed. His anger rose as he thought about someone invading their home, their safe space, their sanctuary; about someone harming their dog; about what might have happened to either of them if they had walked in on the burglary. And then he looked around and saw the devastation wreaked on their lovely home by someone looking for something which was not there. Never, in all his years in the Police, had anything like this happened to him. Sure he had had threats from criminals he had arrested and put behind bars. That went with the territory. But his home and his personal space had never been invaded like this before. It made him reflect that in his younger days as a uniformed bobby he had perhaps not been as sympathetic as he should have been with some of the victims of burglary he had dealt with. You never really understand until you have walked in someone else's shoes. By the time he reached Queen's Gardens Police Station that morning his blood was boiling and he was even more determined to find out who was behind all this and bring them to justice. Mary was waiting for him with fresh coffee brewed. They sat down to review where they had got to so far with their investigation.

"Right," said Mary getting up from her desk to write on the large white board on the wall, "here's what we've got so far. Two suspicious deaths, Billy Bielby and Tommy Bielby. No concrete evidence that either of them was murdered, just a cloud of suspicious circumstances surrounding their deaths. So what links them Frank? Come on, let's think out loud here. No suggestion is too outrageous not to at least think about."

"Well, there's family, obviously," said Frank. "Somebody could be targeting the family. But the deaths are 36 years apart. If somebody's got a vendetta against them and is targeting the family, why wait that long between murders? Why not do them both quickly?"

"OK, said Mary, writing FAMILY on the board and drawing a box round it. "So what else have we got that links them then?"

"Well, this trawler, the Gaul, seems to feature in both cases. Billy, we think, saw something going on aboard the Gaul that he was not supposed to see. Tommy was digging into what happened to the Gaul and investigating some of the conspiracy theories surrounding it. Maybe he found something out that he wasn't supposed to know. Maybe his Dad even wrote something down and Billy found it and was using it in his memoirs? Who knows?"

"Well if that's the case, where is it now? We know somebody did a pretty good job of erasing the memory on Tommy's laptop. But if Billy wrote something down back in the '70s it sure was not electronic. It will have been on a piece of paper or in a book somewhere. Did they find it? There was no evidence of anybody ransacking Tommy's flat looking for something."

"I don't know, Mary. Maybe it's worth getting a team to have another thorough search of Tommy's flat to see if we missed anything the first time."

"Good idea. I'll get onto that," said Mary, again writing GAUL in a box and an arrow leading to SEARCH PROPERTY. "Anything else?"

"Well, I think the murders, sorry "deaths", are linked. I don't mean that the same person carried them out necessarily. But both were pretty professional jobs made to look like accidents. Then there's the fact that somebody has gone to great lengths to make sure that there was very little evidence left for us to investigate in either case. You know what I mean? In Billy's case the potential crime scene, the Newby Wyke, was sent off to Iceland fishing, thus destroying any potential evidence there. In Tommy's case the vehicle that mowed him down was torched, effectively destroying any conclusive proof that it was the murder vehicle, and certainly giving us little chance of proving who was in it at the time. Which reminds me, I don't suppose you have had anything back from forensics on the vehicle yet?"

"No, I haven't," said Mary, writing down PROFESSIONAL in a box, and then CHASE FORENSICS. "I'll do it today but I know they are pretty snowed under at the moment. I'll try and put a rush on it anyway."

"One thing that's puzzling me," said Frank, "is, given they did such a professional job on the murders, why break in to my house and leave such a mess and make it so obvious they had burgled it?"

"It's a warning, Frank. They wanted you to know that they had been in there. They want to unsettle you, and they want to warn you off pursuing the case any further. I'm a serving Police officer so it's a bit more difficult to warn me off. They'd have to put pressure on my superiors and that might arouse suspicion. But you're a civilian. I think they are hoping you might take the hint and back off."

"In that case they don't know me very well Mary. It doesn't scare me. It just makes me very angry and that makes me even more determined to get to the bottom of this. I'm not backing off. Whoever is behind this is just piling one crime on another and I'm not going to tolerate it. I never could stand criminals who were too big for their boots and thought they could run rings round the Police and be untouchable. I'm not going to start being frightened of them now. They are going to be brought to justice, whoever *they* are."

At that moment the phone on Mary's desk rang. She picked it up and answered "DCI Fowler". A lovely lowland Scottish brogue came over the phone and the voice identified itself: "Iain Stewart here, Ma'am, Senior Accident Investigator with the force. I've been looking at that burned out Land Rover that the Traffic boys brought in on Monday. I think I might have found something and they said you wanted to know a.s.a.p. if I did."

"Yes Iain, I did. Thanks for ringing me. Are you at Queen's Gardens Nick?"

"Aye, Ma'am. In the garage out the back."

"Then I'll come down and bring somebody with me who needs to hear whatever it is you have to tell me."

"Okay, Ma'am. See you in a few minutes.

Frank and Mary made their way down to the garage which was very cramped. Here, in this small space, Humberside Police maintained a lot of their vehicle fleet, and also conducted forensic examination of vehicles which had been involved in accidents or crimes. It was not hard to identify the vehicle they were looking for and as they made their way over to it, a figure clad in a white boiler suit made his way over to them. "Iain Stewart, Ma'am," he announced.

"Pleased to meet you Iain. I'm DCI Mary Fowler and this is Frank Fogg who is assisting me with this investigation. Now, what have you got for us, Iain?"

"Well, Ma'am, as you can see for yourselves, the vehicle was pretty comprehensively "trashed", to use a technical term, by the fire. There's no doubt it was deliberate. There are traces of accelerant which I believe to be petrol all over the inside and the outside. So somebody poured petrol all over, in and out, and set it on fire. And they did a pretty good job of destroying any evidence. If you come round here and look at the front of the vehicle" he said beckoning them to follow, "you can quite clearly see the damage to the vehicle bonnet. I can say with a high degree of certainty that that was caused by an impact with a human body. What's more, judging by the evidence from the scene, the size and weight of the victim and the throw distance of the body, I can be about 90% certain that this vehicle was the one involved in your hit and run accident on Hessle Road

on the 3rd. But the fire has destroyed any chance of any forensic evidence, hair, fibres, that sort of thing being left on the vehicle. Which is presumably why it was started. Now, whoever was driving this vehicle went to great lengths to cover their tracks. Clearly they are not stupid. There were no registration plates on the vehicle, so obviously they were removed before the fire started, and presumably taken away from the scene by the driver. That's an obvious move which most criminals are aware of these days. This one went a step further and had filed off the VIN number from the vehicle chassis. We see that quite a bit with professional car thieves who are stealing motors to sell on on the black market. But it's a lot less usual with a vehicle that has been involved in an accident or a crime."

"OK Iain. That's the bad news. But I'm guessing you've got something else to tell us and I'm hoping it might be good news," said Mary.

"Well, I hope so too," said Iain noncommittally. "You see, I don't know if the driver was aware of this, possibly not, but this vehicle was fitted with a GPS tracking device. The owner was obviously careful, and wanted to be able to track the vehicle if it was lost or stolen."

"OK," chimed in Frank, "but we know where the vehicle is. How does that help us?"

"I'm coming to that sir," replied Iain. "So, most of the electronics on the vehicle were destroyed by the fire. But the GPS tracker comes in an extremely durable "black box", a bit like the black box flight recorders that are designed to survive plane crashes. And it is, as far as I can tell, intact and functioning."

"I still don't see how that helps us," said Frank.

"Well, it works like this," explained Iain. "Each of these GPS trackers has a unique digital footprint. It is constantly sending a signal to a remote monitoring station somewhere, even when the vehicle is switched off and inactive. So if we can find out the make and model number of this device we can find out where it is sending that signal to. Now it's pretty damaged on the outside, but I think I can get our tech boys to identify it. If they can do that, the monitoring station will be able to tell us the owner of the vehicle, and probably give us a mobile phone number to which it sends alerts."

"Wow," said Mary. "That's brilliant. Good work Iain. I didn't even know such things existed. Welcome to the modern world of high-tech policing eh? So, please, will you get onto that straight away and ask the techies to let me know as soon as they come up with any information. And tell them not to be fobbed off with any excuses about not disclosing information due to data protection. This was no accident. This is now a murder inquiry and that takes precedence over data protection. If necessary we can get a warrant to secure the information but it's always easier and quicker if they divulge it voluntarily."

"Yes, Ma'am. I'll get onto it straight away."

CHAPTER 19

Monday 12th November 1973

Frank and Tony arrived in the snug at the Black Boy just after seven o'clock. Ye Olde Black Boy was one of the few surviving pubs out of what had once been dozens in Hull's High Street, in a time before the docks were built when the River Hull was the centre of the port of Hull. As they walked in a familiar voice called from the corner: "Now then, lad, what's tha' 'avin'?" followed by "O, hello young Tony, what's yours then?" They sat down with their drinks in the corner, the only occupants of the snug, which suited Frank just fine.

"Now then, you two, what can I do for thee? It all feels a bit cloak and dagger this, meetin' in't pub after work to talk about work. What's up?" Doc Robinson proceeded to take out his pipe, fill it with tobacco and light up, blowing clouds of smoke over them.

Frank was convinced that the Doc affected his broad West Riding accent to emphasise his roots. He liked to come across as a bit of a "character" but Frank knew that beneath the eccentricities he was very good at what he did.

"Look, Doc, I don't want to get you in any bother" said Frank, "so before we begin, if you are uncomfortable with my questions at any point just say so."

"Aye, I will, lad, I will. You know me. Speak my mind and all that."

"Right, well, first off, do you have any idea who brought in the Home Office pathologist to do the autopsy, and why?"

"Nay, lad, I don't. I'm assuming it were't Coroner who made that decision but I don't know why, although I have my suspicions."

"Would you mind telling me what they are?" asked Frank.

"Well, I think Coroner, much as I get on wi' 'im, thinks I'm too cosy wi' you lot. So he thinks that I'll talk too much to you about whatever I find. I think he's probably been got at and somebody wants to keep it all under wraps and produce a nice neat conclusion that ticks the box so the Coroner can say it were an accidental death."

"That's a bit of an insult to your professional capability isn't it?"

"Ey, lad, I don't take it personally. I'm used to having Home Office pathologists take over when it's likely to go to trial and they have to give evidence. I wouldn't want to be standing up in court doing that anyway. No, actually I think in this case it's a backhanded compliment. Coroner thinks I'm too good at my job, too thorough, and I might find something that goes against their foregone conclusion. So he wants me keeping my nose out of it."

"So, what does he think you might find?" asked Frank.

"Well now, it's funny you should ask that, because, as you know, I thought there was something a bit off about the body when it was fished out of the dock, something a bit fishy if you'll pardon the pun. Anyhow, 'e were too muddy and covered in slime to be able to do a proper examination at the scene. But I happened to be in the morgue with another stiff yesterday. I knew by then the technicians would have cleaned our Billy up, so I took the opportunity to take a sneaky peek at him. Oh, don't worry. I haven't tampered wi' the evidence and the Home Office pathologist will never know I've looked. And the morgue technicians are sworn to secrecy. I bribe them with a bottle of whiskey each at Christmas."

"Well, come on then, Doc. Don't keep us in suspense," interrupted Tony. "What did you find?"

"Ah, the impatience of the young" sighed Doc Robinson, deliberately taking his time refilling and relighting his pipe. "Never ruin a good story by getting to the punch line too quick, lad."

"Alright Doc, you've had your fun," said Frank. "Come on. Spill the beans. Don't keep us on tenterhooks all night. We've got crimes to solve you know."

"Alright. Alright," said Doc holding up his hands in surrender. "I give in. It's a fair cop. So I think I mentioned to you at the scene that there was what looked like very faint bruising around his neck. It was a bit more visible, although not very much, once he was cleaned up. It obviously wasn't enough to indicate manual strangulation, or hanging. But it did make me suspicious. So I've been racking my brains trying to think what might cause such marks. The only thing I could think of, and I've seen it once before in a case of autoerotic asphysxiation..."

"You what?" interrupted Tony again.

"Autoerotic asphyxiation, young man. My, you have a lot to learn about the complexities of human nature, don't you. It means strangling or suffocating yourself to heighten sexual arousal and orgasm. It sounds outlandish but it's more common than you think. The only trouble is it more often than not goes horribly wrong. People don't mean to kill themselves. But depriving your brain of oxygen gives you a high. That's what heightens the sexual pleasure. And then when they get to the point of orgasm they may be too weak or have lost too much consciousness to be able to stop the strangling or suffocation and they die.

Anyhow, as I were saying before I were so rudely interrupted" said Doc, winking at Tony as he said it, "I saw this case of autoerotic asphyxiation once. It was called a suicide but I knew it weren't. A young man had put a plastic bag over his head and suffocated himself, apparently. I found out afterwards that the family had found him naked from the waist down and surrounded by porn mags. But they'd dressed him and taken away the mags before they called the ambulance. Anyway the point is, he had similar slight bruising around his neck from pulling the plastic bag tight to stop the air getting in."

"But can't you tell when someone has been suffocated?" asked Frank. "Don't they get that haemorrhaging in the eyes?"

"Ah, well done Inspector. I can see you have done your homework. Petechial haemorrhaging. Well, yes. You would normally expect to see some in a case of suffocation. But their absence is not conclusive proof that it wasn't a case of suffocation. Petechial haemorrhages may be absent altogether, or they may be so tiny they are not visible to the naked eye. I have not had chance to examine his eyes with a magnifying glass, so I can't say for certain that there are none, but I couldn't see any with the naked eye. It'll be interesting to see if our pathologist looks for them tomorrow."

"OK. So what else should he be looking for?" asked Frank. "Because, as you know I am attending the Post Mortem and I want to make sure that I check up on what he is doing."

"Be very careful doing that Frank," said Doc. "They're a touchy lot, Home Office pathologists. He will not take kindly to being told how to do his job by a plod."

"Well, I'm not bothered about his personal feelings. I'm bothered about getting justice for Billy Bielby, that's all," said Frank.

"All I'm saying, Frank, is, be careful how you talk to the pathologist otherwise they'll just clam up on you and you'll get nothing from them and you'll have to wait for their official report, which will probably take weeks to come, especially if you upset them."

"Alright, Doc. Your warning is noted. Now back to my question, what else should I expect them to look for?"

"Well, there's the bleedin' obvious. They should be checking for water in the lungs. Obviously if there is none then he didn't drown and he was dead before he went in the water. Then there are natural causes. Did he die of a heart attack, stroke, brain haemorrhage, that sort of thing? Any of those could mean he was dead before hitting the water. Check for signs of physical assault or a struggle. You know the kind of thing, bruising, wounds etc. Check under the fingernails for skin or blood from an assailant. Then I would of course expect them to check his bloods. You'll find some alcohol in there because we know he was drinking before he died. They need to check for any signs of any drugs, to see if he was drugged in some way before he was overpowered; or if he self-administered anything that might have lead to his death. Come on Frank, you know the drill. You don't need me to tell you all this by now."

"OK Doc. Thanks. I'm just checking to make sure I don't miss anything."

"Can we just go back to the issue of petechial haemorrhaging?" asked Tony. "You suggested that haemorrhages would not necessarily be present in a case of suffocation. Can you estimate how often you would be likely to see them?"

"Ah, good question, Tony. We'll make a policeman of you yet. I would guess about eight out of ten cases they would be there. I'm not bang up to date on the science behind all this. But what I would stress is that petechial haemorrhages are not a reliable guide one way or the other. Just because they are present does not mean the cause of death must have been strangulation or suffocation. There are a number of other conditions that can cause them. And the lack of any evidence of petechiae does not rule out strangulation or suffocation as a cause of death."

"That's brilliant, Doc. Thank you for all your help. Now let me get you another drink, and then I think we're going to have to call it a night."

CHAPTER 20

Wednesday 1st April 2009

That Wednesday evening Frank found himself back at Tim's place at the Charterhouse. He had rung Tim during the day to update him on the events of the previous evening. Tim had insisted that he had more to tell him that was of relevance to the case. Frank was very reluctant to leave Janice again so soon after their home had been invaded. However she assured him that she would be fine. She would get one of her friends to come round while Frank was out, and anyway she was now invested in this matter, having had her home wrecked. So she was now as determined as Frank was that whoever did this would suffer the consequences.

So it was that Frank found himself sitting supping whiskey with Tim again whilst Tim continued his interrupted tale.

"So where was I?" asked Tim.

"I think you'd just finished telling me about the outcome of the second Public Inquiry into the Gaul sinking. From what you told me it sounded like the explanation they came up with was just about plausible and the only one that fitted with the known facts. But it obviously did not satisfy the families and left them with lots of unanswered questions."

"Indeed it did, my friend. Indeed it did. One of the big questions which has never to this day been satisfactorily answered is why on earth it took the British government with all the resources at its disposal so long to find the wreck of the Gaul. They had, or could have had if they had listened to the locals, a pretty good idea of where she would be. An investigative journalist for TV, with no maritime experience, using a few charts and a chartered ex-ferry boat, managed to find it within two days at a cost of £50,000. That rather puts into perspective the government's excuses that they didn't know where to look, it would be prohibitively expensive, there were too many other wrecks in the area etc. etc. That makes you think, and it certainly made the crew's families think, that the government didn't want it found. Now you have to ask yourself why that would be. Although the government have admitted that British trawlers were used in spying on the Russians during the Cold War, they have consistently denied that the Gaul was involved in any surveillance activities on that particular trip. They've also said that such activities had ceased by the time Gaul went missing, although I take such denials with a pinch of salt given their track record of lying and covering up previously.

That leads me on to the other bit of a mystery surrounding the Gaul which some of the families still want explanations for. That is SOSUS cables. What is a SOSUS cable you may ask? It stands for SOund SUrveillance System. It was, and still is, a supposedly top secret US system for the tracking of submarines. It involves the installation of arrays of sonar devices, underwater listening devices, connected by cables to listening stations on the shore. Nobody knows exactly where these listening devices are, but we know of their existence. They were of particular importance during the Cold War in tracking Soviet submarine movements through the Greenland-Iceland-UK gap and into the North Atlantic. Now what has that got to do with the Gaul? Well, when the Dispatches team found the wreck they also found on the seabed what looked like a cable. It was too thick to be a hawser from the boat or one of the trawl cables. Nobody had any idea what it was. Could it have been a SOSUS cable? One theory was that the Gaul got her nets tangled in a SOSUS cable while fishing and got dragged under. That doesn't stand up given the physical evidence from the wreck which suggests she wasn't fishing when she went down. But is it a coincidence that she went down almost on top of what may well be a SOSUS cable? Who knows? And the other strange thing is that this cable was clearly there when the Dispatches Team sent their submersible down there and found the wreck. But strangely a few years later when the Commissioner of Wrecks sent their own cameras down there, lo and behold, they couldn't find any trace of the said cable. All they could find on the bottom around the wreck was trawl gear. They came to the conclusion that the Dispatches Team must have mistaken the cable they saw for discarded cables from trawl gear, which sounds a bit unlikely to me.

So where does all that get us in terms of the mystery of the Gaul, you might ask. The answer, as far as I can see, is not very far. There are still lots of unanswered questions, and I don't see how we are ever going to get any answers unless somebody at some stage raises the wreck. That might get us a little closer to the truth."

"Right. OK," said Frank. "So that's where we're up to with the Gaul. It seems to be leading us into a bit of a cul-de-sac. So, putting my detective's hat on for a minute, it's a pretty fair assumption that for some reason the government did not want the wreck of the Gaul found. And they now want the world to think that the whole issue has been put to bed following the result of the second Public Inquiry which concluded that she sank in high seas. It would appear that Tommy Bielby was murdered because he may have found out something which the government continue to want to keep secret. It would appear, from what we know, that the Gaul has now given up her secrets, apart from the bodies of most of the crew of course. So there's not a lot left about the Gaul to keep secret, is there? Tell me if I'm barking up the wrong tree here. But I wonder if there's something else down there that the government does not want anybody to find?"

"Well, like what?" asked Tim. "If there was a SOSUS cable down there it would appear that there is not any more. So what else might they not want anybody to find?"

"Oh, I don't know, Tim. Maybe a lost submarine? Did you know that there are 11 nuclear submarines sitting at the bottom of the ocean in various places around the world, all the result of accidents which governments don't want you to know about. I know there was speculation at the time that the Gaul might have hit a submarine, but I take it there was no evidence of that on the wreck?"

"No there wasn't. And that was one of the things they looked for. Anyway don't you think if there was another vessel down there the Dispatches Team would have found it?"

"Not necessarily, Tim. Think about it. They only searched for two days and they were looking for one specific thing and they found it. Of course they gave up searching once they found it. Their radar or sonar or whatever it was might have missed anything else, or maybe it wasn't big enough to be of interest. Then they sent the submersible with the cameras down to identify what they'd found and sure enough it was the Gaul. But they only searched the immediate area around the Gaul. The visibility is pretty poor down there so if there was something else on the seabed over a few metres away they would not have seen it."

"But what else would be on the seabed?" asked Tim.

"Well logically, if it is something the government does not want found, it's got to be either something they put there in the first place, which means it's got to be some bit of kit for spying on the Russians; or it must be something that was on the surface, like another ship; or I suppose it could even be an aircraft that ditched into the sea and sank. I don't know. This is all speculation and conjecture. But remember, my dear Watson, what Sherlock Holmes said: 'When you have eliminated the impossible, whatever remains, however improbable, must be the truth.'"

"That's all very well, Sherlock," responded Tim, "but in this case we are not going to get the suspect, the British Government, to sit down and have a cosy chat with us and confess to everything, are we?"

"That's very true, Tim," said Frank with a grin. "Perhaps what we need is our very own Mycroft at the heart of the government to find out what we need to know. Although the Mycroft Holmes of the stories would probably have told us it was a matter of national security, and was on a 'need to know' basis, and we don't need to know."

"That reminds me," said Tim, "I was talking to one of our residents earlier on today. He's only been with us a few weeks. He's a retired trawler skipper, Charlie Broom. We got to reminiscing about the old days, as most of us in here do. Charlie skippered the Gaul a couple of trips when she was sailing out of North Shields and he said it is perfectly plausible that she lost her buoyancy because water got in the hold through the duff and offal chutes. He remembers those well. What he objected to was the conclusion of the inquiry that it was the crew's fault and in particular the skipper, for not making sure the hatches were secured properly before the seas got too high. He remembered a trip to Iceland with the Gaul. They were fishing and the seas got really high so they had to haul in the nets and start dodging the waves. He says they were well aware of the danger presented by seawater coming down the duff and offal chutes and they made sure they secured the hatches. But after about half an hour the coxswain who was on the helm reported that she was getting a bit sluggish and unresponsive. They asked the Second Engineer to have a look and see if there was anything wrong with the steering gear and he reported back that the hold was awash with seawater. Apparently the hatches on the duff and offal chutes had come unfastened. He said they had a hell of a job getting them fastened again because of the wind and the waves, and nearly lost one of the crew overboard in the process."

"Why didn't he give this evidence to the Inquiry?" asked Frank.

"He was going to, but unfortunately he had a massive stroke a couple of weeks before the Inquiry opened and he was rendered speechless for months. By the time he got his speech back, after lots of therapy, the Inquiry was all done and dusted and had reached their conclusions. He didn't think at that point there was anything he could do to make them change their minds, so he's just kept quiet about it. But he feels really bad that the skipper and crew got blamed for it. I think telling me about it was by way of a confession, you know, getting the whole thing off his chest."

"Yeah, I can see that. So that in a way confirms that the Gaul sinking was an accident, not deliberate. Did he have anything else interesting to say?"

"Oh, yes. He said that when he was skippering he was approached by the owners about spying on the Russians. He flatly refused. He said he was too well aware of what might happen, not just to him but to the crew, if they got caught by the Russians. He didn't want to take responsibility for his crew all ending up in a Siberian gulag for the rest of their lives, or worse still, getting shot, for the sake of a bit of information the Navy could get in some other way. He was fortunate because the owners were understanding and didn't press the issue. Some of the other trawler owners would have blacklisted him and said you're never sailing with us again. He was within his rights of course because once that boat leaves port the skipper is entirely responsible for the ship and its crew and their safety. His word is law at sea. But not all the trawler owners were so understanding."

"This Charlie sounds like an interesting guy. I'd like to have a word with him and see what else he remembers, especially about the spying stuff. Do you think he might be willing to sit and have a yarn with me?" asked Frank.

"I can ask," replied Tim. "I don't see why not. He seems a friendly and talkative kind of chap. He'll probably be pleased to have the opportunity to have a yarn about the old days with somebody."

"OK. Thanks, Tim, for all your help with this. I really do appreciate it. Now I really should get going, make sure that Janice is OK. I don't want to leave her all evening in the present circumstances."

"No, no. Of course not. You crack on mate. Good to see you, as always, and I'll see you soon. I'll ring and let you know what our friend says about seeing you."

"That's great Tim. Thanks. See you." And with that he was off.

CHAPTER 21

Tuesday 13th November 1973

Discretion was the better part of valour, Frank decided, as he waited outside the morgue for the Pathologist to turn up. So he would sit in a corner and observe and say nothing. He'd got Jim Dunlop to spin the Coroner a yarn about him needing to be at the autopsy for professional development purposes. The Coroner seemed to have bought this. Whether the Pathologist would was another matter. As he was musing on this a large saloon car swept around the corner into the car park, a Bentley Corniche, if he was not very much mistaken. The car stopped and out stepped a short, very dapper man, dressed in a camel overcoat, what was clearly a Saville Row suit, dicky bow tie, and some very expensive looking Italian shoes.

Frank thought he had better go and introduce himself so he walked up, holding out his hand, and said: "Detective Inspector Frank Fogg, sir, pleased to meet you."

"Professor Sir Charles Jamieson," the other responded in a plummy voice. "So you must be our policeman who wants to observe my autopsy. I don't know if I should be flattered by that or not. What do you think?"

Don't respond to that, thought Frank to himself. He's fishing for information, trying to find out why I'm here. "I thought it would be beneficial for my professional development sir. It's not every day we have an autopsy performed by a Home Office Pathologist in this neck of the woods. So I thought it would be a good opportunity to learn a little more about the process from a skilled professional. I hope that's alright with you. It would be really helpful to me if you could talk me through what you are doing as you go along so that I can take some notes for future reference."

"Just like having the medical students in one of my autopsies, eh, except that they have to invest the time coming to my lectures beforehand so that they can recognise what I am doing without me having to talk them through it. Well, OK my dear fellow. But I'm rather afraid you are wasting your time with this one. From what I have been told in advance you are not going to learn much from this corpse – a pretty straightforward case of either drowning or natural causes I would say."

Frank was sorely tempted to ask if it wasn't just a teeny bit premature to come to such a conclusion before even seeing the body. But he held his tongue. He just made a mental note to remember this remark for later. He wondered what the Professor would say to one of his students who made such a remark.

Frank went to sit on one side during the autopsy, armed with his packet of trusty Fisherman's Friends. He was not bothered by the sight of blood and guts. He had been 'blooded' early on in his career as a detective when his DI had sent him to his first autopsy. He had found that he could distance himself from the cutting up of a body. If you imagined it as a slab of meat at the butcher's rather than something that had once been a human being, it helped. What always got to him and made him feel queasy was the smell. Decomposing human flesh has a particular odour which once smelled is never forgotten, and it is an odour which lingers in the nostrils long after the presence of the offending article has been removed. Of course this smell got much worse when a pathologist opened up the stomach and intestines. A much older DC had given him a tip after his first experience: "Always take a pack of Fisherman's Friends with you lad. That way you can't smell a thing." And it was true. It worked for him.

Anyhow, having decided to behave himself, Frank took a seat to one side of the Autopsy Room to observe and listen to the Pathologist. Having scrubbed up and dressed appropriately Jamieson came in and handed a Dictaphone to one of the assistants, asking him to hold it up so that he could dictate notes whilst he was working. He then proceeded to give the body a thorough and meticulous external examination, beginning at the feet and working his way upwards. He noted that there were signs of decomposition due to being in the water for approximately three days. He said that it would be impossible to give a time of death with any exactitude since the body was not discovered for several days after having entered the water. He paused at the neck and Frank was interested to see what he would make of the bruising but he simply noted that there was some very faint bruising barely visible to the naked eye. He then examined the face and noted some signs of congestion in the facial tissue.

Jamieson then carefully examined the eyes. Frank knew that this was partly because changes in the eye can be an important indicator of the time of death. But he also surmised that he was checking for petechial haemorrhaging. This assumption proved to be correct when Jamieson announced for his notes that there was no sign of any haemorrhaging. Although Frank noted that he had only looked with the naked eye. He then asked for the body to be turned over and conducted an equally careful examination of the back. Again according to his dictated notes he appeared to find no particular cause for concern. The fingernails, toenails and hair were all examined for traces of anything such as skin or dirt under the fingernails. Given that the body had been in the water of the dock for several days it was unsurprising that there was no trace evidence of anything except the contents of the water in the dock.

Having completed his post-mortem examination Jamieson then turned to the autopsy proper, the dissection of the body. Frank tensed a little as Jamieson picked up his scalpel and made his Y-incision in the front of the body. The body was opened up and the ribs cracked. The upper internal organs, the lungs, heart, oesophagus and trachea were all removed, examined, weighed and set aside for possible dissection if need be later. Frank could tell from the way Jamieson handled the lungs that there did not appear to be any water in them, which suggested Billy had not drowned.

Jamieson then moved on to the organs from the lower abdominal cavity, the liver, spleen, kidneys, stomach and intestines. A slice of each organ was taken for examination. It always amazed Frank just how much stuff was packed into the inside of a human body. By now the smell was getting stronger and stronger. Frank knew that when the pathologist opened the stomach to examine the stomach contents it would be too much for him.

Fortunately Jamieson turned next to the head. Making an incision across the top of the scalp from one ear to the other he proceeded to take the scalp from the top of the skull and down across the face revealing the skull. Taking his bone saw he made a wedge shaped hole in the skull to reveal the brain. The brain was then carefully removed, weighed and set aside for possible dissection.

At this point Frank decided he had had enough and needed some fresh air. Even his trusty Fisherman's Friends were not enough to prevent the stench beginning to turn his stomach. He wished he had passed on breakfast this morning. As he made to get up the pathologist turned to him with a slight sneer on his face and said: "All getting too much for you, is it Inspector? I thought you northern men were made of tougher stuff."

"As a matter of fact, Professor," said Frank with the emphasis on the word Professor, "it is. I'm going outside for some fresh air for a few minutes. I would be very grateful if you could spare me a few minutes when you have finished, sir," he said returning to respectful mode, "just to let me know your preliminary thoughts on a time and cause of death. It would greatly help my investigation if I could know as soon as possible. I appreciate that I will need to wait for your full report but preliminary conclusions are always helpful."

"Of course, of course my dear fellow," said the Professor affably. "That's no problem. I'm sure I can save you a lot of time. I will give you a shout when I have finished with the body and am writing up my notes."

"Thank you, sir," said Frank and, breathing a sigh of relief, left the room.

He walked through the main doors of the morgue and went to stand outside. The weather outside suited his mood. It was overcast, cold and damp. There was not a breath of wind and the water just hung in the air. It was one of those days when a strong smell rose from the Humber and blanketed the whole of the city with a foul smelling miasma. His excuse of needing some fresh air was only partly true. Actually what he really needed was a cigarette. Lighting up, his thoughts turned to another occasion when he had felt as queasy as this.

On his one and only trip on a trawler as a deckie learner and cook, at the age of 16, by the time they had passed down the Humber and rounded Spurn Point and were travelling north past Bridlington Bay, he was convinced they were in a major storm and he already felt seasick. The rest of the crew had just laughed at him and given him knowing looks that said "wait til you get further up north and you'll see what heavy seas are really like." And he had. Eventually the seasickness had passed and he had found his sea legs and got used to the constant motion beneath him. Which was just as well because he had had to endure almost three weeks in the icy storm-battered Arctic waters.

CHAPTER 22

Tuesday 13th November 1973

His reverie was interrupted by the outer door of the morgue crashing open and Pete, the mortuary assistant, barging through. "Ah there you are Frank. I thought I might find you out here having a crafty ciggie. His Lordship asked me to tell you that he's finished with the body and is in the office writing up his notes if you would care to join him. Blimey, he's a right snooty one isn't he?" And with that he was gone as quickly as he had arrived.

Well, I suppose I'd better get back to it, thought Frank, crushing out the remains of his second cig. Going back into the morgue he entered the autopsy room and knocked on the open door of the tiny little cubicle which served as an office. Professor Jamieson was in there, writing up notes longhand from his Dictaphone. "Come in, come in, detective," he said. "So you wanted to know my preliminary conclusion. This is of course subject to the usual caveats, about needing the results of blood tests and so on. But my preliminary conclusion is that you have been wasting your time. Isn't that a criminal offence, wasting Police time? Perhaps you should arrest yourself!" he said in a feeble attempt at humour.

"Now seriously, Inspector, I have concluded that he died sometime between the hours of around 6.00pm on Monday 5th

November and around 8.00am on the 6th. I cannot be more precise than that because as you know the body was in the water for some time which really messes with the evidence."

"Well that fits with what we know about his movements" said Frank. "The last time anyone saw him alive was around 9.00pm on the 5th, so that at least confirms that he likely died that night."

"It does indeed Inspector. Now as to the cause of death, I can be 99.9% certain that this was natural causes. Of course, being the inquisitive soul that you are, you will want to know my reasons for reaching that conclusion. And they are as follows. Firstly there are absolutely no external signs of foul play. Secondly, there was no water in his lungs. I found a tiny bit of what I would guess is dock water in his stomach which would have happened when he went in the water. But my considered opinion is that he was already dead when that happened. He certainly did not drown, which rules out an accidental death. Thirdly, when I cut open his lungs, there was evidence that he was in a fairly advanced stage of a disease called pneumoconiosis, more commonly known as miner's lung. It is a form of emphysema, a degenerative disease of the lungs, in this particular form usually caused by working amongst coal. Do you know if that was the case, Inspector?"

"Yes, sir, it was. In his younger days Mr. Bielby served as a stoker on steam trawlers, shovelling coal into the fire to fire the boilers that drove the engines."

"Well there you go, Inspector. That will be the cause of his lung disease. On top of that I would say there is evidence that he was a fairly heavy smoker. Not a wise thing to do when you have emphysema. It makes it ten times worse.

Then there is the drinking. Judging by his stomach contents he had consumed a fair amount of beer on the night of his death. His liver was enlarged, with some scar tissue, which suggests he had been a heavy drinker for quite a long time."

Well of course he was a heavy drinker, thought Frank to himself. He was a trawlerman. He thought back again to his trip, when, as a 16 year old, they had plied him with alcohol. When they went off shift it was the normal practice to have a "can and a dram" and the bo'sun had insisted he have his, he'd earned it. Then when they came home from fishing as "three day millionaires" most of the trawlermen drank heavily, spending a lot of their earnings in the pub. He knew this from his days as a young beat bobby, having had to sort out many a drunken brawl amongst the men when they had had a few too many.

"Hello, Inspector," Jamieson interrupted his thoughts, "are you still with us? You know it's very rude to daydream when someone is conversing with you, don't you? Do they not teach you any manners up north? Anyhow, where was I? Ah, yes! The stomach contents. So, as well as a fair amount of alcohol in his stomach, which I am sure will be reflected in his blood alcohol level, there was also evidence of having consumed a fish and chip supper on the evening of his death. Put all this together, Inspector, and you have evidence of someone who was already very ill, and continuing to live a very unhealthy lifestyle. Be warned of the dangers of smoking and drinking, Inspector. It will bring you to an early grave.

So my conclusion is that the cause of death is a myocardial infarction, a "heart attack" in common parlance. This will have been primarily caused by his lung disease. It is very common in emphysema patients. Because the lungs are processing insufficient oxygen into the blood stream, and especially to the brain, the heart works overtime to try to pump the blood faster around the body and especially to the brain which is crying out for oxygen. By the way, Inspector, this oxygen starvation in the brain can cause the patient to behave in strange and uncharacteristic ways, and even on occasions to hallucinate. So I would not set too much store on anything that people may have told you Mr. Bielby said or did in the weeks prior to his death.

This additional strain on the heart will cause any existing

minor defects in the heart, such as those caused by a long term unhealthy lifestyle, to become major defects very quickly. And then bang, the heart just stops. I hope I have explained my conclusion and my reasoning in sufficiently clear terms for you to understand. Of course the full reasoning, in correct medical terminology, will be in my final report, which I shall submit to the Coroner as soon as possible. Naturally, it is up to the Coroner to make a determination of the cause of death. However there is little doubt in my mind that this is a clear cut case of death by natural causes and that is the view I shall be expressing to the Coroner."

"Alright, thank you, Professor. You have indeed explained it in terms which even I can understand." The irony seemed to be lost on Jamieson. "I do have one question which is bothering me, though."

"Well, fire away, Inspector. That's why I'm here, to soothe your troubled breast."

"OK. Well when we took Mr. Bielby's body from the water, it was pretty filthy as you can imagine, but there appeared to be some slight signs of bruising around the neck. It was hard to tell what they were or what caused them, but they were definitely there. They appear to have faded a bit now but you can still see some evidence of slight bruising. Can you tell me what might have caused that?"

"Certainly, my dear chap. It's simple. A shirt with a collar which is too small and top button fastened. Possibly even with a tie which is tied too tight."

"Well, he wasn't wearing a tie when we found his body, and I really don't see how a tie could possibly come off in the water. If anything surely it would become tighter around the neck as the body bloated. Nor was his top button fastened up. That's how we were able to see the bruising in the first place."

"When you say we, to whom are you referring?" asked Jamieson.

Frank had not wanted to drop the Doc in it, but now felt he had no option but to come clean. "It was myself and the Police Surgeon who examined the body at the scene and we both noted the bruising Professor."

"Ah! Don't tell me. Let me guess. And now the hick amateur Police Surgeon, who has not had half the training which I have had, nor ever done any research into Forensic Pathology, has some half-baked theory, no doubt, about how the bruising got there. Well, I am telling you Inspector, in no uncertain terms, that that bruising was caused by a shirt which was too small. Check the evidence. Check the collar size on the shirt he was wearing when you found him, and I can tell you what collar size he actually is. Compare the two. You will definitely find they do not match."

"If that's the case, Professor," shot back Frank, "how do you explain the fact that his top button was not fastened when we found him."

"Inspector, you really are making a meal out of this when it is a very simple hors d'oeuvre. That's quite straightforward. When the heart stops you get some congestion in the blood vessels, especially in the upper part of the body, in the face and the neck. You can see quite clearly the congestion in his face. This leads to swelling. So, quite clearly, when his heart stopped his face and neck became swollen. His shirt button, which was fastened and which caused the bruising, then popped due to the pressure caused by the swelling in his neck. Hence when you found him it was unfastened.

Now I really do not have the time to answer any more of your frivolous questions, Inspector. I am a busy man and I have other cases to attend to, and I need to be leaving here very shortly. So I really must bid you adieu." With that he waved Frank out of the room in a gesture of dismissal.

Frank left the tiny office feeling like he had when he had been at school and been sent to see the Headmaster. You pompous, arrogant, condescending git, Frank really wanted to say to Jamieson. But he refrained. Best keep this professional he thought, or I will be in even more trouble with my bosses. As he was leaving, he lingered for just a moment in the autopsy room, gathering his thoughts. It was only a second or two, but it was long enough for Frank to hear Jamieson picking up the phone and dialling a number. That's odd, thought Frank. I wonder who you are ringing. I thought you were in such a hurry to leave that you didn't have time for any more questions. But obviously somebody somewhere wants to know immediately the outcome of the autopsy, and perhaps what kind of questions the nosy policeman is asking. Well, this nosy policeman is far from satisfied with this concocted load of baloney and is going to keep on asking awkward questions.

CHAPTER 23

Tuesday 13th November 1973

F rank arrived back at the Station. He was still fuming at his treatment at the hands of Jamieson. But it wasn't so much his condescending attitude that irked Frank. It was the fact that he knew in his water that something was going on and that the Professor was clearly part of the cover-up. And yet he also knew, very frustratingly, that there was going to be absolutely nothing he could do about it. So to make himself feel a little better he let rip with some of his anger when he got into his office.

He was cursing and swearing under his breath when Tony knocked on the door. "Come in Tony," he said.

"How'd it go, boss?" asked Tony.

"Do you know what, Tony, I don't want to sound as if I've got a great big working class chip on my shoulder. But this country is run by toffee-nosed entitled a***holes who think that because they went to the right public school and the right Oxbridge College they know better than everybody else and can look down on us mere mortals because they have a divine right to rule."

"I take it you didn't like the Pathologist then, boss?"

"Didn't like is putting it mildly, Tony. I couldn't stand the man. He's a condescending, pompous, self-righteous prick if you ask me. And as for finding anything useful from the autopsy, we can forget that. He wants us to believe that Billy died of natural causes. He had a heart attack brought on by his emphysema putting extra strain on his heart and not helped by his unhealthy lifestyle, smoking, drinking and unhealthy eating. I'm surprised I didn't also get a lecture about the evils of sex and drugs and rock'n'roll as well. Now it all sounds very plausible, as it is meant to. They've thought about this very carefully.

But he did get a bit twitchy when I asked about the bruising round the neck. I think he was hoping I hadn't noticed that. Anyhow apparently that means nothing. He must have been wearing a shirt that was too small for him with the collar fastened and that's what caused the bruising, so says our learned Pathologist. And who am I to differ? The fact that when we found him in the water his collar was undone is of course due to swelling of the neck after his heart attack, which must have popped his shirt button open. Of course. Why didn't I think of that? Can you believe this tissue of lies? By the way, one thing I do want you to check, Tony, is the collar size of the shirt he was wearing which should be in the evidence received from the mortuary. And check with his family, see if anybody can remember what collar size he normally took. Because I want to prove that Professor High and Mighty's theory is a load of boloney."

"I can do that boss. But what do we do now? Surely if he's going to put in his report that it was death by natural causes, isn't the Coroner going to run with that as a verdict and then we'll have no case to investigate? Not that we've got much of one now mind. But isn't there any way you can ask for a second opinion, you know like you do with doctors?"

"I wish, Tony, I wish. Firstly the Coroner would have to ask for that because he is the one who brought in the Pathologist. Secondly he's not going to do that on the say so of a humble Detective Inspector. It would need someone much higher up the food chain than me to make that request. And guess what?

Those higher up the food chain are part of the conspiracy and are the very people who have been trying very hard to stop us investigating. So we've got absolutely no chance of that happening. No, I'm going to have to go and see the DCI and get his take on this situation. Because I can't for the life of me think where we go from here."

"OK boss. Well good luck with that. Are you going to try and see him now?"

"I am Tony. Might as well strike while the iron is hot, as they say."

But he was out of luck. When he rang Jim's number he got no answer. And after asking around he found that Jim was due in court all day on a high profile case and would probably not be back in the office that day. Cursing his luck, he sat down and tried to think through what his next step might be. But thinking would not come, so he decided to try his usual trick of going out for a smoke to create some thinking space.

As he meandered around Queen's Gardens, now on his second cigarette, he passed one of the benches. He heard a croaky voice call out: "Mr. Fogg!" Looking around to see where the voice had come from he noticed on the bench he had just passed what looked like a bundle of rags. On closer inspection it turned out to be a person, dressed in a huge old army trenchcoat, with underneath what appeared to be filthy rags wrapped around him. Frank turned and made to go towards him, but was stopped in his tracks by the stench of alcohol and stale urine.

The voice said again: "Mr. Fogg!" It was a surprisingly cultivated voice, and it was unexpected coming from a down and out. But Frank immediately recognised it. "Captain Albert Baker, if I'm not very much mistaken," he said. "How are you Albert? And what on earth are you doing here? This is not your usual beat, is it?"

Frank knew Albert from of old. He was a regular on his beat on Hessle Road as a young bobby. Albert was generally no trouble. He occasionally got himself arrested for vagrancy or being drunk and disorderly, mainly Frank suspected so he could get a night in the cells and a decent breakfast. Frank also knew some of Albert's back story and had a bit of a soft spot for him. Like Frank, Albert had been born into a fishing family; his Dad too had been a trawler skipper. Like Frank, Albert had not taken to the fishing life and wanted to do something else. But his something else had been very different. He had gone to school and college and then served his time as a merchant seaman, all the while studying for his master's ticket. He had then plied his trade as master of a merchant ship, mostly crossing the North Sea from the Baltic countries to Newcastle, Hull and Immingham. This was during the 1950s when the North Sea was still littered with old munitions from the Second World War. His ship had the misfortune to run into a sea mine and be fatally damaged. They had managed to get off a distress call but with no sign of help on the way the Captain had given the order to abandon ship. The crew had set off in the lifeboats and in the time honoured fashion the Captain had stayed with the sinking ship. At this point a rescue helicopter had shown up and taken the Captain off the sinking ship, but of the lifeboats they could find no trace. An empty lifeboat turned up a couple of months later but what happened to the crew was never known.

Unfortunately for Captain Albert the loss of both his ship and his crew, and his guilt at surviving without them, was too much for him. He took to the bottle and had a serious breakdown. As a result he lost his job, his family, and eventually his home. He took to the streets and became a regular vagrant in the Hessle Road area where he had grown up. He also often frequented the Fish Dock, where he was well known to the Transport Police.

In response to Frank's question Albert asked his usual question which was: "Can you spare me a couple of bob for a cup of tea Mr. Fogg?"

"Oh come on, Albert. We both know it's not tea you're wanting. So no, I can't spare you a couple of bob. What are you doing here? I don't think I've ever seen you in this neck of the woods. You're taking a risk if one of the city centre lads thinks you're stealing his pitch aren't you?"

"I came," said Albert slurring his words slightly and then hiccupping, "I came to see you Mr. Fogg."

"Then why didn't you come into the Police Station and ask for me Albert?"

"Now Mr. Fogg you've got to be joking. Look at the state of me. Do you really think the desk Sergeant is going to give me the time of day, let alone take seriously a request to see you. I'd have been told to sling my hook in double quick time. So I thought I would just wait out here. I knew you would come out eventually. I see you're still on the ciggies. Can you spare one for a poor old man?"

"Come on, less of the old, Albert. You're only a few years older than me." Although it was true that the weather and his lifestyle had aged Albert beyond his years. "Anyway, of course you can have a cig. Here you go," said Frank taking one out of the packet and handing it over and then flicking his lighter to light it for Albert.

"Now was there a particular reason why you wanted to see me, or is this just a social call for old times' sake?"

Albert looked at him with a sly grin. "Buy me a breakfast and I will tell you. I have important informashion that may be of use to you."

"You sly old fox Albert. You'll have to do a bit better than that to get a breakfast out of me. What sort of information? Pertaining to what?"

"Let'sh jush say it relates to a cashe you are currently inveshtigating" said Albert, slurring his words more and more.

"Alright Albert, you've got me hooked. I'm intrigued now. But don't you dare go falling asleep on me. Come on, let's go over to the café and get you some strong black coffee and some food inside you and then we'll see if you make any more sense."

"You're a good soul Mr. Fogg and I thank you. You will not regret it. This is pure gold this informashion."

Fortunately Frank was a regular at the café, preferring it to the Police canteen, and so he knew the owner Betty pretty well. Which was just as well because he had to do some really smooth sweet talking to get her to let Albert in. Normally she would have seen him off the premises before he had set a foot in the door, and Frank couldn't blame her. It wasn't good for business having Albert there, nor was it pleasant for the other customers. Frank sat Albert down with a strong black coffee and ordered him a full English breakfast, and his own usual bacon sandwich.

Having got them settled he sat across the table from Albert and looked him in the eyes and said: "Now what's this all about Albert? It must be something pretty important to drag you away from your normal beat and bring you up to town looking for me."

"Well, it's like this Mr. Fogg. I heard on the grapevine that you were the one investigating Billy Bielby's death. And I've also heard them saying that it's going to be ruled as a death by natural causes. That's the word on the street. I liked Billy. He was always kind to me. And I know that his death was no accident. Somebody murdered him and they need to pay for it. And I thought, if Mr. Fogg is investigating he might actually listen to me. Most of your lot, coppers I mean, won't give me the time of day, but you're different."

"OK, Albert. So I'm listening. But how do you know his death was not an accident or natural causes. You can't just say that. There has to be some reason why you think that."

"Because I was there, Mr. Fogg. I saw what happened."

"What? What do you mean you were there Albert?"

"It's like this, Mr. Fogg. I was dossing in the doorway of Stanton's. It's a good place to sleep because it's sheltered from the weather as long as the wind's not in the north. I'm always careful not to make a mess, so they don't mind me sleeping there. And as you know they open up pretty early in the morning and sometimes when Mick or Beryl are first in they take pity on me and give me a cup of tea and a bacon sandwich.

Anyway so there I was trying to get some kip in Stanton's doorway. I was happy as Larry. I'd had a few cans of Special Brew and I'd managed to blag a bottle of Bells so I was on cloud nine. I don't remember exactly what night it was. But I know I'd settled in cosy like for the night. Then I had to get up and go and answer a call of nature. I was just getting to my feet, which is a bit of a struggle these days, and I saw some movement on the boat nearest to me. I didn't give it much of a thought. I thought it was probably the night watchman doing his rounds. But then I heard a noise like somebody was falling over something and then a voice. It was speaking quietly, but there was no wind that night, it was very still, so I could hear it clear as a bell. "Ouch. Damn it!" That made me look. And then I saw these two black clad figures run up behind the night watchman who was just turning round to see what the noise was. They ran up behind him and quick as you like put a plastic bag over his head. They held it there for ages until he went limp. Then they laid him down on the deck and looked like they were checking for a pulse, making sure he was really dead like. Then they picked up his body and carried it to the stern where it was really dark and they threw him in the dock."

"Did you see him go in the Dock Albert?"

"No, but I saw them disappear towards the stern carrying the body, then I heard a splash, then they came back with no body."

"Right Albert. You do realise, don't you, that this is a very serious allegation you are making? So you're sure this is what you saw, and not just the Special Brew and the Bells talking?"

"Mr. Fogg, I swear on my daughter's life it's all true. I saw it clear as daylight."

"And why didn't you report this at the time, Albert?" asked

Frank.

"Because I knew I would get exactly the reaction from the Dock Police that I've just had from you. They would not have believed me. And they'd have thrown me off the dock. And anyway I was scared. I'd just watched two blokes murder another one. If they had found out I was watching they would have come after me next. I hid behind the bins and waited and waited until I thought the coast was clear and they'd gone. Then I scuttled off up the dock towards the Fish Meal Factory, just in case they came back looking for me."

"Now Albert, this is really important. Can you describe these men to me?" asked Frank.

"Well I can't tell you what their faces were like because they were both wearing black balaclavas. But one was pretty tall, I would say about six foot four and skinny. The other was average height, about five foot eight maybe, and he was well built, muscular you know."

"Did you see which way they went?"

"I think they headed off in the opposite direction, up towards the lock gates."

"Have you told anyone else about this Albert? I believe these men are really dangerous and if they find out that they were seen they will come after you. You were right to be scared of them. And it's really important that you don't tell anyone else what you've told me."

"Yes, Mr. Fogg. I understand that and I haven't told another soul. Does this mean you believe me then?"

"Yes, Albert, I believe you. From what I already know your story sounds very likely. But, Albert, I might need you to make an official statement at some point so don't go disappearing on me will you?"

"Who me, Mr. Fogg? I've got nowhere to go, as you know. I've got nothing and nobody in this world and that's just the way I like it.

I can't hurt anybody else if I don't get involved with them. You'll find me where you always find me if you need me."

"Alright Albert. Thank you for coming to find me. You've given me really valuable information. You were right about that. As a thank you, here's a couple of bob for a cup of tea" said Frank fishing out his wallet and placing a fiver on the table.

"Mr. Fogg, you're a gem. I knew I could rely on you. I've got to go now," said Albert finishing the last of his breakfast and hastily stuffing the fiver in his coat pocket. "Be seeing you Mr. Fogg."

And with that Albert was gone. Obviously the money was burning a hole in his pocket.

CHAPTER 24

Friday 3rd April 2009

On Thursday Frank had had a call from Mary to say that she had arranged for a further search of Tommy's flat to take place the following morning. She had obtained the keys, and the services of three of her best detectives to form a search team to tear the place apart. Would Frank like to be there? Well of course Frank would like to be there, wild horses would not keep him away. So it was arranged that they would meet at Tommy's flat at nine a.m., and it would take as long as it took.

He had then had another call, this time from Tim to say that Charlie Brooks was willing to meet him and have a yarn with him. So he arranged to do that in the afternoon, as soon as he could get there. Things were moving apace. There was a lot of activity, although it didn't feel like they were getting very far in cracking this case.

So Frank turned up as arranged at Tommy's flat on the Friday morning. They tried to get in incognito as they didn't want nosy neighbours banging on the door and peering through the windows and then gossiping about the Police having been there. This successfully achieved, they proceeded with the search. It was a Council flat in one of the tower blocks on the Thornton Estate. It was not the most salubrious part of town, although Frank knew worse places. The flat was quite small and Frank did not think it should take the search team too long to do a thorough going over of the place. There was a bedroom, living room, bathroom, and a tiny kitchen.

They began with all the obvious places, turning out all the drawers and cupboards. The search team had asked what they were looking for but Frank and Mary could not be very specific. Anything out of the ordinary they said, and papers, notebooks or anything that might store information from a computer such as CDroms or a USB stick. Having drawn a blank with drawers and cupboards, they started to try less obvious places – on top of a wardrobe, under a mattress, underneath all the furniture looking for anything taped to the bottom, inside the toilet cistern. They looked underneath carpets and lino. They would have taken floorboards up if there had been any but the place had concrete floors. Starting to despair of finding anything of any interest, they were just starting to consider calling off the search when one of the search team suggested that they try taking the plinths off the kitchen units and the bath, just in case. That was when they struck gold. They took the front panel off the bath and one of the team got down on the floor with a torch and made a thorough inspection under the bath. And there, taped to the wall at the back of the bath, was an envelope. They took it off the wall and opened it to find a USB stick inside.

"This must be something important that Tommy didn't want found," said Mary. "Someone's gone to a lot of trouble to hide something. I think we might just have struck lucky here and Tommy might be about to reveal his secrets." It was with some frustration that they realised that there was no laptop in the flat as it had been taken into custody to be searched. They would have to contain their excitement until they got back to the Station.

"Well thank you gentlemen," Mary said to the search team, "I think we may have got what we came for. You can all get on with the rest of your work now. I'll see you back at the Station and I'll let you know if we find anything of interest on here," she said holding up the USB stick. Frank and Mary made their way back to the Station, both impatient to see what was on the USB stick. They got back to Mary's office and plugged it into her computer, but they would both have to contain their impatience a little longer because they found it was password protected.

"A careful man, our Tommy," remarked Frank. "It wouldn't surprise me if he's also encrypted the contents. Do you think the techie guys will be able to get anything off it?"

"They'll certainly be able to crack the password, that's for sure. Whether they can decrypt the contents if they are encrypted, I don't know. We'll have to ask them."

She was about to pick up the phone and do just that when it rang.

"Ma'am, it's Iain Stewart here again," said the voice when she answered the phone.

"Yes, Iain, what can I do for you? Have you got some good news for me?"

"I have indeed Ma'am. We've managed to track down the registration number of your burnt out vehicle from the GPS tracker. I have a name and address for the registered keeper. The only trouble is that it is registered to a limited company, not an individual, so I can't give you an address for the driver. However I can give you the company's address."

"That's great work, Iain. So spill the beans. Give me the information over the phone and I'll make a note of it, and then if you could follow that up with an email that would be great."

"I have to tell you Ma'am, it was reported stolen on Friday 20th March. There is a record on the system. Not that that necessarily means it was stolen. Criminals have been known before to report a vehicle stolen before then using it in a crime and getting rid."

"OK. Thanks for the heads up Iain. So let me have this name and address and we will go and pay the company a visit, to follow up on this report of a stolen vehicle."

She jotted down the name and address, put down the phone, and said to Frank: "Ha, gotcha."

"Is that what I think it is?" asked Frank. "A name and address of the owner of a certain burnt out Land Rover Discovery?"

"It certainly is. Now I feel like we're getting somewhere. Want to come and pay a visit with me?"

"Whereabouts is it?" asked Frank.

Mary glanced at her piece of paper. "A place called Scotton. I don't know where that is but it's got a DL9 postcode."

"Well DL is the Darlington area," explained Frank. "So it's got to be way up the top end of North Yorkshire. I think it might be somewhere in the Catterick area. That's going to take a couple of hours to get there from here. You're not in London now you know where you can just nip across town. Things are long distances apart up here."

"Just nip across town?" exclaimed Mary. "When did you last visit London and try driving in London traffic. You don't just nip anywhere in London unless you're going to blue light it and clear everybody out of the way."

"Well anyway, I have an appointment with a retired trawler skipper this afternoon, who may have information pertinent, so I'm going to have to pass on your kind offer. Why don't you take John Townsend with you if you're going today? Give him a trip out and you can update him on the case on the way – see if he has any wisdom to add to solving our mystery."

"OK. Do you know anything else about this Scotton place?"

"Well, if it's where I think it is, it's next door to Catterick Garrison, which is the largest army base in the UK. I don't know if that's significant but it will be interesting to know what kind of business this company is in. Chances are it's something to do with the military. Are you going to give them a call to make sure someone is in before you go? It's a long way to go for nothing."

"Yes. I'll give them a ring. After all it's not like anyone is a suspect, yet," said Mary. "I'll spin them a yarn about investigating a major car theft ring who are stealing top of the range cars to order. That'll explain why a DCI is following up on their car theft report. I'm a bit puzzled as to why, when the theft was reported, they didn't tell us the car had a GPS tracking device on it. I thought that was the whole point of those things, so you could track your car if it got lost or stolen, and recover it."

"OK, well, good luck with the interview. I'll see you when you get back, and we can compare notes. I can let you know how I get on with my trawler skipper, and you can update me on Mr. Stolen Car."

"Yeah. It sounds like I'm going to be quite late back and it's Friday so the traffic will probably be horrendous. We'd probably better put off that pleasure until tomorrow. Oh, that's Saturday, isn't it? I keep forgetting you're a civilian. You don't work 24/7 like us coppers when we're on a murder hunt. Do you mind a Saturday meeting?"

"It's OK with me" responded Frank. "I'd better just check and see whether Janice has got anything planned for me, but if not I'll be here. I'll let you know. And Mary, be careful. As you know, I already have my suspicions about who is behind all this. But this possible military connection makes me even more wary. I can't for the life of me find the thread that ties it all together, but it's there somewhere and I think the closer we get to finding it, the more dangerous this is going to be."

"That is duly noted Frank. John Townend is firearms trained, so I will get him to check out a weapon and go carrying just in case. Now I've got to just get this USB stick into the techie boys and then I must be on my way. Bye Frank."

CHAPTER 25

Friday 3rd April 2009

Frank set off once again for the Charterhouse. It was only five minutes walk from the Police Station. When he got there he went in search of Tim who was not in his house. It turned out he was in the Chapel, getting ready for Sunday morning's service. The Chapel, to Frank's surprise, was stunning. It was a classical piece of Georgian architecture, and he wondered why, in all his years of living in Hull, he had never discovered this place. Built around 1780 the Chapel reflected the religious vogue of the time. Entering by a door in the South wall, Frank found himself facing in the North wall a double decker pulpit. To his left were the pews for the residents and to his right at the east end was an altar. The whole place was light and airy, a great contrast to the gloom of many later Victorian churches which had been built during the Gothic revival.

He announced himself and Tim stopped what he was doing and greeted him. "Come on over to the house, Frank. I'll pick up Charlie on the way. He's expecting you. We can go and sit in the sitting room and have a cup of tea and you two can talk."

They called at Charlie's flat on the way and he answered the door. Frank was slightly taken aback because Charlie was much older than he had been anticipating. He had expected someone a few years older than himself, perhaps early seventies. But Charlie appeared to be in his late eighties. He had weathered well for someone who had spent a large part of his working life at sea.

They sat down with a cup of tea in Tim's sitting room, and Charlie began: "So what can I do for you young fella?"

"Well," said Frank, "when I was a young copper, a Detective Inspector, years ago now, I had to investigate the death of a trawlerman called Billy Bielby. This was back in 1973. There were rumours flying around then about our fishing fleet being involved in spying on the Russians. It turns out, from what Tim here has told me, that these rumours were true and the government eventually admitted it. Now Tim tells me that you knew a bit about this. I always thought Billy's death might be connected in some way, but I've never been able to figure it out. I thought you might have some background information that might be useful to me."

"Billy Bielby, eh?" said Charlie. "What did you say your name was?"

"Me? I'm Frank Fogg. Why?"

"Well I never. Fancy that, after all these years, Davey Fogg's lad turning up here. I remember you when you were nobbut a little bain."

"I take it you knew my Dad then?" asked Frank.

"Knew him? I'll say. I sailed with him. I was first mate on the Kingston Jade. He was the best skipper I ever sailed with. He was firm but very fair with the men. Straight as a dye he was. If he thought you was wrong he would tell you. But if you was in the right he'd back you to the hilt. A proper gentleman, your Dad were. And a bloody good skipper. Man, could he find fish? I learnt everything I know about fishing from him. I was so sorry when I heard he'd been lost at sea. I were even more sorry I weren't on that last trip with him and didn't get to see him one last time."

"I'm really sorry, Charlie," said Frank. "I don't remember you at all."

"Aye, well, you were in shock after he died. I saw you at the funeral. You looked totally lost."

"I was. It took me years to get over losing him. I always felt cheated out of some of the best years of his life. But you know, that's the hand life deals you sometimes. You've got to get on and make the best of it haven't you."

"Well, well, I can't get over bumping into you again after all these years. Anyhow you didn't come here to talk about me and your Dad. You wanted to talk about Billy Bielby. Anything I can do to help Davey's lad, I'm all yours. I knew Billy. He were a nosy little sod, always poking his nose into other people's business. So, you're still trying to find out what got him killed. The word at the time was he died of natural causes – a heart attack was what I heard."

"That's right. That was the verdict the Coroner came to, based on the Pathologist's report. But I never believed it."

"Nor me. It were all a bit convenient, if you know what I mean. Now I do know that Billy was very nosy. And he'd got his teeth into something to do with this spying business. Did Father Tim tell you that I was asked to do it and I refused. I didn't want to be responsible for getting my crew arrested and hauled off to some gulag in Siberia or shot."

"Yes, he did, Charlie. Can you tell me anything about what Billy thought he had found?"

"Not really, no. I only know the stuff that's been talked about since. You know, that Naval Intelligence were placing people on our trawlers to spy on the Russians, pretending to be getting seagoing experience. And, if you agreed, they would give you cameras and recognition charts and such like to record the comings and goings of Russian vessels. Of course we talked about it in the pub, as skippers did, sharing our experiences. Everyone knew it were going on.

I also know that there was summat else going on, that they

didn't want us to know about. It were all a bit of a mystery. But it had summat to do with a company called British Fishing Company. They were only a tiny company. They had an office in the White Fish Authority building, do you remember that, by the lockpit?"

"I do Charlie. Every fishing family remembers the lock at Fish Dock don't they? It's where we would go when we knew our Dad was on his way home from sea, to get a glimpse of him coming in."

"Aye, well, anyway this company were a bit of mystery as I say. They only had one boat operating out of Hull. Now what was it called? It'll come back to me ere long. Anyhow, one of the strange things was that they never used local crew. They always used to bring in their own crew from away. And they didn't look like fishermen. They looked more like Navy types to me. You could tell from the haircuts and the way they stood to attention and so on. Don't get me wrong. They were definitely fishing. They used to come back with a catch and sell it on Fish Market. But you never knew where they were fishing. They never were part of the main fishing fleet.

I heard tell that they always fished in the White Sea. Now I'm not saying that's not a good place to fish at certain times of year. But most of us used to vary where we went to get a good catch. And of course you will know that the White Sea is just off the north coast of Russia. It made me wonder why someone would always want to be fishing so close to Russia."

Charlie paused for a moment, thinking.

"This is all good stuff Charlie," said Frank. "Why don't we take a cig break while you see what else you can remember. Tim, is there any chance of another cup of tea?"

"I've had to give up smoking," said Charlie, "but I'll come outside with you and what do they call it, passive smoke, if that's all right. Another cup of tea would go down well, thanks Father."

"No problem," said Tim. "Would you like something a bit stronger, a wee dram, to go with it?"

"That would be great," they both responded. "Thanks."

As they were standing outside Charlie said: "It's just come back to me, the name of that boat that fished out of Hull, that belonged to British Fishing. It were called the Catscope. Strange name, I always thought, for a trawler. But there was never any telling where the owners thought up the names from."

When they were back indoors, Charlie continued with his tale.

"So where was I? Oh yes, British Fishing. Like I just said to Frank here, I remembered the name of the trawler they ran out of Hull. It were called the Catscope. Don't know what it means. It was a new one on me. She looked like a normal sidewinder on the outside. But I remember some of the bobbers telling me she had a really small fish hold so she never came back with a big catch 'cos she didn't have room for it. That puzzled me a bit as well. Why would you build a trawler with a really small hold. All the owners I ever worked for were all about profit, profit, profit. And they got plenty of that didn't they. Just look at the big houses they all lived in and the fancy cars they all drove. They weren't short of a bob or two. So why would you build a normal size trawler but only have a little hold in it. What else was in there that they didn't want anybody to know about?"

"Charlie, this is like gold, this information. I wish I'd had it all thirty six years ago. I might have got closer to finding out what happened to poor Billy."

"Oh aye. Let's not forget poor Billy. I'm telling you he must have found out something he wasn't meant to know. You mark my words. He was a nosy bugger and who knows what he saw doing them night watchman duties."

"Is there anything else you can think of that might help me Charlie?" asked Frank.

"Well only that I heard tell that British Fishing operated out of

Grimsby and Fleetwood as well. I don't know how many boats they had there, but I thought it was a bit strange when you're only a small company to have three operating bases. Why not base all your trawlers in one place?"

"That's brilliant Charlie," said Frank. "Thank you so much for all your help. If I need to, can I come back and ask some more questions?"

"Of course, lad. You know where I am. Like I said, nought is too much trouble for Davey Fogg's lad. Let me know if you find out anything more. You've got me intrigued now thinking about it all. It was all a long time ago, but it only seems like yesterday to me. I'll see you soon, lad."

With that Charlie took his leave.

"What did you make of all that, Tim?" asked Frank.

"I don't know. But we always knew there was something hush hush going on that was connected to the Fish Dock. We've never before got this close to finding out what it was. There is one interesting thing I picked up from Charlie. You know he said that this British Fishing Company had an office in the White Fish Authority building. Well, according to that documentary about the Gaul that I told you about, that's where Commander Hardcastle, the Naval Intelligence officer in charge of recruiting trawlermen to spy on the Russians, was based. It could be just a coincidence. But it was, after all, a government building, so where else would government people operate from?"

"So I'm going to go away and do some digging into historic records to see what I can find out about this British Fishing Company and the trawler Catscope. Thanks for your help Tim. I'll keep in touch."

"OK Frank. I'll see you soon."

CHAPTER 26

Wednesday 14th November 1973

The next day Frank tried again to see Jim Dunlop, the DCI, only to be told that his evidence had been delayed and he had had to return to court that morning as a witness. Trying to contain his impatience Frank shared with Tony what he had been told by Albert Baker. Tony was excited.

"This changes everything doesn't it, boss? Now we've got an eyewitness they can't possibly try and bury this any more."

"Let's not get ahead of ourselves Tony. What I haven't told you, and you will not know unless you happen to know him is that Albert is a vagrant, derelict, down and out, whatever you want to call him. He has no job. He has no fixed abode. And he's a chronic alcoholic. He's hardly the most credible witness ever. I dread to think what a good defence barrister would do under cross examination to destroy his credibility."

"Well yeah, boss. I see that. But still, surely they've got to let us carry on investigating it now. If we've got one eyewitness that confirms it was definitely murder, who's to say we might not turn up another one, or some other evidence, that might actually stand up in court."

"I appreciate that is the theory of how police work is supposed to be done, Tony. But don't rely on it in this case. I am rapidly learning that this case is not going to be solved by the book because there are people who don't want it to be solved at all."

With that they both got on with some other work. They had to show willing after all. They were not even supposed to be investigating Billy's death on Police time.

Eventually, after what seemed like an eternity, Frank's phone rang. He picked it up. "DI Fogg" he grunted into the phone.

"Frank, where's the fire? It's Jim Dunlop. I understand you've been trying to get hold of me as a matter of urgency."

"I have, sir. Have you got a minute or two to spare to see me."

"Of course, Frank. Come on up. I'll get some coffee on.

Frank breathed a sigh of relief. He really felt that he needed his superior officer's advice about where to go next with this case. He'd felt that after the autopsy and before he had bumped into Albert Baker. Now he felt it even more.

He knocked on Dunlop's door and was greeted with a cheery: "Come in Frank. Have a seat. Black, no sugar, isn't it? Now, sit down and tell me what's on your mind."

So Frank went through his experience of the autopsy, his jousting with the pathologist, using slightly less spicy language than he had used to describe it to Tony, his belief that the bruising around the neck was of significance and was being downplayed by the pathologist, and his disbelief at the explanation provided by the pathologist for the bruising.

Jim listened without interrupting, and then responded to Frank: "I believe you are probably right Frank. I have already been told by the Super that the verdict is going to come in as Death by Natural Causes, so obviously someone has had contact with the Coroner's Office who have had an advance briefing about what is going to be in the Autopsy Report. The thing is Frank, I'm not sure there's anything I can do about it. Those above us may be engaged in a cover up. But maybe they have good reasons for doing that. I don't know. I'm sure if I asked I would be given some baloney about national security. That is what it reeks of to me."

"OK sir. Well here's the thing," said Frank, and dropped his bombshell about having an eyewitness.

Jim said: "Well why didn't you say so. That changes everything. Who is this eyewitness?"

Frank went on to tell him about Albert Baker, and what he claimed to have seen.

"Frank, are we talking about the Albert Baker here? Captain Albert Baker, the gentleman of the road, who hangs about shop doorways on Hessle Road, and is mostly three sheets to the wind?"

"The same, sir."

"Come on, Frank. We can't possibly put him up as a witness. He would have no credibility in a witness box. I'm not sure that I even believe his story, do you?"

"Yes sir. I do. I've known Albert a long time. And he's a creature of habit. He never strays from his beat up and down Hessle Road and onto the Dock. He'll go up Hessle High Road and sleep under the trees on the verges there sometimes, or in the railway yards at the back. But I've never ever seen him in the city centre before. So something important made him go out of his normal routine. Something was bothering him and he needed to tell someone about it. Again, that's not like Albert. Normally he doesn't talk to anybody except to beg from them."

"Alright. Well, let's say he is telling the truth and he really did see this event and not imagine the whole scenario, he's still not much use to us as a witness is he? We could never put him in court. His evidence would be rubbished from the get go."

"Sir, I see that totally. But as Tony said, if we've got one eyewitness, who's to say there isn't another out there who would be more credible in court; or some other evidence that we haven't found yet. Don't forget we haven't had chance to get forensics to go over the crime scene yet because it's still at sea.

We just can't shut down this investigation yet. It would be a total travesty of justice if we do."

"Look Frank, I see where you're coming from. I really do. But my hands are tied. I've had orders from the Super not to investigate this at all until we have had a verdict from the Coroner. It sounds like that verdict is going to be pretty cut and dried, Death by Natural Causes. Once that comes in officially there will be absolutely nothing I can do. So you can carry on investigating for now, off the books as we agreed. But I reckon you've got about 48 hours before that Autopsy report lands officially on the Super's desk. At that point I will not be able to cover your back any longer. Is that understood Frank?"

"Yes, sir. It is. Alright, well if I've only got 48 hours I'd better get on with it sir, if that's alright with you."

"Fine. You carry on Frank. Let me know if you find anything useful" said Dunlop, with the emphasis on the word "useful".

Frank left his office feeling even more disgruntled and frustrated than he had entered it. He didn't know what he had been expecting. He respected Jim Dunlop as a copper, but he had to accept that he was part of a hierarchy and that he was under orders from others above him.

He decided to go out for a smoke to try to calm himself down. Last time he had tried that, an eyewitness had appeared out of nowhere and he had thought he was at last making some progress with this case. Clearly he had been mistaken. Unfortunately he was not to get so lucky this time. And by the time he had finished his smoke he was still as confused and frustrated as before.

CHAPTER 27

Friday 3rd April 2009

Mary had no clue where Catterick was. She was pretty sure she had never been further north than Hull before. Frank had told her that Catterick was in Yorkshire so she didn't think it could be that far away. She thought Frank must have been exaggerating when he said it would take her a couple of hours to get there. So she was taken aback when she Google mapped it to find that it was a hundred miles away. She had no idea Yorkshire was so big. It was a straightforward enough journey, west out of Hull on the M62 and then north up the A1. But the map said it would take an hour and 45 minutes, and that was without road works, heavy traffic, or breakdowns. Frank had been right. She was glad she had decided to take John Townsend, her Sergeant, with her. That meant they could share the driving.

She had rung ahead to let them know she was coming. The phone had been answered by a female voice which said: "BFC. How may I help you?" Mary explained what she wanted and the voice said: "I think you will need to speak to Major Farquharson, our Managing Director. Let me just see if he is free." She was put on hold for what seemed like ages, and then a very upper class voice answered: "Major Stewart Farquharson here, Chief Inspector. Yvonne tells me that you wish to pay us a visit. Well, you are very welcome I'm sure. But I'm rather afraid you will be wasting your time. I cannot tell you anything which I have not already told the local police."

"Sir, I think you need to let me be the judge of that. We are investigating a major crime ring which appears to be stealing top of the range motors to order. It's very important that we gather as much information as we can in order to stop this criminal gang."

"Very well, Chief Inspector. If you insist, we would of course be very happy to see you. I shall be here until 5.30 this evening and then I shall have to leave as I have an important dinner engagement to attend. Posh do, you know. Can't let the side down and all that. See you later."

Mary had taken an instinctive dislike to this man during the phone call. She knew that she always reacted badly to upper class accents. She had grown up on a Council Estate in Tottenham in North London and knew that she had a bit of a prejudice. She tried to put that to one side and deal with everybody equally. But she also disliked people with pretensions, and anyone who was not a serving Army Officer who continued to call themselves Major was sure to rub her up the wrong way.

Mary and John Townsend set off through the early afternoon traffic and made good progress until they had almost reached Ferrybridge where they would turn off for the A1. Then the entire westbound motorway, all three lanes, ground to a halt and they were stuck. They could see smoke billowing across the carriageway some way ahead of them and it was obvious there was some kind of fire. And then the flashing blue lights and sirens arrived, screaming along the hard shoulder. Three fire engines suggested it was something quite serious. Then the Traffic cars arrived. After waiting for what seemed like hours, but was probably nearer 45 minutes, a PC in a high vis jacket appeared walking along the lines of cars explaining to the waiting motorists what had happened. It turned out that a chemical tanker had caught fire on the carriageway ahead of them. The fire was emitting toxic smoke across both carriageways of the motorway and nobody would be moving anywhere until the Fire Brigade declared it safe to do so.

Mary identified herself and explained that they were on a mission to interview a possible suspect in a murder inquiry. That got the PC's attention. She asked if there was any way he could extricate them from the traffic and get them off the motorway so they could continue their journey. "I'll speak to my Sergeant," said the PC. A few minutes later a Traffic car came tearing down the hard shoulder in the wrong direction, with the said Sergeant at the wheel. He got out and spoke to the PC, who then started asking the cars behind to back up to create a gap so that Mary could swing around and follow the Sergeant's car down the hard shoulder. "If you follow me, Ma'am," he said to her, "I'll escort you back to the A19 junction and then up the on ramp. From there you can start travelling north on the A19 and then you'll have to use your satnav to get back on the A1."

"Thank you, Sergeant," she replied. By the time they got onto the A19 after that little adventure they were running over an hour late and the satnav was estimating their arrival time at just after 5.00pm. "Oh, for some blues and twos eh, John," she said to her Sergeant sitting next to her and with that she put her foot down and poor John had to endure a hairy journey in the passenger seat the rest of the way to Scotton. Even so by the time they got there it was 5.15pm.

Arriving at the address they had been given they found it was on what could best be described as a Business Park. There were various industrial units and a small block of offices which were obviously in multiple occupation judging by the number of business name plates outside.

Jumping out of the car they went to the door and found the appropriate buzzer on the intercom. Mary pressed it and a voice which was obviously Major Farquharson himself answered and let them in. The Major turned out to be almost a caricature of a retired army officer. He had sandy hair and sported a regulation military moustache and haircut. He wore a tweed jacket and cavalry twill trousers and looked every inch the part.

Mary began with an apology. "I'm so sorry we are late Major. We ran into a major incident on the motorway on the way here and were totally blocked in. We got here as quickly as we could."

The Major grudgingly accepted their apology but said with some asperity: "Now look Chief Inspector, I explained on the phone that I have to leave here at 5.30. Yvonne has gone home already as she finishes at 5.00 so I'm afraid I can't offer you any refreshment, unless you'd like a gin and tonic or a scotch."

They both declined this offer. "Right then, Major, let's get down to business since we are short of time. You reported a vehicle which belongs to this company as stolen on..."she consulted her notes,   "Friday 20th March. Could you tell me about the circumstances of the theft, please."

"I did tell all this to the local Police. Don't you people talk to one another?"

"I would just like to go over it again with you, Major, please, just to check that we have the details correct."

"Oh very well. As I told the other officers it was my company car. I use it for business and to travel from home to the office and back. It was stolen from outside my house sometime between the hours of about 6.00pm when I returned home from work and parked it on the driveway and around 11.00pm when I was doing the rounds checking doors and windows before going to bed and I noticed it was missing."

"Does the vehicle have an alarm, sir?" asked John Townsend.

"It does, but I didn't hear it go off. So I assume the thieves were professionals who had some means of disabling the alarm system."

"I see, sir. I don't suppose you have any CCTV at your home?"

"No Sergeant, we don't. We live in a very quiet area with a very low crime rate. I have never seen any point in spending money installing something which we don't need just to line some alarm company's pocket."

"Could you just give us your home address from where the vehicle was taken, sir?" continued John. The Major reeled off a local address and John made a note of it, then glanced at Mary to continue with the questioning.

"Would you mind telling us what sort of business you run here Major?" asked Mary.

"Well I can tell you a little, but some of what we do is highly confidential Chief Inspector."

"Perhaps you could start by telling us what BFC stands for, Major. I assume it is short for something."

"The company started off as the British Firearms Company, supplying, obviously, firearms to the military. In those days it used to manufacture firearms. But then, as competition from overseas in that market became fierce, it diversified into the military supplies business. These days we supply anything and everything that is needed by the forces, including food, uniforms, bedding, fuel, ammunition, small arms, you name it, we can supply it."

"If you don't mind my asking sir, this seems a very small office for such a major operation. I presume you have warehouses somewhere where you stock all these supplies."

"No, no, Chief Inspector. Don't misunderstand me. When I say we supply the military, what I mean is that we procure on behalf of the military. Or job is to buy the equipment and supplies they need at the best possible price and arrange for them to be delivered where and when they are needed. We don't actually handle the goods. We're a kind of middle man, if you like. It's the way of the world these days. Everything is outsourced. Gone are the days when the military employed it's own staff to do purchasing. We can do it for them cheaper and more efficiently."

"Now Chief Inspector, as I have said repeatedly, I am pressed for time and I fail to see how these questions about my business have any relevance to my stolen vehicle. I am the victim of a crime here and yet I feel like I am being treated as a suspect. So, if you have no more questions relating to my stolen vehicle, I suggest that this interview is over."

"I will decide when this interview is over, Major. Unless you are refusing to answer any more questions, which would constitute an obstruction of justice." Mary knew she was skating on thin ice here, but sometimes such a suggestion helped to secure the co-operation of unwilling witnesses.

"No, no. Of course not Chief Inspector. So, what further questions do you have relating to my stolen vehicle, then?"

"Well, we found it, sir."

"You did?" Farquharson seemed genuinely shocked at this. "But how?...where?" he asked. "I thought you said it had been stolen by a criminal gang who were stealing vehicles to order for export."

This was the story which Mary had spun him on the phone, that vehicles were being stolen and shipped out through Hull in containers to Poland, the Baltic countries and Russia. It was not entirely fictional. There was indeed a gang of car thieves operating in the area, but as yet North Yorkshire Police had no idea where the vehicles were disappearing to.

"That was indeed what the local Police suspected, sir. We were as surprised as you are when we found it abandoned in the Humberside Police area. Have you any idea how it got there, sir?"

"No, of course not Chief Inspector. Does this mean I can have my car back then?"

"I'm afraid not, sir. You see when we found it, it was totally burned out. We believe someone had set it on fire deliberately.

Criminals only do that normally when they are trying to destroy evidence that the vehicle has been used in some sort of crime. You wouldn't know anything about that, would you sir?"

"I'm not sure I like the tone of your questioning, Chief Inspector. Am I being accused of something here? Do I need my lawyer present?"

"That's entirely up to you, sir. That is your right of course, but you are not being interviewed under caution." Mary nearly added "yet" but kept that thought to herself.

"Look here Chief Inspector, you are barking up entirely the wrong tree here. Clearly, what you thought was a theft by a criminal gang was merely a case of joyriders taking the vehicle for a ride and then abandoning it and setting fire to it for fun as they often do."

"That is certainly a possibility which we need to consider, Major, but in my experience joyriders do not usually remove the number plates from a vehicle and file off the VIN number so it can't be identified, before sending it up in flames.

No, I think, Major, that someone wanted us to think it had been stolen by the car theft gang, someone who was well aware that they were operating in this area, someone who lives locally and will have seen the news in the local paper and on the TV warning people to be extra careful."

"Well there you have it Chief Inspector. Obviously it was a local criminal who stole the car for use in a crime in your area, and then did not want it to be traced back to this area. May I suggest that you need to be looking into the local criminal fraternity?"

"Oh believe me we will, Major, we will. Well I think we have taken up enough of your time and we need to be on our way, as do you. So, thank you for your help and co-operation. We will ask the local Police to inform you when we have finished with what remains of your vehicle, sir."

With a nod to John she signalled that the interview was over. As they were getting up to leave, Major Farquharson said: "There is just one thing that is puzzling me, Chief Inspector."

"What is that sir?" asked Mary.

"How on earth do you know it is my vehicle you have found, if it had no number plates and no VIN number? It could be any Land Rover Discovery."

"Ah, did I not mention, sir? It was the tracking device fitted to the vehicle that led us to you."

Farquharson was shocked. "But we never…." he began, and then quickly corrected himself. "Of course, Chief Inspector. I had totally forgotten about that."

"Well, I assumed you must have done, sir, otherwise you would have told the local Police about it when you reported the theft. Once again, thank you for your time, sir. Now we must leave you to get to your important dinner engagement."

And with that they left.

CHAPTER 28

Saturday 4th April 2009

On the way home John and Mary had compared notes. John had made a copious record of the interview, so Mary drove so that John could consult his notes, which she would not have been able to read. They had both agreed that Major Farquharson would make a pretty good poker player. He obviously knew far more than he was letting on, but he had hidden it pretty well.

He had a good line in misdirection. Reporting the car stolen in the first place was an obvious move to make. But since he must have known there was a gang of car thieves operating in the area he must have been pretty confident the Police would never find the vehicle and assume that it had been shipped abroad somewhere. They would put it down as just another crime statistic. Then he had tried to point them in the direction of joyriders. And when that did not work he had pointed the finger at a local criminal. Mary was pretty sure she knew who that criminal was – but getting any proof would be difficult.

Where Farquharson had let his mask slip slightly, and showed his hand, was when he learned that the car had been found. Clearly he was not expecting that and it took him by surprise. Then he had not been able to resist asking how they had traced the car back to him. He was obviously taken aback by that. The shock on his face when they had said it had been fitted with a tracking device was entirely genuine. He had not been aware of that, both Mary and John were sure of that fact. Not quite knowing what to make of all that they had drifted off into silence in the car.

Eventually Mary had asked John if he minded if she put some music on. Receiving no reply she had turned to look at him and found he was fast asleep. She envied him the ability to fall asleep just like that. When she was on a case like this her mind worked overtime and would not let it go, and sleep was very hard to come by. She had reached over and taken out her favourite Eagles CD, Hotel California. She loved the guitar work, especially on the Hotel California track. When it came to the number Lying Eyes she had thought of Major Farquharson and thought "yes Major, you can't hide your lying eyes, and your smile is a thin disguise."

John had agreed to come in the following morning when she was due to update Frank. So Saturday morning found the three of them drinking coffee in Mary's office. She had had little sleep, mulling over all that had happened in the last week and pondering how it all fitted together, trying to find some common thread which would pull all this disparate information together. The tiredness showed in her eyes. Frank on the other hand looked fresh as a daisy and was raring to go, anxious to find out how their interview had gone, and desperate to share with them the news of his chat with Charlie Broom.

"So who's going to go first?" asked Mary. "Shall we tell you about our mysterious Major?"

"Yes. You go ahead. I'm all ears," said Frank.

So Mary and John recounted their tale of the dashing Major and his mysterious company which was engaged in some "highly confidential" business. They supposed that could mean that they were supplying stuff which was classified to the military, although from the way he had described it they couldn't quite see what would be classified about food, fuel, uniforms, bedding or whatever else it was he had mentioned.

They both shared their opinion that he was lying through his teeth and definitely had something to hide. They thought it was probably the fact that he, or someone known to him, had used the car in the hit and run, which had been planned in advance, hence the removal of the VIN numbers. They had then driven the car out to Barmby and torched it and been picked up by an accomplice. So there was more than one person in on this crime. They described his attempts to misdirect them during the interview and his genuine surprise when they had revealed they had found the vehicle, something he obviously was not expecting. And then the shock on his face when Mary had said the vehicle was fitted with a tracker and how he had just for a moment betrayed his shock by saying: "But we never..." before rapidly trying to recover the situation by pretending he had forgotten about the tracker.

Frank was intrigued by all of this, especially by the information about the tracker. "I suppose it makes sense," he said. "Because surely you wouldn't go to all that trouble to try and make your vehicle anonymous so it couldn't be traced back to you, and then forget that you had a tracking device on it. That would just be really dumb, and it doesn't sound like your Major Farquharson is that stupid. But then that leaves us with the question of who was tracking his vehicle and why? Once again this sounds like the kind of activity the spooks engage in."

"Yes, but why?" asked Mary. "That's what I keep asking myself. If Farquharson works for British intelligence, then who is spying on him? Is it some foreign power? Or maybe he's spying for somebody else like the Russians, and MI5 is onto him. I don't know. The world of spooks is so complicated."

"Maybe it's both, Ma'am," interjected John.

"What do you mean?" asked Mary.

"Maybe he is a British agent who has been turned by somebody like the Russians and is a double agent and he's being tracked by counter-intelligence, you know the spook's equivalent of internal affairs."

"Now you're doing my head in John," said Mary. "I think you've been reading too much John le Carre."

"Well now, all this speculation is all fine and dandy," said Frank "but we need some facts, some proof, some evidence. So let me tell you about Mr. Charlie Broom and then we need to make a plan of action to set about getting the proof we need."

"I take it he was quite co-operative then, Mr. Broom?" asked Mary.

"Oh yes. It turns out he was an old mate of my Dad's, literally. He worked as first mate on a trawler of which my Dad was the skipper. So he was very anxious to help me. He confirmed what we already know is in the public domain about the Navy using British trawlers to spy on the comings and goings of the Russians around the Barents Sea. He was actually approached to do a bit of spying when he was a skipper, but he refused, and got away with it.

Anyway, he told me about this trawler company called British Fishing. They operated one trawler out of Hull called the Catscope. But he thought there was something "fishy" about them, if you'll pardon the pun. They were a small company but they operated out of three places, Hull, Grimsby and Fleetwood. They brought in their own crews from outside of Hull for the Catscope and Charlie said they always looked like navy types. They had an office in the White Fish Authority building which is where Commander Hardcastle, the trawlermen's spymaster operated from, which was a government building. And there was something odd about the Catscope. It always fished in the White Sea, which is just off the north coast of Russia, and although they came back with a catch and sold it on the market, it was only ever a small catch because the fish hold was much smaller than a normal trawler. Now I don't know about you, but that all sounds mighty suspicious to me. It sounds like our friends the spooks were up to no good. I don't quite know what they can have been doing but obviously this was no normal trawler. They went to great lengths not to let the locals on board and it was clearly fitted with some kind of special equipment they didn't want anybody to see. Maybe they were spying on Soviet submarines somehow, I don't know. But it all sounds worth doing some more digging into, don't you think?"

They all agreed that it did and so they set about coming up with a plan of who would do what. It was agreed that John would do some desk research, looking into this British Fishing Company and its history, and see what he could find out from public records about the trawler Catscope. He would see what he could find online from Companies House records and Lloyds Shipping Register, and if necessary go to the Hull History Centre which kept extensive archives of fishing industry records.

Mary was going to see what she could find out about Major Farquharson's military supply company, BFC. She also agreed, without much hope of success, to try to ferret out some information about his military service record. And Frank had agreed to contact Adrian Hill, the local historian, who he knew quite well, to see if he could shed any light on the information Charlie Broom had given them.

Before they agreed to go their separate ways Frank had a thought. "What did you say Farquharson's company was called?"

"BFC," responded Mary. "It stands for British Firearms Company apparently although they use the short version because they are no longer solely in the business of supplying firearms. Why?"

"Well, surely it can't be a coincidence, two companies with the same initials, British Firearms Company and British Fishing Company, and they are both involved in something dodgy by the looks of it. I don't believe in coincidences."

"Nor do I," said Mary. "Well spotted Frank. We'll have to see if there is any connection between them."

"By the way, one more thing before I go," said Frank. "Have you heard anything back from the tech boys about Tommy's USB stick?"

"Wait a minute," said Mary, "I think I did see an email from them but I haven't had chance to read it yet. Yes, here we are," she said scrolling through her emails. "OK. So they have cracked the password, no trouble. Unfortunately the contents are encrypted. They think they might be able to crack the encryption but it's going to take some time, and they can't give me an estimate of how long. It's a case of trial and error to see how it's been encrypted. Hey, but guess what? The password Tommy used was catscopecustoscrespion3. That doesn't mean a lot to me, but the first part of it sounds familiar doesn't it? I would say there is going to be something of interest on there if they can crack the code, don't you think."

"I certainly do," said Frank. "Just a thought, John," he added, "while you are trawling through trawler records, just see if you can find any record of a vessel called custoscrespion, or possibly two vessels, custos and crespion or some combination of those letters. If the first part of the password is a trawler name, it's likely that the rest will be too."

"OK," said Mary. "Thank you gentlemen. That has been a fruitful session. Let me know as soon as you come up with anything interesting, and we'll speak soon, hopefully."

CHAPTER 29

Friday 16th November 1973

It was Friday morning, about 40 hours after Jim Dunlop had estimated he had two days before the Autopsy Report arrived and the investigation was officially shut down. The clock was ticking and no new leads had come in. Frank was praying that the report would be delayed until Monday so that he could at least have the weekend to turn up something.

The phone on his desk rang. Frank picked it up and to his surprise it was Tim on the other end. "Frank, I'm sorry to bother you at work but Albert Baker has turned up at the Vicarage. He's pretty far gone in drink and not making a lot of sense, but he seems to be talking about two men who are out to get him, and he's asking for you. I haven't a clue what he's on about but I think it might reassure him if you could come and see him."

"Right Tim, is he indoors now?"

"Yes, of course."

"OK. Keep him out of sight of the windows. Don't let him drink anything more, if you can. And see if you can get some black coffee down him. I'm on my way."

By the time Frank got there Albert was fast asleep on the tatty old sofa in Tim's sitting room which he used for Parish meetings.

"So Tim, what exactly did he say before succumbing to the Land of Nod?" asked Frank.

"Only that he'd seen the two men he told you about and that they were "after him" as he put it. I don't know if that means they were following him or if they'd actually tried to assault him. But I can tell you he was scared. I've never seen him like this before. I'll tell you how scared he was. Normally when he calls at the Vicarage door I invite him in for a cup of tea and a sandwich. But he always refuses. He says he doesn't like houses and being indoors. This time he was begging to come in, as if the Hounds of Hell were after him. Then he asked if I could contact you. "Get Mr. Fogg, he'll know what to do" were his exact words. After that I couldn't get anything more out of him."

"He looks like he's been on a proper bender," said Frank looking in a slightly guilty manner at Albert and thinking about the fiver he had given him.

"Look Tim, since Albert has involved you in this I'd better tell you what's going on. A couple of days ago Albert accosted me in Queen's Gardens…"

"Queen's Gardens," interrupted Tim. "That's way off his normal beat. What was he doing there?"

"Come to see me apparently. He was scared then. He told me he'd witnessed Billy Bielby's murder. He was kipping in Stanton's doorway and he saw two men in black wearing balaclavas put a plastic bag over Billy's head and suffocate him and then dump the body in the dock. He didn't think they had seen him because he kept well out of sight in case they came after him. But he was itching to tell someone what he had seen and get it off his chest. So now I'm wondering if perhaps they did see him and have come looking for him."

"There is an alternative scenario," said Tim. "Have you told anybody you have an eyewitness?"

"Only my Sergeant Tony and I trust him with my life…and my DCI. But I can't believe he would be a mole. Oh damn, Tim. I bet you're right. I bet he's told the Super and the Super's fed that information back to whoever wants to stop this investigation."

"So, what do we do with Albert now?" asked Tim. "We've got to keep him safe somehow."

"Well, I can't offer him Police protection because this investigation doesn't exist officially, until the Coroner rules on it. And I'm pretty sure that ruling is going to be Death by Natural Causes. It's no good taking him into Police custody and putting him in the cells. It sounds like he might not be safe even there. They'll probably find a way of getting at him and making it look like suicide or something."

"I could get him to stay here," offered Tim. "I can stay with him until he wakes up. I'm not needed anywhere else. When he's awake and can move under his own steam there's a connecting door from the Vicarage into the church and I've got somewhere I can hide him away there."

"Well, I suppose beggars can't be choosers Tim. It's the best offer I've got. But please be aware these are very dangerous people and if they are looking for him they will stop at nothing to get him. Please do not answer the door to anyone you don't know."

"What you don't know Frank is that I am quite handy with the cricket bat I keep hidden by the front door just in case."

"Tim," said Frank, shocked. "I didn't think you were capable of such violence."

"Only ever in self-defence Frank, or in this case in defence of an innocent."

"Alright. But remember there are at least two of them. Any worries call me or Tony. As a last resort call the local nick. You've got the number haven't you? It's just round the corner. They can have somebody here in two minutes. I'll alert them that there's been some trouble at the Vicarage and to keep an eye on the place."

"OK Frank. Thanks. I'll give you a ring as soon as he wakes up and we'll see if we can get anything more out of him, like a description of the people who are after him."

"Good idea. Thanks for letting me know he was here. And thank you for agreeing to give him sanctuary."

"That's what the Church is for, Frank. You should try it sometime."

"Aah. Don't go trying to convert me just now my old friend. Just take care of yourself and Albert."

Frank didn't quite know what he was expecting to get from Albert when he awoke. However, as he made his way back to the office he was on tenterhooks, waiting for a call from Tim. He thought, with a lot of luck Albert might have been pursued and have seen his pursuers and be able to give a good description of them. Then, with even more luck and a fair wind, they might be able to catch them and get them to confess. Aye, and pigs might fly he thought to himself. Anyway, his main concern was to keep Albert safe, whether or not he might be useful as a witness later. These men had killed once, because somebody knew too much about their business. He had no doubt they would not hesitate to kill again.

When he did finally get a call from Tim, about 5.30pm, to say that Albert was awake, he breathed a sigh of relief. At least he was still safe. He rushed down to the Vicarage and knocked on the door.

"Everything OK, Tim?" he asked when Tim answered the door, having carefully checked, Frank noted, to see who was there.

"Fine," said Tim. "Come on in. I've just made him some soup which he seems to be wolfing down gratefully. I'm trying to persuade him to take a bath and put on some fresh clothes but he's having none of it at the moment. I suggest when he's finished his soup we get him moved into the church. There's a little room at the back of the altar that we use as a private prayer space, and I use it for counselling sometimes. There are a couple of armchairs in there. We can make him comfy for the night in there.

There is one thing, though, Frank. The way he is at the moment I don't think he's going to let us leave him on his own. If somebody is watching the Vicarage and knows he's here, it's going to look a bit suspicious if I'm not in here tonight. And I have to be in church early in the morning to celebrate Mass, which would mean leaving him on his own. Is there any chance you can stay with him overnight?"

"Yes, of course," said Frank. "That's no problem. I'd only be going home to my flat to spend the evening on my own. I don't mind keeping Albert company. I might even get some more useful information out of him. You never know."

"I suppose we don't know how long this situation is going to go on for, so I propose that I make a phone call tonight to a mate of mine who is a Vicar in a tiny village out Selby way. He lives in a big Vicarage on his own. I think he might be willing to take Albert in for a few days until this all blows over. How does that sound?"

"Excellent Tim. Thank you so much. If you can sort out somewhere for him to stay for a few days, I can get him there. Since I'm not officially on a murder inquiry, and tomorrow is Saturday, I don't need to be at work, so I'll drive him over myself."

With some effort they managed to get Albert up from his reclining position on the sofa. They tried to help him walk through to the church but he was having none of it. "I'm not in my dotage yet, young man," he said to Tim. "I'm perfectly capable of walking by myself thank you."

Frank was pleased to see some of Albert's spirit returning. They got him through to the Prayer Room and Tim switched on the three bar electric fire to try to get some warmth to penetrate the cold of the massive brick building they were in. Albert seemed oblivious to it, but then he was used to sleeping rough in all weathers.

"Now Albert, I'm going to stay with you tonight," said Frank. "We can bunk down in the armchairs and have a natter and then try to get some kip. And in the morning, all being well, we will get you out of here and get you somewhere safe for a few days."

"Thank you, Mr. Fogg, and you Padre. You're both true gentlemen. I don't mind telling you I am scared to go out there tonight. Those two fellas properly gave me the willies."

"Can you tell us what happened, Albert, now you've had a sleep?" asked Frank.

"Well, I was minding my own business, as usual, walking down Hessle Road. I'd had a bottle of White Lightning, and I was going to go onto something stronger because I came into some money," he said winking at Frank. "I saw this big black car coming slowly up the road behind me. I'm not too good on cars, never having owned one, but I think it might have been a Rover. I didn't think too much of it. I thought I'd go in the chip shop and get six pennyworth of chips – sometimes they take pity on me and give me them for free. Anyhow, I got my chips and when I came out, there was this car again. I started walking and it started following me again – gave me the creeps it did."

"Could you see the driver, Albert?" asked Tim.

"No padre. It had those, what do you call them, the dark windows. Anyhow I started to get a bit worried, you know with what happened the other night and all, so I ducked down the tenfoot at the back of the shops. The car tried to follow me but I knew the tenfoot would be full of bins for the shops so they wouldn't be able to drive down it. One of them got out. I'm pretty sure it was the smaller burly one from the other night. I couldn't see him too well. My eyesight's not what it used to be when I was at sea. He definitely had dark hair cut short, you know, military style, and a black moustache. He started following me down the tenfoot but I had a pretty good lead on him. The car disappeared, and I knew he would be going round the other end of the tenfoot to cut me off. Fortunately, as you know, I know Hessle Road like the back of my hand. I knew that halfway down the tenfoot there's a snicket that goes through to the next street. In fact it crosses all the streets at the back. I know all the snickets," he said with a little smile to himself and then a nod at Frank. "I've had to use them often enough to get away from your lot, no offence Mr. Fogg. Anyway I managed to disappear down the snicket and I don't think they knew where I'd gone. But I thought, I've got to get off the streets, where can I go? And then I thought of you, Padre, and I was just praying you would be in when I knocked on the door. So that's how I ended up here. Now I don't suppose you've got anything with which I can whet my whistle, have you Padre? I'm very dry."

"I'll see what I can do Albert," said Tim. "I might be able to find you a couple of beers, but I'm not giving you anything stronger. I don't want you passed out on me when we try to move you in the morning."

"Aw, God bless you, Padre. You're a good 'un."

Tim came back a little while later with a four-pack of beers which Albert eyed up hungrily. Tim didn't really want to give him any alcohol but he knew it would be really dangerous to expect Albert to stop drinking just like that, cold turkey.

Albert sat in his chair by the fire with his beers and luxuriated in the unaccustomed warmth. He rambled about his days at sea – more to himself than anyone else – and then eventually nodded off to sleep again.

"Now that he's off," Tim whispered to Frank "I'll fetch you a dram. It might help you to sleep in this cold damp room."

"Thanks Tim. You're a star."

CHAPTER 30

Saturday 17th November 1973

The night passed uneventfully, apart from Albert moaning and shouting in his sleep about abandoning ship. Frank slept fitfully, aware that he needed to stay on alert. Being November there was hardly any dawn to speak of, just a gradual lightening of the gloomy sky. Tim popped in to see them to let them know that he would be saying Mass in the church and ask them to stay quiet. When he had finished he would come and get them and make some breakfast and then they could be on their way.

After they had breakfasted Frank brought the Cortina, which he had left on the street so as not to draw attention, into the Vicarage driveway. They hurriedly loaded Albert and his two carrier bags with his few possessions in them into the car. Tim was coming with them, using the opportunity to see his friend Charles, and to help guide Frank since it was an out of the way place.

Charles lived in an early nineteenth century Vicarage in a little place called Aughton, right on the western side of the East Riding of Yorkshire, on the banks of the River Derwent. It was very rural, at the end of a dead end road, and quite difficult to find, which suited their purposes fine. Frank set off eastwards across the city and then took the road north and east as if heading for the sea. He was on the lookout in his mirrors to see if they were being tailed. A couple of times he thought he saw the same black Rover some way behind them but it was difficult to tell in the urban traffic.

When he got to White Cross he turned westwards to head towards Beverley and deliberately slowed down to see if the Rover would appear behind them. It did, but it kept its distance, matching their speed. When Frank speeded up, so did the Rover. So when he reached Beverley Frank decided to try to throw them off the scent and turned north up the road towards Malton. When he reached the turn off for South Dalton he had a bit of distance between himself and the tail, it was just appearing around the corner about a quarter of a mile behind. So he took the sharp left turn at high speed, the Cortina almost going round the corner on two wheels. Then he put his foot down. He knew that if he could make the short distance into South Dalton in double quick time there were several different ways he could go from there. Provided the tail didn't see which way he went they would have to choose one route, hopefully the wrong one.

Frank's ruse worked and they managed to cross over the Wolds and drop down into Pocklington without seeing any more of the Rover. Confident that they could now proceed to their destination unobserved they continued on to Aughton. As they got out of the car Frank apologised for the bumpy ride. Albert grinned at him and said it was the best fun he had had in ages.

They got Albert installed in the Vicarage and then bid their goodbyes to him and Charles and were on their way home. "So," Frank said to Tim, "I need some advice now. I need to bounce this off somebody, and you are my best friend. And you have now been involved in this affair whether you like it or not. So here goes. I've got a difficult situation. By the end of Monday at the latest, I am expecting the Autopsy Report to have come in on Billy. The Pathologist made it very clear to me that he thought it was death by natural causes so I fully expect that is what will be in his report. At that point my Superintendent is going to say that we have nothing to investigate because the Coroner will rule it natural causes. My investigation will be well and truly shut down then.

I didn't believe the Pathologist's story about the marks on Billy's neck being caused by wearing a shirt with a collar which was too small. And that was before Albert came forward with his witness statement. That just confirmed what I and Doc Robinson suspected, that he was suffocated with a plastic bag over his head.

Now Albert's statement, in a sane and rational world, should be enough to instigate a murder inquiry. But it's not, mainly because of who Albert is. My DCI didn't believe it when I told him about it. And Albert's testimony would never stand up in court. But I do believe him. I believe that the Police are colluding in a miscarriage of justice, trying to cover up a murder and make it look like something else.

So that's my first issue. What on earth do I do about it? I mean, I'm only a DI. At the end of the day I have to obey orders or they will just get rid of me and I'll be out of a job and I don't know what else I could do."

"OK," said Tim. "Let's deal with that one first. You know what you have to do Frank. You are an officer of the law. You are sworn to uphold law and justice. You have the strongest possible reasons for suspecting that a murder has been committed. You have to investigate that to the best of your ability, even at the risk of losing your job. If they stop you doing it during working hours, you wouldn't be the first copper to do a bit of private investigating in your own time, now would you?"

"Alright, well my second issue is we have not even had chance to look at the crime scene. Albert's evidence has confirmed what we already suspected, that Billy's death actually took place on the Newby Wyke. Now under normal circumstances, even if the Pathologist was saying it was natural causes, we would check the scene. There might not be any evidence of foul play on the body but sometimes a crime scene will show up contra-indicators. Now my crime scene was sent off to fish off Iceland and I was stopped from getting it back. In the normal course of events she will be due back next week. I still want to have a look at her, and ideally get a Scene of Crimes team to examine her for evidence. The chances are there won't be any after she's been at sea for three weeks but you never know. But how am I going to do that if the investigation has been closed?"

"Can you get advance notice of when she is due in?" asked Tim.

"I could ask Harry Beadle to let me know, unofficially, on the QT, I suppose" said Frank.

"Well, why don't you do that and then arrange for your scenes of crime team to get on board as soon as she's in. You know they always come in and unload in the early morning to catch the market. You could get on board and have a good look before any of your senior officers are even in work, couldn't you?"

"Tim, you're a genius. That might just work, you know. Thanks."

"Now my biggest question," continued Frank, "is who on earth is doing this and for what reason? I'm sure you must have been wondering about that?"

"Of course I have Frank. And I want justice for Billy just as much as you do. I want it even more now that they have started coming after Albert. Neither Billy nor Albert would have ever done anything intentionally to hurt another soul. So what have they done to deserve this?"

"So," Tim continued, "let's start at the beginning and see what we know, shall we?"

As Frank drove, Tim reeled off the points they knew, counting them on his fingers. "So firstly, we now know for certain that Billy was murdered, in the early hours of the Tuesday morning, on board the Newby Wyke – fact.

Why was he murdered? We don't know for certain. This is speculation, but it's likely that he saw something which he was not supposed to see and the only way to keep him quiet about it was to get rid of him."

"Don't forget," interrupted Frank "that we had a report of some riggers working on a vessel nearby. Oh," he said, suddenly realising that Tim was not as up to speed with this case as he was "you wouldn't know that. But we did. Alan Wilson, who was the last person to see Billy alive, said there were some riggers working on the next boat. Interestingly, Alan has now disappeared after talking to us. We don't know where he is. I'm hoping he's gone to ground and not something worse like nearly happened to Albert. Now as far as we can find out the only trawler tied up next to the Newby Wyke that night was the Gaul. So we're assuming they were working on the Gaul, but the company denies all knowledge of their existence."

"OK," said Tim. "So, that's fact two. Some riggers doing something unknown on the Gaul. There's a possible reason for Billy getting more interested than he should have been and perhaps getting himself killed.

Fact three. We know that somebody somewhere does not want you investigating Billy's death. And it is somebody with some influence, since they seem to be able to put pressure on senior Police officers to stop the investigation, and on the Coroner to bring in a Home Office Pathologist who will come to the conclusion they want.

Fact four. These same people now know that Albert has talked to you. They can only know that from a source within the Police. They are desperate to prevent Albert from saying any more and they don't want him to be available as a witness. So either they were intent on kidnapping him, or even killing him. We've seen that for ourselves.

Does that about sum it up, Frank?"

"Yes. Pretty much. Now all we've got to do is find out who. Easier said than done," said Frank.

"Patience, my friend. We may yet find a way. Have a bit of faith."

"Ha. That's easy for you to say. It's your job."

CHAPTER 31

Monday 26th November 1973

As is the way of these things, nothing significant happened to reveal any further information during the next week. As Frank had expected, a copy of the Pathologist's Autopsy Report to the Coroner arrived on the Monday. Frank was not even given the courtesy of seeing it. The copy was sent straight upstairs to Superintendent Walker, who immediately asked to see Frank and Jim Dunlop in his office. When they arrived he did not ask them to sit down. He simply waved a copy of the Pathologist's report at them and said: "There you are. I told you so. Complete waste of Police time investigating what happened to your Mr. Bielby. The Pathologist says it is quite clearly a case of death by natural causes. Now I gave you both an order not to waste any time on this until we had some confirmation that it was a suspicious death. I know that you have actively disobeyed that order. I know that you, Inspector Fogg, against my orders, attended the autopsy. I also know that you have been questioning potential witnesses. That will stop now. That is an order. Is that clear enough for you? There is nothing to investigate. Do you need that in writing Inspector Fogg? I'll be happy to do so, so that when you are up on a disciplinary charge there is a record of my instruction."

"No sir," replied Frank. "That is perfectly clear, thank you sir."

"And you, Chief Inspector Dunlop," he continued. "I expect you, in the future, to make sure that the members of your team carry out my orders instead of trying to undermine me by turning a blind eye to what they are doing. Is that understood?"

"Yes, sir," replied Jim.

"Right then. I do not want to hear any more about this Billy Bielby business. It's over and done with. That'll be all. You're both dismissed."

As they were both leaving, he added: "Oh, by the way, Fogg, what happened to that potential witness?"

Frank turned to look at him, and feigning ignorance said: "I have no idea sir. I haven't seen him since he approached me in Queen's Gardens with his story. But that's not surprising sir. The man is homeless. He wanders the streets and sleeps in shop doorways mostly. He could be anywhere by now."

"H'mm," said the Superintendent. "Alright. Get out of here both of you."

As they were going down the stairs Jim said to Frank: "You know you really are going to have to leave this alone now, Frank. You're risking your career, and mine by the way. I know Walker. He will carry out that threat to have you on a disciplinary if he finds out your still on the case. So just drop it for both our sakes."

"OK, Jim. I understand," Frank had responded noncommittally.

Having received this bollocking Frank decided he had better keep his head down for the time being. He passed the message on to Tony that Walker was on the warpath and told him not to stick his head above the parapet.

At the same time he was still determined to pursue this as far as he could. He wondered why Walker was so interested in the whereabouts of his witness, given that he did not believe the witness statement and probably thought it was a product of Albert's fevered drunken imagination.

Arriving back at his office he decided to take Tim's advice and ring Harry Beadle and ask him about the progress of the Newby Wyke. Apparently she was still fishing and was not expected back until early the following week. He asked Harry to give him the heads up when she was expected in port and he agreed to do that. Frank did not tell him the investigation was now officially closed, only that they needed to do a crime scene survey as a matter of normal procedure.

He then went to see the lead Scene of Crimes Officer, Dan. They were old mates, having joined the force together and gone through their basic training and their probation together, and shared a few boozy nights in the pub over the years. Frank explained what he needed. He would need a team to be ready to go in the early morning either Monday or Tuesday the following week to board a trawler as it returned to St. Andrew's Dock. He explained that it had been at sea for three weeks but was a possible murder scene. He also put Dan in the picture about Superintendent Walker's orders not to pursue the investigation and how he suspected a cover-up was going on. Dan would have no reason to be aware of Walker's order since it was given only to Frank and Jim Dunlop. So Frank would ask him to investigate a crime scene as he would in any other murder case and Dan would respond to that request. If there was any comeback it would be entirely on Frank. Dan readily agreed to this and said that he would have a team on standby waiting for Frank's request.

Frank finally got the call from Harry Beadle late on Sunday evening on his home phone. The Newby Wyke was in Bridlington Bay heading for Spurn Point. She would be in dock in time for the fish market in the early hours. Frank thanked him and put through a call to Dan at home who said he would activate his standby team to be there for 4.00am. Frank thought he had better try and get some sleep but it would not come. Eventually he dozed off in his armchair with a glass of Lagavulin by his side, listening to Pink Floyd's Meddle album. He slept fitfully.

His alarm roused him at 3.00am and he had a quick shower and change of clothes and then set off in the pitch black and freezing fog of a November night. He flashed his Warrant Card at the Transport Policeman on the Dock Gate who waved him through. This time he headed for the wet side of the Dock, the north side, where he knew the Newby Wyke would be unloading her catch. True to his word he found Dan and his team ready and waiting to board. Frank strode on board and headed for the bridge where he found the skipper just packing up his belongings ready to go home.

He showed his Warrant Card and explained what they were about to do. "Help yourself mate," said the skipper, "she's in dock now. She's not my responsibility. Best tell the Ship's Husband what you're doin'. I'm off home." and with that he picked up his bags and was off. Having already spoken to Harry Beadle, Frank did not feel the need to do so again so he set about instructing the search team where to look. The bobbers were still unloading fish from the hold and the gulls were screaming around their heads. He told the search team whereabouts on the deck, based on Albert's description, the murder had taken place and asked them to examine that first, and then the area between there and the stern where they thought the body had been tipped over.

To no one's surprise, they found absolutely nothing of any use. There were fingerprints everywhere, of course. But sorting out Billy's, and then Alan Wilson's, who had been on the bridge with him that night, from the departing crew's, and possibly the crew before that, would be a nightmare and virtually impossible. The chances were the murderers had worn gloves anyway, so it was a bit of a pointless exercise to collect any prints. After several hours of painstaking work, the search team were finishing up examining those parts of the boat which they hadn't already looked over.

It was about 9.30. The tugs were just getting ready to tow the

Newby Wyke over to the dry side for repairs when Frank heard the wail of a siren, and saw a Police Rover come screaming onto the dock with blue lights flashing. He said to Tony, who had joined him, "Better make yourself scarce, Tony. This looks like trouble. There's no point in both of us copping it in the neck. I've got to take the flak for this one." Tony promptly disappeared below decks.

The Police car screamed to a halt and Superintendent Walker emerged in full uniform. He must have some event on at lunch time Frank thought. It was rare to see him in uniform at work. He did not look a happy bunny. He jumped out of the car and caught sight of Frank on the deck. He strode up to the side of the boat and yelled at him: "Fogg, get off that ship, right now."

Frank corrected him automatically: "Boat, sir. It's a trawler. We call her a boat, sir, not a ship."

"Whaat?" screamed Walker, looking apoplectic, his face purple and spittle running down his chin. "Do you think I give a flying fig what is the correct way to describe a trawler. Get here now. And get that search team off this ship. You are suspended from duty as of this moment, pending a disciplinary inquiry into your conduct. Give me your Warrant Card, get in your car and go home now."

Wow, thought Frank, I wasn't expecting that. I suppose I have been pushing my luck a bit, but immediate suspension seems a bit extreme.

However there was nothing for it but to do as he was told and leave. All that for the sake of nothing. They had not turned up anything of any use.

CHAPTER 32

Monday 6th April 2009

Andy got to it straight away on the Monday morning, digging around in Companies House records to see what he could find out about a British Fishing Company. His initial search was to prove fruitless. He searched the database for the company name and came up with nothing. As he did not have a registration number for the company he was then at a bit of a loss. It was possible it had existed and closed down, in which case he would have to contact Companies House and get them to search through old records. He knew that this would take some time and it was time they didn't really have.

So, on a whim, he thought he might try searching by Director's names. But who would the directors be? Now, what was the name of that Naval Commander, he thought, who was masterminding the trawlers spying? The name was on the tip of his tongue but it just wouldn't come. He was sure he'd written it down somewhere so he dug out his notebook and searched through it and there it was....Commander Hardcastle.

He put the name Hardcastle into his search of Directors and, not surprisingly, came up with hundreds of them. He trawled through the names of the companies of which they were directors, and after an hour of painstaking hard work he struck gold. C. Hardcastle was listed as a former director of the British

Firearms Company. Hang on, thought Andy, that wasn't what I was looking for. I was looking for British Fishing Company. When he dug some more he found that the company now called British Firearms Company had previously traded as British Fishing Company. It had changed its name in 1990. Going back through its accounts he discovered that the company had traded through the 1960s and early 1970s as British Fishing Company with a registered office in the White Fish Authority Building, St. Andrew's Dock, Hull. During this period it had frequently made losses but seemed to have occasional injections of large sums of cash from somewhere which kept it solvent.

It had ceased trading late in 1973 and become a dormant company before being revived and changing its name in 1990. Since then it appeared to have been trading quite healthily, not making vast profits, but enough to stay afloat. So Major Farquharson had been lying through his teeth when he said that the company used to manufacture firearms. It did not appear that they had ever been in the manufacturing business.

One other thing Andy noted was that the current directors were listed as one David Hardcastle, and Stewart Farquharson. Interesting, thought Andy. This is obviously not the same Hardcastle. It was always unlikely to be given the age which Commander Hardcastle would now be, if he was still alive. However it looked as though there was some sort of family connection there.

He thought he had better just give Mary a ring to let her know what he had found out. It would save her looking into British Firearms Company and finding out exactly the same information that he had. That done he turned to tracking down the mysterious trawler Catscope.

He found that the Lloyds Register of Shipping for the years he wanted was not online. They were slowly scanning their archives and putting them online but they years he wanted were not yet available. So that would mean a trip to the library or the

Hull History Centre to access a copy.

He also discovered that every commercial fishing vessel has to be registered with the UK ship register, part of the Maritime and Coastguard Agency. Whilst the information he wanted was not online he thought if he gave them a ring they would probably be quite co-operative with the Police in a murder investigation. So that is what he did. He asked for any information they might have on a fishing vessel registered in Hull called Catscope. While he was at it he mentioned the other two names Frank had suggested, Custos and Crespion. Whilst they could not give him the information straight away they promised to ring him back and let him know what they could find before the end of the day. Andy was impressed. Not every government department was as helpful, co-operative and efficient in his experience.

Meanwhile Frank had been busy on the phone and arranged to meet Adrian Hill, the local historian, for coffee that morning so that he could pick his brains for any information about the Catscope and British Fishing Company. After exchanging pleasantries and asking after each other's families Frank decided to dive straight in.

"Adrian, I'm working on a bit of a mystery right now, and I thought you might be able to help."

"Go on," said Adrian, intrigued.

"Well, I'm trying to find out what I can about a company called British Fishing, and a vessel called the Catscope. I know you have a comprehensive knowledge of most of the local fishing companies and their history, so I thought you might be able to help."

"Ah, well now, there you've got me Frank. Ask me about any of the other fishing companies and I can give you chapter and verse about when they were started, by whom, which ones merged with or were taken over by others, and so on. But British Fishing is, as you say, a bit of a mystery. It just seemed to pop up out of nowhere in the 60s and then it equally mysteriously disappeared in the mid-1970s. It was when the bottom dropped out of deep sea fishing after the UK Government did a deal with Iceland to end the Cod war in 1973.

So I can't tell you a lot about the owners, but the Catscope is another matter. I can give you some facts and some gossip and hearsay about that. I'll tell you what I told Tommy Bielby...."

"Wait a minute," said Frank, "are you telling me that Tommy Bielby was also asking questions about the Catscope and British Fishing?"

"Yes Frank, he certainly was. Don't tell me that's what got him killed? Oh, you're probably not going to tell me that because it's confidential Police business. I thought you were retired Frank?"

"I am Adrian. I'm just assisting the Police with what we these days call a "cold case". And as the politicians say: 'I can neither confirm nor deny your supposition that that information is what got Tommy killed.' In fact the Police don't even know for certain if his death was deliberate. It could have been an accident."

"Oh, yeah. Come on Frank, maybe pigs can fly. We both know it wasn't an accident."

"Anyhow, so what do you know about the Catscope? Come on, spill the beans."

"Well, as you know I am a bit of an engineering nerd. I had heard that the Catscope was an unusual design for a trawler, with a rather small fish hold and something else taking up a lot of space in the hold. So I thought I would try to find out where she was built and see if I could get any of the naval architect's drawings for her. And I drew a total blank. Nobody could, or would, give me any information about where she was built, which company built her, and I certainly could not get hold of any drawings. I didn't think much of it at the time. I just thought the owners were being excessively secretive about some bit of new technology she must have on board that they didn't want the competition to find out about.

Then years later I heard something from somebody who had actually worked on her. You know the company were very secretive about her. They always provided their own crews who were not from around here. And they brought in their own maintenance staff, you know, shipwrights and fitters, riggers, electricians, all of those trades. But I found out that on one occasion Catscope needed some emergency electrical repairs. They couldn't get hold of their own electrician in time so they used a lad from one of the local companies. I know this because he told me about it. Now apparently half of what would normally be the fish hold was taken up by a large generator. That was what they were having a problem with that they needed him to fix. He wondered at the time why an ordinary trawler would need this massive extra generator on board, but he was sworn to secrecy. He was told not to tell anyone about anything he saw on board. It was only years later that he told me, long after the Catscope had been scrapped. And that's the other strange thing I know about Catscope."

"What's that?" asked Frank.

"Well she was allegedly scrapped. But people who saw her being prepped before her last trip swore that she was making ready to go to sea. You know, she took on a full load of fuel, and provisions, and ice for the fish hold, and when she left she had a full crew. You don't do that if you're going to a breaker's yard somewhere. And then she just never came back. Now it's possible that she could have been on a fishing trip and then landed her catch at some other port and then been sent for scrap. But it's unusual. Normally when a boat went for scrap she would go to her home port first and be cannibalised of anything useful that the owners could use on another boat. Once they had finished stripping her then she would go for scrap, and not under her own steam. She would be towed by a tug to her last destination. So as I say, it's all a bit odd, like everything about Catscope."

"One more thing, Adrian, and this could be really important. Do you know when this took place, her alleged last voyage?"

"I'm afraid I can't pin that down, Frank, other than to say it was towards the end of '73, probably November/December time. But there will be a record somewhere, if it's that important. It'll be in the old Harbourmaster's Office records."

"Adrian," said Frank, "as always you are a fount of local knowledge. You have been really helpful. I am going to have to go but please give my love to Andrea, and Janice said she would like to invite you both round for a meal since we haven't seen you properly for ages. I'll get her to give Andrea a ring and arrange it."

"OK. Good luck with whatever it is you're working on Frank. And take care. You're dabbling in murky waters, my friend."

When Frank got back to the station he went in search of Andy to see how he had got on with his research. By this time Andy had had a return phone call from the UK Ship Register with the information he had been seeking. A trawler called Catscope had indeed been registered in Hull, owned by a British Fishing Company. They had also owned two other trawlers, one registered in Grimsby named Custos, and another in Fleetwood called Crespion. They were all registered as having been scrapped in December 1973. He was also able to share what he knew about the British Fishing Company and how it had morphed into what now called itself BFC.

Frank was intrigued and felt that they were getting closer to putting some pieces of the puzzle together. The overall picture, however, remained tantalizingly hidden. Mary, when they shared their news with her, was of the same opinion.

CHAPTER 33

Tuesday 7th April 2009

The next day Mary was a little surprised to receive a phone call around lunchtime from Detective Chief Superintendent Brooks asking her to go and see him as a matter of some urgency at Priory Road Police Station, the Force HQ. She was surprised because she already had an appointment to update him on the progress of the case on Thursday so she couldn't quite understand the rush.

When she got to Priory Road for her 3.00pm appointment Brooks waved her into his office and apologised for dragging her down there at short notice. "The thing is Mary," he began, "I've had a summons to see the ACC at 3.30. Now so far she has let us get on and investigate this without interfering. So I'm wondering what has sparked her sticking her nose in now. I have asked if you can come in with me because you are up to speed on the detail of the case. But I'd like you to update me before we go in so that I don't get any nasty surprises sprung on me."

"Yes, sir, of course," said Mary. So she quickly brought him up to speed on their tracking and tracing of the vehicle used in the hit and run, which led them to Major Farquharson and his company. She told him about her and Andy's interview with the Major. And then about their digging into the history of BFC in both its incarnations, and the mysterious "trawlers" owned by the company.

Brooks said: "This all sounds like major spook territory to me. I have no doubt something has set alarm bells ringing with them and they don't want us asking too many questions. It may be your questioning Farquharson which has got them worried. Or it may be that digging into the past of BFC has sent up some red flags. Anyhow, I'm pretty sure we're going to be given the gypsy's warning. But I don't want you to worry about it Mary. This is on me, OK? I am the SIO. I take full responsibility for whatever happens on my watch."

"I suspect you're right sir," said Mary. "It sounds like it is out of their playbook. It happened to Frank when he did too much digging into Billy Bielby's death. They tried very hard to get the Police to shut down his investigation. From what he's told me he was even suspended from duty and threatened with disciplinary action for disobeying a direct order from his Superintendent."

"Well, it doesn't seem to have done too much long term damage to his career does it Mary? So let's not worry about it. Alright, let's go and see what Ma'am has to say shall we?"

"I'm all ears, sir," responded Mary.

Mary had not met the ACC before. She thought she had probably met her type in the Met, though. She was in her mid-fifties, wearing an immaculate uniform, hair cut short. Her office was pristine. A large wooden desk, clearly her own addition, not a Police regulation issue desk, dominated the room. On the desk was a name plaque which said: "Assistant Chief Constable Melanie Forbes." Mary wondered irreverently if this was because she forgot her own name frequently and needed to remind herself. She decided it was more likely a power thing, to remind those sitting opposite her desk just who she was. The desk was immaculate. Not a piece of paper in sight anywhere. A computer monitor was positioned on a separate desk to one side so that she could swivel round in her chair to use it, thus keeping the top of her beautiful wooden desk free of clutter. Mary was not a great one for amateur psychology, but she thought she recognised the signs of controlling behaviour when she saw them.

The ACC welcomed them to her office. "Chief Inspector Fowler. I have not had the pleasure so far of meeting you. Welcome to the Humberside Force. How are you finding our rural way of life up here? A bit different from the Met, eh?"

"I'm enjoying it so far, Ma'am, thank you. In some respects it is very different but we get our fair share of murders, crimes of violence, sexual assaults and all of that. Especially in Hull. So it's not so different Ma'am. The biggest difference I am having to get used to is how big the area is and how far apart everywhere is."

"Yes. Well, anyway, you two have been ringing alarm bells in the intelligence community with your investigation into the death of this Thomas Bielby."

"Tommy, Ma'am," interrupted Brooks. "His given name was Tommy."

"Well that's a little stupid. Who calls a child Tommy. Anyway stop trying to throw in red herrings Jim. The fact is you are treading on the toes of the intelligence community and they don't like it. They have let me know in no uncertain terms that they want you to back off. They are saying that Tommy Bielby's death was an unfortunate accident which was not meant to happen, but it occurred in pursuance of a matter of national security. They cannot reveal any more about it because it may prejudice an ongoing investigation of their own. But they most definitely do not want us looking any further into this matter. We could jeopardise years of intelligence work if we persist."

"Sorry, Ma'am, and you bought that load of BS?" interrupted Jim.

"Chief Superintendent, if I want your advice about how to do my job, I will ask for it. Meanwhile, I am giving you an order to cease and desist from this investigation. And you can take that retired ACC, what's his name, Fogg off it as well. I am not going to be responsible for jeopardising a major intelligence operation."

No, thought Mary, what you don't want to be responsible for is jeopardising your glittering and so far spotless career path to Chief Constable somewhere. Everyone knew that, whilst Chief Constables were technically appointed by the Police Authority for the area, if you blotted your copy book with the Home Office you would never even get on the shortlist for such a post.

"May I ask, Ma'am," said Mary, "who it was that gave you this information from the intelligence community about their operation?"

"No Chief Inspector, you may not. I am not at liberty to divulge that information to you. And unless you want your career with this Police force to be much shorter than you expected you will stop asking stupid questions. Is that clear Chief Inspector?"

"It is Ma'am, yes," responded Mary, taken aback by her brusqueness.

"With all due respect Ma'am," Jim chimed into the conversation again, "we have good reason to believe a serious crime has been committed here, the most serious in fact. We can't just leave it alone on the say so of some unnamed intelligence officer. Even the intelligence services do not have a licence to go around murdering British citizens."

"Oh, Chief Superintendent, don't be so naïve. You are well aware of the situation we have found ourselves in since 2001 and even more so since the London bombings in 2005. We are on a much heightened level of alert against acts of terrorism being planned in this country. The security services are working flat out to try to prevent those. Occasionally that may mean things happen which were not intentional but bring harm to British citizens who are in fact enemies of the state. So don't bleat to me about the human rights of such people. They don't deserve any rights once they step outside the rule of law and plan acts of violence and mass murder."

"And how can you be so sure, Ma'am, that that is what happened in this case? Because if it is not surely we have a duty to investigate and prosecute wrongdoing to the full extent of the law."

"Of course we do, Chief Superintendent. But I have been assured by the security services that this was an unfortunate accident in pursuance of an investigation into terrorism related activities. Now if that assurance is good enough for me, it had better be good enough for you, or you may have to find another Police force to work for, one that is more suited to your delicate sensibilities.

Now that is enough. You are dismissed, both of you. I have other pressing matters to attend to."

As they left and walked back to Jim's office Mary said: "What an obnoxious piece of work she is. Pardon me for calling a senior officer like that, but is she always like that?"

"She can be a bit prickly sometimes but I've never known her to be so aggressive before. I would say she must be under a lot of pressure from somewhere to suppress this investigation."

"So what are we going to do sir?" asked Mary.

"We, my dear Chief Inspector, are going to call in the cavalry. I think she has just made a mistake. She mentioned that this is terrorism related. Now of course that is a very convenient smokescreen currently for the intelligence services. But it's very far-fetched to expect us to believe that Tommy Bielby was involved in anything to do with terrorism. We have found no evidence of that at all, and there are none of the usual indicators. He hadn't converted to Islam. He didn't have any connections with Ireland. He wasn't involved in any far-right or extreme left wing activities that we have been able to find. So terrorism, my arse. But we'll take Ma'am at her word. So we are not going to continue with this investigation.

But I have a good friend who is a Detective Chief Super with the Met. We were on the Superintendents Course at Bramshill together and have remained firm friends ever since. He is now in charge of Anti-Terror policing in the Met. And as such he has connections in the intelligence community. So I am going to give him a ring and ask him to put out some feelers to see what he can find out about this big intelligence operation that we are so in danger of screwing up. I think that may put the cat among the pigeons. Or maybe it will prove that our dear ACC is right and we should not be putting our noses in. We shall see, shan't we."

CHAPTER 34

Wednesday 8th April 2009

Mary was due to catch up with Frank the next morning. So she updated him on the latest development with the ACC having effectively taken them off the case. She did not mention at this stage Jim Brooks' plan to effectively go over her head. She thought she had better keep that confidential until they knew what the outcome was going to be.

"So, I'm sorry Frank. But I have been ordered to stand you down. I want to thank you for all your hard work on this and to assure you that we are not simply going to let this drop. We are pursuing other avenues to try to find out more about what's going on. But at this stage I am afraid I must ask you to leave the whole thing alone for now."

Frank had a sense of déjà vu. He remembered as if it was yesterday those days and weeks he had spent on suspension after Supt. Walker removed him from the investigation. His strongest memory was of the boredom. He had sat at home listening to his music. He must have gone through every Pink Floyd album they had released up to that point, Led Zeppelin I to IV, assorted Cream albums, Yes, Deep Purple, Wishbone Ash and several others he remembered. At least this time he had a life outside of his job. Having prepared himself for retirement he had made sure that he had other interests to turn to once that happened. So at least he could now get back to his garden which was sorely in need of some attention at this time of year. It was planting season for vegetables, and the weeds would be running riot with the mixture of rain and sunshine they had been having.

As he was about to take his leave Mary's phone rang. It was one of the techies who had been working on trying to decrypt Tommy's USB stick. He wanted to know if he could come and share with her where they had got to so far. They had apparently made some limited progress with the task. Mary readily agreed and did not tell him that technically the investigation was closed. It would after all be a bit harsh to tell him that all that time had been wasted.

"Frank, did you hear what that was about?" Frank nodded. "Well since you've been with me this far on the journey and this may well concern your cold case, you might as well stay and hear what he has to say."

"OK, Mary. If you're sure. I don't want to get you into any bother."

"Oh, Madam high and mighty can go f*** herself," said Mary. "I still want to know what has happened. And I don't buy her guff about it being a matter of national security. Somebody is trying to hide something and I want to know what it is. So if Tommy found something out I need to know."

"OK. Well if you do, then so do I. Let's do it."

The techie, whose name happened ironically to be Mac, arrived at Mary's office. They all gathered around her computer screen and he explained that they had managed to break the encryption of the first part of what was on Tommy's USB stick. The rest of it appeared to be have been encrypted using a different tool and they were still working on that. However this first part appeared to be a transcript of some notes which Tommy had discovered which his father left. They were a bit disjointed and sparse because, as Tommy explained in his introduction, Billy had never learned to read and write very well. It wasn't clear from Tommy's note whether Billy had written these notes down himself or got somebody else to do it for him.

But what was clear was that Billy had been quite busy snooping around and ferreting out information. There was quite a lot in there that they already knew. Billy had found out that some trawlers were being used for spying on the Russian fleet; that skippers were being issued with special cameras to record their sightings; and with recognition charts so that they could tell which class of warship or submarine they were looking at. All of that they knew already because most of it had been made public by the Channel 4 documentary about the Gaul.

But then they got to the interesting bit because Billy had found out that there was something suspicious about the trawler Catscope and had done some digging into that. Perhaps he had made the connection between Commander Hardcastle recruiting skippers to spy, and the office of British Fishing being in the same building. This was not clear from the notes. But Billy had got as far as identifying that the Catscope was not a normal trawler, and that she was fitted with a massive generator in the space where half the fish hold would normally be. Billy had gone on to speculate about what the purpose of this might be and had come to the conclusion that it was something to do with radio equipment. He had noted that the Catscope was fitted with extra wireless antennae. But obviously not knowing a lot about radio he had not known whether these were for receiving signals, maybe listening in to Russian naval communications, or possibly for transmitting signals.

It was interesting to Frank that Billy had noted all this down before he was killed. That meant that he must have discovered all this before his last shift as night watchman on the Newby Wyke. There was no way he could have noted all this down on that last night and it have come into Tommy's possession. He must have written these notes and hidden them somewhere prior to his last night. Frank knew this because there had been nothing on the body they had fished out of the water. And they had searched the Newby Wyke thoroughly when she eventually returned to port. Billy could not possibly have hidden something there which subsequently found its way to Tommy. They would surely have found it in their search.

So that meant that Billy knew all this before his fatal final shift. Which set Frank off thinking that perhaps Billy had been trying to find out exactly what the purpose of this equipment on the Catscope was. He was sure they were missing something here.

"Penny for them?" asked Mary when Frank appeared to be lost in thought. So he shared what he was thinking. "Wait a minute," said Mary. "Didn't you tell me that you thought Billy must have seen something suspicious on the Gaul which was moored next to the Newby Wyke?"

"I did, yes," said Frank. "Why?"

"Well what if it wasn't the Gaul that Billy was snooping around? What if it was the Catscope?"

"Do you know Mary, you might be onto something there," said Frank. "We always assumed it was the Gaul because she was the vessel that was moored ahead of the Newby Wyke. So she would have been visible from the windows of the bridge where Billy was keeping his station as night watchman. But we never checked to see if there was another vessel moored astern of her. It would have been possible to see something astern but only from the bridge wings. So Billy would have had to make a very deliberate effort to look. We never even considered that possibility. That's my fault. A bit of lax detective work there."

"I wonder if there is any way of finding out, after all this time, if there was a vessel moored astern of the Newby Wyke," Mary mused.

"Well, there may be a possibility. I know that the harbourmasters kept records of which vessels were moored where. I just don't know if those records would still exist now, all these years later. But it might be worth looking into. If only we had not been taken off the case."

"Sorry, Mac," said Mary to the techie, "just pretend you didn't hear that, OK?"

"It's alright with me Ma'am," said Mac. "Could I just make a suggestion? You could try the Local History Centre. I believe they kept a lot of maritime records, especially of the fishing industry. They are in the process of digitising all of them but it's going to take a long time. But you could give them a call and see if they might have a hard copy of those records which you could go and consult."

"Thanks, Mac. Yes. I'll follow that up," said Mary.

"But I thought the ACC had instructed you to drop this case?" queried Frank.

"She instructed me to drop the current case looking into Tommy's death, because it might jeopardise an investigation which was of importance to national security. She told me to lay you off. But she didn't specifically state that we should drop the cold case investigation into Billy's death. So until I am told otherwise I am going to pursue any possible new leads we may have on that. I'm a Police officer and as far as I know, the last time I looked, there is no statute of limitations on the crime of murder in this country."

"If it would help, Ma'am, I'm a bit of a local history nerd and I have a good drinking buddy who works at the Local History Centre. I could ask him to have a look, strictly on the QT."

"Oh, thanks, Mac. That's great. Do that and let me know what you find out."

CHAPTER 35

Sunday 2nd December 1973

I t had been less than a week since his suspension and Frank was already going out of his head with boredom. He had already listened to most of his record collection. He had even attempted, without success, to fix the dodgy heater on his Cortina, that was how bad it was. His suspension meant that he was not allowed to be in touch with any of his work colleagues. The only person he had left to talk to was Tim.

So he was greatly relieved when Tim had said to him: "Why don't you come round on Sunday evening? I'll take the evening off. My curate can take care of Evensong with Benediction." (Frank didn't even know what that meant). "It'll do him good to get the experience of taking the service without me. I'll cook us a meal and we can sit and chat for the evening."

Not only would this relieve his boredom, but Frank knew that Tim was a good cook. And living on his own and working long hours, he rarely ate properly. So he looked forward to a good meal when one was on offer. Frank arrived at the Vicarage and was welcomed in and offered a beer. Tim had gone through to the kitchen to attend to his cooking leaving the sitting room door open. Frank heard the front doorbell ring and heard Tim go to answer the door. He couldn't see who was there, but he heard a voice quite clearly say: "Good evening padre. You're going to come with us for a little drive and show us where you have stashed that tramp we've been looking for." Frank heard Tim reaching for what he assumed was his trusty cricket bat by the front door, and then the sound of a scuffle.

Frank knew his way around Tim's Vicarage and knew that there was a connecting door from the sitting room to the dining room through which he could get, unseen by anyone at the front door, to the back of the house. Going as quietly as he could through the back door, he crept around the house down the side passageway to where he had a view of the front door. He could see two men, one very tall and skinny with sandy hair, and the other about average height but very well built with a mop of dark hair. They were engaged in a scuffle with Tim, trying to subdue him and take a cricket bat out of his grip, whilst Tim was putting up a valiant struggle.

Frank thought he had better even up the odds a bit. So moving as silently as he could, he broke into a run, head down, and did his best rugby tackle on the well built man. He ran into his middle, knocking the wind out of the man and tumbling him over. As the man tried to get up Frank kicked him to try and make sure he stayed down. Meanwhile Tim had managed to free up his hands and took a swing with his cricket bat at the tall sandy haired one, hitting him in the ribs with a cracking sound.

Mr. Dark Hair was on his feet again by now and coming for Frank, but Frank managed to side step him and give him a shove as he went past, crashing him into the wall of the Vicarage. Winded he took a moment to recover his breath. Frank was about to go after him again when a look passed between the two men and they both turned and legged it into the night. Frank was tempted to go after them but thought he had better see if his friend was alright first.

Tim was breathless and slightly nauseous, having taken a punch directly in the stomach and then an uppercut to the jaw. Frank urged him inside and got him to sit and put his head between his knees until he stopped feeling dizzy. He looked into Tim's eyes, checking for any signs of concussion. He seemed to be OK, just temporarily winded.

"I'll tell you what, Tim, if your swing had connected with the ball that was a definite six. As it is, it's a couple of cracked ribs at least. I heard them go. Nice shot."

"Yeah, thanks Frank. But what do we do now? Should we go after them?"

"No that's a waste of time. They'll be long gone by now. They will have had a car parked just outside. Probably even left the engine running so they could make a quick getaway with you in tow. And there is one good thing."

"What's that?" asked Tim.

"At least we know they haven't found out where Albert is. They wouldn't have come here looking for you if they already knew."

"All the same, I think I'm going to ring Charles and tell him what has happened and ask him to be extra vigilant."

"I think that's a very sensible precaution, Tim. Now are you sure you're feeling OK?"

"Yes Frank. I'll be fine. I've had worse injuries on a rugby pitch. I can take a couple of fisticuffs. All the same it has shaken me up. I wasn't expecting them to come back looking for me."

"No. I didn't see that one coming either. Perhaps I should have done. I'm supposed to be the one with a suspicious mind. At least we both got a good look at them this time. They fitted the description Albert gave us of the men who were after him, and the ones he saw on the Newby Wyke the night of Billy's death. So we now have two suspects, and a pretty good description of them. Although, of course, nothing happened that night. Billy died of natural causes according to my Superintendent and the Home Office."

"So what do we do now, Frank? Should I report this incident to the Police?"

"I am the Police, Tim. And I already know about it. I was there, remember. No, seriously, I'm not sure we should report it. I'm not sure you would be believed, especially because I was here. If we report it, Walker's going to put it about that we made up this story so that I could get the case reopened. So I think we'd best keep schtum about this for the time being. But these people make me very angry. Who do they think they are, going around trying to kidnap law abiding citizens on their own doorsteps?"

"My guess is," said Tim, "that they are people who think they can get away with it, who think they are immune to investigation and prosecution. And that means that they are people with some friends in very high places. That means this probably goes higher than your Superintendent Walker and it is going to be very difficult to do anything about it."

"There is one thing we can do," said Frank. "Do you know Levi Abrams?"

"Sir Levi, why yes. He's one of my Ward Councillors. But what's the Leader of the Council got to do with this?"

"Because, my friend, he is also Chair of the Police Authority. Now that does not mean that he has any authority over our Chief Constable. The Chief is operationally independent and solely responsible for operational matters. However our friend, Sir Levi, has regular meetings with him to discuss matters of mutual concern to the Police and the Council. If we were to tell him about our suspicions, and maybe even about our witness, maybe he could raise it as a matter of concern with the Chief and ask him to look into it. At least that would flush out the Chief and we'd find out whose side he is on."

"I like that idea Frank, but maybe you should stay out of this. I don't want to bring any more manure on your head from a great height. I can go and see Sir Levi at one of his surgeries and raise our suspicions with him confidentially. If he agrees to say something to the Chief Constable I can ask him to keep it anonymous and just say it was a resident of his ward who raised the issue."

"OK, then. Let's do that. It sounds like a plan. In the meantime, forgive me for inviting myself, but I am going to stay here for your protection, just in case our friends decide to pay you another visit."

"That sounds good to me Frank. I think I will sleep better at night knowing there is someone else in the house. Thanks."

"Now I think we could both do with a stiff whiskey inside us after all that excitement. And then we should see if we can rustle up something to eat."

"Aaah, the dinner. I'd totally forgotten about that. I'll go and sort it out."

"Alright, but I'll come with you and give you a hand this time. We don't want any more alarms and excursions."

CHAPTER 36

Friday 10th April 2009

It was Good Friday. Mary's partner, Claire, was on school holidays. Mary always tried to make some time to spend with her during the holidays and so she had decided to take at least part of the Easter Weekend off. She was entitled to take all of it off but they were embroiled in a murder case and normally she would work 24/7 on that, pausing only to sleep. She knew that time was of the essence in cracking most murders. However she didn't feel too bad about taking some time off. After all they had been warned off and told to stop digging too deeply.

So it was that Mary and Claire found themselves preparing to go out for a drive. They were taking a picnic and were going to see where the road took them. The day had dawned bright and sunny with a cloudless sky, a beautiful spring day. The forecast had said the temperature would be in the low twenties. They loaded up their Fiat 500 with their picnic, walking boots, and coats just in case the weather turned, and off they went. Claire was driving and she was good company. Mary felt herself starting to relax and enjoy herself.

Claire chattered away. She was a history teacher and knew a lot about local history. She told Mary all about how the land on which Hull was built had originally belonged to the Monks of

Mieux; how they had founded a little settlement called Wyke upon Hull at the mouth of the River Hull where it emptied into the Humber, to serve as a port for exporting the wool from their lands. She went on to tell how King Edward 1 had bought the town from the monks in 1293 and subsequently given it a Royal Charter as a city, renaming it Kingstown upon Hull; and how it had served as an important staging post for military supplies and troops for the King during the First Scottish War of Independence. Mary found all this quite fascinating because, since moving to Hull, she had had little time to learn anything about its history.

After they had been driving rather aimlessly for a while, Claire said: "I know. Why don't we go and see the sea? It's such a beautiful day, I can show you some of the lovely East Yorkshire coastline."

So they started to head east, towards the sea. Claire said: "I know just the spot for a picnic on such a gorgeous day. We'll go to Tunstall." This was a tiny village just to the north of the seaside resort of Withernsea. It boasted very little apart from a large caravan park and a lovely sandy beach.

Claire started to chat about how there was a lost prehistoric forest under the sea just off Tunstall. It was called Sand Le Mere and had given its name to the large caravan and holiday home park there. Sometimes, when the tide was very low, remains of the trees could be seen in the water. As she chatted about things hidden under the sea she went on to tell Mary about Yorkshire's own lost city of Atlantis. This was a little further down the coast towards Spurn Point and was called Ravenserodd. Legend had it that the church bells could still be heard ringing at some states of the tide.

Tunstall itself, Claire explained, apart from its holiday village, was also popular with fossil hunters. They came to gather rocks on the beach and split them open to find fossils. The rocks were washed down from the boulder clay cliffs which were gradually being eroded by the sea, revealing their ancient secrets.

Arriving at Tunstall they found it was very quiet, even though it was a bank holiday. They pulled off the road leading down towards the Holiday Park and parked at the top of the cliffs. They were intending to get out and take a walk down past the Holiday Park to the beach with their picnic.

"Oh, it's so beautiful here," said Claire. "Why don't we just sit here and eat our lunch and enjoy the view. Then we can have a walk on the beach."

It was true. It was beautiful. The tide was high. The sun was dancing off the waves, the breakers foaming white. Seabirds were wheeling above the breakers. Out to sea a couple of yachts, probably out of Bridlington Harbour, were racing one another across the bay. Further out to sea they could see a couple of merchant ships wending their way northwards up the North Sea. Mary did not like heights and looked somewhat nervously at the flimsy wooden post and rail fence which separated them from the thirty foot drop into the waters of the North Sea. Somewhat reluctantly she agreed to Claire's suggestion.

They took off their seatbelts and reached into the back seat to get their picnic. They sat there happily munching their sandwiches, Claire staring intently out to sea to try to identify the various seabirds she could see and keeping up a running commentary. Suddenly they felt a lurch and their car started moving forward towards the cliff edge. Mary glanced behind briefly to see a large black 4 wheel drive vehicle with tinted windows right behind them pushing their car towards the sea. She tried to get out and screamed at Claire, "Jump, Claire." Too late she realised that, being the safety conscious Police Officer that she was she had automatically put on the child lock to stop anyone getting in the vehicle. Unfortunately that also meant she could not open the passenger door from inside until she had released the child lock. By the time she had done this their car had crashed through the fence and was beginning to tip over the cliff edge down towards the sea.

She just had time to say to Claire, "I love you" and to say a prayer in her head: "O God, don't let this be how it all ends." Then the car crashed into the water and everything went black.

When Mary awoke she found herself wrapped in something and a strange clattering noise going on all around her. She struggled to get out of whatever was wrapping her up and to sit up. A strange voice said: "It's all right Miss. Just lie still. You're in the Rescue helicopter. We're taking you to Hull Royal Infirmary. We had to wrap you in the emergency blanket because you were suffering from hypothermia when we fished you out of the sea. You've had a pretty severe blow to the head and it looks like you've got two broken legs. So you just need to lie still. We've given you something for the pain."

It was only then that Mary noticed the severe pain in the lower part of her body, as well as the throbbing in her head. She wanted to ask something but couldn't quite think what it was. Then she succumbed to unconsciousness again.

An eagle eyed early season holidaymaker from the Holiday Park had been on the beach and seen their vehicle come over the cliff and had had the good sense to immediately call 999. That triggered a response from HM Coastguard. The Inshore Lifeboat was called out, along with the Air Sea Rescue Helicopter from RAF Leconfield. Although the helicopter was quickly on the scene, unfortunately by the time it got there a wind had got up coming from the east and blowing the waves onto the foot of the cliffs.

A quick risk assessment by the crew deemed it too dangerous to bring the Inshore Lifeboat so close in to the foot of the cliffs. A winch rescue was also ruled out as too risky. So they landed the winch crew on the clifftop and the helicopter took up position in the air above the wreck. By this time the Fire Brigade were also in attendance and in consultation with the senior Fire Officer it was decided that the best way to reach the car, which was resting nose down on the sandy beach, half covered by the rising tide, was for a rescue crew to abseil down the cliffs. This would be a dangerous undertaking at the best of times because the crumbling boulder clay was apt to break off in large chunks and fall into the sea. A fall triggered by the climbers could bury the car in tons of heavy clay.

Keeping their vehicles well away from the cliff edge so as not to add extra weight on the top of the cliff, the climbers secured ropes and set off gingerly over the cliff edge and down to the wrecked car. When they got there the water was up to the necks of the occupants and rising rapidly. They decided they would have to act quickly otherwise the poor souls would drown. They quickly decided there was nothing they could do for the driver of the car. She was not breathing and they could not find a pulse, and it looked like her neck was broken. So, deciding to prioritise the passenger, who did show some signs of life, they tried to lift her out of the car and onto a body board. However her legs were trapped in the remains of the car where the dashboard had crumpled over them. The rescuers then had to get one of the Firefighters to come down with some cutting gear to try to free Mary's body from the wreckage. The Firefighter had seen this many times with road traffic accidents. She guessed the passenger's legs would at least be broken. In a worst case scenario she had seen legs severed or partially severed and having to be amputated at the scene to free the victim.

Standing chest deep in rapidly rising sea water, the Firefighter raced against time to try to free Mary. It was not an easy task since she was now having to use her pneumatic cutting gear under water which meant having to duck her head under the water to see what she was doing. The water level had by now reached Mary's mouth and would soon be at her nose. The water sloshed up and down with the waves and Mary was beginning to ingest seawater, still unconscious. They clapped an oxygen mask over her nose and mouth in a desperate attempt to keep her alive. It was touch and go but finally the Firefighter had cut the vehicle body in all the right places and they were able to lift away a section of the front. They gently eased Mary's unconscious form onto a body board and secured her there for the trip up the cliffs. The winchman from the helicopter volunteered to go up with her and was clipped onto the line which was waiting there for them. Then the bodyboard was secured to the line and the winchman grasped it and gave the order to haul them up. The Fire Engine very gently turned its winch and slowly and steadily hauled them up the cliff.

When they reached the top Mary's bodyboard was unfastened from the winch line and they signalled the helicopter to come down and pick her up for transport to the hospital. Whilst the chopper whisked her off to hospital the winchman prepared for another trip down the cliff to join the firefighter in rescuing Claire's body. The last thing they wanted was for the rising tide to somehow free the body from the car and then float it out to sea as the tide receded. After some difficulty they managed to get the body out and winch it up to the cliff top. Claire was pronounced dead at the scene by the attending medic and an ambulance was summoned to take the body to the morgue. With that the Fire Engine and assorted other emergency vehicles left the scene, leaving only the attending Police officers to tape off the scene of the "accident" and start trying to get witness statements to see if anyone saw what had happened.

The car would have to be recovered and forensically examined. But it would have to take its chances with the sea until the tide went down and they could recover it from the beach. The Fire Officer had categorically ruled out winching it up the cliffs as much too dangerous, and likely to cause a major cliff fall.

CHAPTER 37

Sunday 12th April 2009

They had eventually found Mary's Warrant Card in the car and identified her as a Police officer. The message about her accident eventually found its way to Chief Superintendent Brooks who immediately arranged for an armed guard to be placed outside the door of the room in which she lay in the Intensive Care Unit at Hull Royal Infirmary. He then, as a matter of courtesy, rang Frank to let him know what had happened, including the news about Claire. So it was that Frank and Janice, having completed their Easter Sunday duties at church, found themselves in that same room.

Mary was all wired up and hooked up to beeping monitors and drips and so on. She was breathing on her own, which was a good sign. She was barely conscious. Her head was swathed in a bandage, both of her legs were in plaster and held up in the air by traction wires. She gave them a weak smile when she saw them. They sat beside the bed and Frank held her hand and said: "I'm so sorry, Mary, that this happened to you, and for the loss of Claire. Words are never adequate in this situation but please know that we are thinking of you and you are in our prayers."

"Thank you," mumbled Mary.

"No, please don't try to speak, there's no need."

"Need to tell you something," Mary whispered.

"Mary, it can wait."

"Black Range Rover," she mumbled, and then once again drifted off into sleep.

"Did she just say 'black Range Rover'?" asked Frank.

That's what it sounded like to me," replied Janice.

"What do you think she's talking about?"

"I don't know, Frank. It must have been something she saw I guess. It's obviously important to her."

"Can you just stay here for a few minutes, Jan, while I go and see if I can get Jim Brooks on the phone. I've got a feeling this was no accident and she may have seen something important. I need to make sure they keep the site of the accident cordoned off and guarded. It could be a crime scene."

"OK Frank. You go and do what you need to do."

The use of mobile phones was strictly forbidden in the ICU. So Frank decided to go outside and make his phone call. If he was honest, seeing Mary in that state had shaken him up. He had almost given up smoking since he retired and confined his habit to a few small cigars a week. But now felt like the time for one of them. Deciding not to wait for the lift, which could take for ever, he went down the stairs and out through the doors to the front of the hospital. Although it was a bright sunny day, there was, as always here, a keen wind blowing around the bottom of the hospital tower block. Frank always thought of this place as somewhere that levelled up humanity, because this was where all the smokers gathered, patients and visitors alike. They were to be seen in hospital gowns, some in wheelchairs or on crutches, the drug addicts and alcoholics mixing with the "nice" people who also came out here to smoke, the poorest of them even trying to bum a cigarette from others.

He lit up his cigar and made his phone call. Jim Brooks picked up quickly. When Frank told him what Mary had said he was very interested. "To be honest, Frank, I suspected some kind of foul play here. I don't see how that car could have gone off the cliff on its own. So we've already got it sealed off as a crime scene. I've got forensics and some uniforms doing a fingertip search of the area and I've asked the Traffic lads to work their magic and see if they can reconstruct what happened from any marks on the ground. That's also why I had the armed guard put outside Mary's room, just in case they find out she survived and come for another pop at her. I'm kicking myself though, Frank. I should have seen something like this coming. These people are totally ruthless and seemingly will stop at nothing."

"It's not your fault, Jim," Frank tried to reassure him. "I did try to tell Mary to take great care, and impress upon her how these people work, especially after they broke into my house. So what are you going to do now Jim? Mary said ACC Forbes had told you to drop this case."

"I've got a plan, Frank. And now that Mary is out of the picture, for the time being at least, I need to share it with you because I'm going to need your help. But I'm not going to tell you over the phone. Let's meet up later. Can you come over to my place at seven?"

So it was agreed they would meet up later. Frank ended the call and went back upstairs to see Janice. When he got back to Mary's room Janice reported that she had not stirred and appeared to be sleeping, so they decided to just leave her a little note to say they had been, in case she didn't remember when she woke up, and then they left.

They drove home in silence, and when they were almost there Janice broke the silence with a question. "Who's next Frank? Are they going to come after you? I'm really worried about you now, after seeing Mary like that. If they can do that to Mary and poor Claire it makes you wonder what they won't do."

"I know my love. I'm very aware of that. The thing is I'm in this up to my neck now anyway. Even if I stopped investigating now, I already know too much for my own good. So if they are going to come for me they will. I'm not blase about it Jan, and I am being very careful. I'm trying not to go anywhere on my own, and make sure somebody always knows where I am. But if they really want to have a go they will. Look, let me see what this plan of Jim Brooks' is and then we can make a decision about how to go forward. I'm probably more worried about your safety than you are about mine but let me see if I think Jim's plan will work to bring an end to all this. And if not, then we'll have to think of a plan B to protect ourselves, OK?"

"It'll have to be Frank, won't it? We don't have any other options."

They had a cup of tea and then Frank drove over to Jim's place, reflecting on the way that he had never seen Janice this rattled about anything before. She was a very strong woman who had been through a lot in her life and she didn't deserve this in his retirement. The sooner this was all ended the better.

"Come in, Frank, come in," Jim greeted him when he rang the doorbell. "Sit down. Do you want a drink? Tea, coffee, or maybe something stronger? I could use a whiskey."

"That'll do me nicely, thanks Jim."

When they were settled with drinks Frank asked: "So, what's this plan of yours Jim?"

So Jim outlined his thinking. He had already made contact with his friend Detective Chief Superintendent Trevin Jones and given him a brief outline of the problem he was facing. Trevin had asked him to leave it with him for a couple of days and he would put out some feelers and see what he could find out.

"But," said Jim, "now that all this has happened what I was proposing to do, if you are in agreement, is to set up a meeting with Trevin where we can give him chapter and verse about everything that has gone on. I would obviously have taken Mary with me to that meeting but now that she is hors de combat, you would be the obvious choice because you know more about this affair than anyone else. But I will only do that if you are in agreement. I totally understand if you want to back away and have nothing further to do with this."

"Tempting as that may be, Jim, I can't unknow what I already know. If that makes me a target for these murdering bastards, well so be it. Besides I want to get even with them for breaking into my house and making my dog disappear and scaring the living daylights out of my wife. And then there's the small matter of some justice for Mary and Claire, and let's not forget Tommy Bielby. So, no, I'm not backing out or backing off, not now, not ever."

"Great. OK. That's what I was hoping you would say, Frank. So is it alright with you if I give Trevin a ring now whilst you're here and we will try to set up a meeting?"

"I've just got one question before you do that, Jim."

"Go on, what is it?" asked Jim.

"Do you trust him? Because I'm beginning to think that I can't trust anybody with all this smoke and mirrors stuff that has been going on for, when you think about it, a very long time now."

"I trust Trevin with my life Frank. There is no one you would rather want at your side going in to battle. The man is straight as a dye, totally incorruptible, and a lawman through and through. If anyone can get to the bottom of this he will."

"Alright then. Go ahead. Make your call," said Frank.

So Jim did just that. He told Trevin about the new development at their end. They agreed to meet somewhere neutral to avoid any information getting back to ACC Forbes. Trevin said that he would like to bring someone with him, someone from the "government". And they agreed to meet at a Service Station on the M1 half way between London and Hull.

CHAPTER 38

Monday 10th December 1973

T im had rung Levi Abrams the following day and asked if he could see him to discuss something confidential. Levi had readily agreed and asked Tim to come to his home. However he was a busy man, being leader of a large Local Authority. So he had not been able to make space to see Tim until the evening of the following Monday.

"Tim, my boy, how are you?" Levi greeted him at the door. "Or rather I should call you Father Tim, shouldn't I, these days. I keep forgetting."

"And I should call you Sir Levi, shouldn't I sir. I'm very well thank you."

The two had known each since Tim's school days when Levi had been one of his teachers and attempted to teach him history, not very successfully. Although he was not a big man Levi had an imposing presence. Tim supposed that was from decades of imposing his presence on classes of unwilling and uninterested schoolboys, and then being a high profile local politician.

"Well, come in. We'll go in the sitting room and Hannah will make us a cup of tea and you can tell me what is on your mind."

When they were seated with their tea Levi started: "I must say Tim, before we begin, that I am very proud of you. It is a great joy to see one of my students not only do so well academically, but then to put their scholarship to use by contributing something to the community from which they come. It gladdens my heart."

"Well thank you, sir," replied Tim, "but it is my pleasure and my privilege to serve in this community. Now I have something to tell you in confidence which concerns this community. I have reached a dead end with it and don't know where else to turn and I'm hoping you may be able to be of some help."

"Go on, my boy. Now I'm intrigued. Of course if I can be of assistance I will do my best."

So Tim went on to describe the events of Billy's death, how the Home Office Pathologist had insisted it was from natural causes, how Frank had come across a witness in the form of Albert Baker who had then been the subject of a determined attempt to discredit and then get rid of him. And finally the knub of the problem which was that Frank was not being allowed to investigate Billy's death as a murder and had now been suspended from duty by his Superintendent.

"This is all very interesting and fascinating," interrupted Levi, "but I'm not clear how I could be of any assistance in this matter."

"Well, sir, the problem as I see it is like this. There has obviously been a determined attempt to cover up what is clearly a crime. This runs to high places. Clearly the Home Office is involved, and somebody very high up in the Police Force. Now it may be that there are genuine grounds of national security for trying to suppress this information. Although I have to say morally I find it repugnant that, even on grounds of national security, the state can sanction the murder of a human being. But, leaving that aside, the only other rational explanation is some sort of corruption at a very high level. So I am asking you if you can do anything to help us firstly to clarify whether this is a national security issue, and secondly to bring about some justice for the death of one of the residents of your city and your ward.

I appreciate that as Leader of the Council you have no formal involvement in the criminal justice system."

"Now let me just stop you there," said Levi. "That of course is true. I only have influence rather than any formal powers. But don't underestimate the influence of my office. Unfortunately my party is not in government at the moment, otherwise my influence would be greater. However, I can still ask questions informally of the Home Office, and even ask our local MPs to get more formally involved if necessary. Their ultimate power is to ask questions in public in the House of Commons, questions which are covered by Parliamentary privilege, and which can be very embarrassing for a government. So I can certainly ask questions in the right places."

"That's great, sir. If you can do that that would be much appreciated. The other way I thought you might be useful is in your role as Chair of the Police Authority. I understand that you meet regularly with the Chief Constable to discuss items of mutual interest. I thought you might be able to raise this matter informally with the Chief Constable."

"Again you need to appreciate that my powers in that respect are very limited" said Levi. "The role of the Police Authority is to raise funding locally from rates to supplement Home Office grants to the Police, and to appoint the Chief Constable when there is a vacancy. Once appointed the Chief Constable, quite rightly, is totally operationally independent from local politicians. I always think that is a good thing because when you look down the years at some of the scandals involving local politics it is right and proper that the Police should have powers to investigate anyone and everyone without fear of interference. However, I do have a good working relationship with the Chief Constable, and I can certainly ask him a question to see if he is aware of the situation. I hope you are not suggesting that the Chief Constable might be complicit in any corruption. That would be a very serious accusation to make."

"I am not suggesting anything, sir. I am merely trying to find out more information to try to get to the bottom of what is really going on here. And by the way, sir, I would really appreciate it if you could keep Frank's name out of this as much as possible. He is in enough trouble with his higher ups as it is. I don't want to bring any more bother raining down on his head."

"Alright my boy. Well, you're going to have to leave this one with me and I will see what I can do. I can't make any promises. But I can certainly ask some appropriate questions in the right places."

"Thank you, sir. That's all I am asking."

"Right, well, it's been good to see you again, even if you are landing problems on my doorstep," Levi said with a wry smile. "Keep up the good work Tim."

And with that his time was up and the interview over.

CHAPTER 39

Tuesday 25th December 1973

A ll had been quiet on the Western Front for a couple of weeks. No further alarms and excursions had occurred at the Vicarage and Frank had reluctantly agreed eventually to go back to his flat. He didn't like the idea of Tim being alone in that Vicarage, but he was a big boy and could take care of himself. If Tim was really honest he had to admit to himself that he breathed a small sigh of relief when Frank left. They had been friends since school and they got on very well but sharing your home with someone was something else. Tim was accustomed to living on his own and having his own space and he quite liked it that way. It would have been easier if Frank had been at work but he was still suspended and was bored and like a bear with a sore head. Tim had resorted eventually to getting him to do some odd jobs around the church and the churchyard to try to stave off his boredom and give him something useful to do.

They had however agreed to keep in regular touch and Tim had invited Frank for Christmas dinner.

"Why don't you come over for the Christmas morning service and then you can stay on for dinner?" he had asked.

"Still trying to convert me are you Tim? Am I being invited to dine with your usual collection of waifs and strays on Christmas

Day?" Frank had asked.

"Now Frank Fogg, perish the thought that you should have to share a table with a collection of riff-raff. I didn't have you down for a snob."

"I'm not Tim. It's just that I have probably arrested most of them at some point in my career. It might make for an uncomfortable meal that's all."

"No, you're all right Frank. My Curate has the privilege of hosting them at his place this year, so you'll be safe."

"In that case it sounds like an offer I can't refuse," said Frank.

Frank had heard nothing further about his suspension. He was suspended on full pay, so money was not an issue. But boredom was. He wanted to be back at work. He had done virtually nothing else most of his adult life except work. Even during his brief courtship and marriage he had found it hard to switch off from work. Perhaps that was why the marriage had been a mistake and hadn't lasted he reflected ruefully to himself.

Finally on the Monday, on Christmas Eve, he had a call from his DCI Jim Dunlop to say that the disciplinary proceedings against him had been dropped, no further action was to be taken, and he was free to return to work. "There is one condition though, Frank!" he had said. "What's that sir?" Frank replied. "We drop the investigation into Billy Bielby. It's death by natural causes. Is that understood Frank?" Frank felt he had no choice at that point so he responded "Yes, sir."

Frank was all for going in that day to catch up on what he had missed during his absence but Jim persuaded him to at least take Christmas off. So it was agreed that he would go in the day after Boxing Day. Frank was in equal measure elated that his suspension had been lifted and he could return to work and puzzled about what it meant.

He could hardly wait to tell Tim but then he realised that it was Christmas Eve. Tim would be busy with a Crib Service in the afternoon and then Midnight Mass later on. He would be seeing him tomorrow. It could wait until then.

Frank duly and dutifully turned up for the Christmas morning service and somewhat to his surprise actually quite enjoyed it. There were lots of bells and smells which were not really to his taste, but he enjoyed the music led by a very good organist and choir. After the service Tim told him to go on over to the Vicarage and help himself to a drink while he greeted all the parishioners.

Frank did as he was told and eventually Tim arrived, changed out of his robes, and wearing his black suit and clerical collar. "Let me take this off," he said indicating the collar, "and fix myself a drink and then we can talk." When Tim was settled with his drink Frank said to him: "I have some news, Tim."

"I think I may already know, Frank. I had a call from Levi yesterday. He said that your situation had been sorted out, which I took to mean that you were going back to work. Apparently your Superintendent Walker, who instigated the disciplinary against you, is taking early retirement."

"Now that I did not know," said Frank. "I was just told to come back to work and that the charges had been dropped, on condition that the matter of Billy's death is closed."

"Yes, well that was the other part of Levi's message to me. He said that he had done everything he could in the matter and that it was now closed. So I asked for mercy for you, which has been granted. But I also asked for some justice for Billy, which has not. Levi said that he had used as much influence as he could and there was nothing further he could do. And he also said that he couldn't tell me anything more about the matter. So I'm assuming that's a coded message to say that it is indeed a matter of national security."

"Ah, but is it Tim? We still don't know that. Nobody has come out and said it. And even if they did, how do we know it's true. And even if it is true, it doesn't justify cold blooded murder in my book. Whatever Billy had done, and I suspect it was simply knowing too much about something, doesn't justify murder. If he broke the law in some way then he deserves to pay for it through the proper channels, being investigated and tried and having his day in court like anyone else. Even the security services can't become judge, jury and executioner."

"So what are you going to do now Frank?"

"I don't know Tim. It seems like I don't have much of a choice do I? I'm being invited to go back to work where they can keep an eye on me and keep me under control and make sure I don't do any more digging into this matter. If I choose not to do that then I'm out of a job, with no source of income, and I don't know what else I would do. I could continue investigating on my own, but without the powers of a Police officer and the resources of the Police Force behind me I'm not going to get very far. And they know it."

"I agree with your analysis of the situation Frank. I don't think you have got any option but to go back to work, and obey the order not to investigate further, or at least to appear to obey it. What I don't quite understand is why they appear to be backing off now. I can see they have got you where they want you. But a couple of weeks ago they seemed determined to hunt down and get rid of the witness. Now it just seems to have blown over and they want it all swept under the carpet. Why?"

"I don't know Tim. I don't know. Speaking of witnesses I almost forgot to ask, how is Albert?"

"Oh Albert seems to be having a fine old time. When he arrived at Charles' place he said that he couldn't stay in the house, he didn't like houses, never had done. So, do you remember the outbuildings at Charles' Vicarage, the old stables? Well Charles let him have the run of the stable block and Albert has decked part of it out like a sea cabin and is living in there.

One thing I didn't tell you about Charles is that he was a Captain in the army before going into the ministry. He commanded a Bomb Disposal Squad who were clearing up unexploded munitions after the war. He knows what it is like to lose members of your team to unexploded ordnance. He has his own demons of guilt about that to deal with."

"You sly old fox, you didn't tell me or Albert any of that when we took him there."

"No. I thought I would leave Albert and Charles to get acquainted with one another and share their life stories. It seems it may have been some help to Albert as well. He has cut down on his drinking apparently. He's letting Charles cook him ship's breakfasts and he is going for long walks, or should I say shambles, around the local countryside. So it seems my prayers for Albert may be being answered and he is beginning to come to terms with his own demons and learn to live with them."

"Wow. Well that's good news. That's a proper story of redemption for Christmas. I'm glad there is at least some good news."

"Oh Frank, don't despair about Billy's case. I know you. You are persistent and tenacious. You're like a terrier. When you get your teeth into something you don't let go. I know this is a temporary setback. But I also know that one day you will solve this Frank. Have a bit of faith. It is Christmas after all. Now have another drink and I'll go and sort out our Christmas Dinner."

And that was where Frank had had to leave it..... for the next thirty five and a half years.

CHAPTER 40

Monday 13th April 2009

S o Easter Monday saw Jim Brooks and Frank driving down the M1 to Trowell Services near Nottingham. Trevin Jones had booked a meeting room in the Travelodge there to give them some privacy, and refreshments were waiting for them. They appreciated the forethought. Moments after they arrived Trevin walked in followed by another man neither of them knew. Trevin cut an impressive presence. He was a big man in every way – about six foot four tall, broad across the shoulders, with a thick bull neck, slightly stooping stance, piercing blue eyes and a huge balding shaven head. He looked as if he should have played rugby for Wales and probably did at some point. He exuded an air of calm confidence. The other man with him was more nondescript, average height, average build, wearing a grey business suit, but nevertheless with an air of authority.

"Hello Jim," said Trevin in his beautiful Welsh lilt, grasping his hand. "How are you? It's really good to see you. And you must be Frank Fogg, retired Assistant Chief Constable," turning to Frank and shaking his hand in turn. "I've heard a lot of good things about you, sir. Now let me introduce Mr. Holmes. Mr. Holmes works for the Government and is very interested in what you had to tell me, so I brought him along to hear it from the horse's mouth, as it were."

"Ah, so you're my Mycroft, Mr. Holmes, said Frank.

"I beg your pardon," said Holmes.

"Oh sorry. It was a private joke with a friend of mine. We were discussing some of the matters you want to talk about and he joked that I was Sherlock Holmes and he was Watson and what we needed was a Mycroft at the centre of government to unravel some of this mystery."

"I hope you have not been discussing state secrets with members of the public, Mr. Fogg," said Holmes, only half joking.

"You will see as the story unfolds that my friend Tim has not only been involved in the original events of over thirty years ago but has been instrumental in shedding some light on current events. And don't worry. He is very discreet."

"Right then," said Trevin, "well I see you've helped yourselves to coffee. That's good. So let's get down to business. We need you to tell us chapter and verse from the beginning. Try not to leave anything out. We have got as long as it takes, so just take your time."

So they began at the beginning with Billy's death, the attempts to make it look like natural causes and stop Frank's investigation, the discovery of a witness and the determined attempts to get rid of him. They outlined Tim's part in all this. And then Frank's suspension which was mysteriously lifted, Superintendent Walker retired, and the whole thing was put on ice. Frank outlined his suspicion that Billy had seen something which he shouldn't have seen, that it might have been on the Gaul, or there may have been another vessel moored astern which they had not managed to trace.

They paused for breath and to get more coffee. Then they continued with the story of Tommy's "accident" some thirty five years later and how that had led them back to the events of 1973. They talked about Tommy's doctored memoirs on his laptop. They described the finding of the vehicle involved in the accident, how it led them to Major Farquharson and BFC through the tracking device; how they discovered that BFC was linked to the British Fishing Company which operated the three mysterious trawlers Catscope, Custos and Crespion which were all scrapped at the same time around the end of '73. They related how Jim and Mary had been warned off their investigation by ACC Forbes. And they mentioned their discovery of Tommy's USB stick which they had only managed to partially decrypt but the part they had showed that Billy had been very interested in radio equipment on the Catscope.

At the mention of the USB stick Mr. Holmes's ears pricked up and he said: "I don't suppose by any chance you have brought that USB stick with you, Chief Superintendent, have you? You see I have access to people with specialist skills in decryption, and computer software which is not available to your Police technicians. I may be able to help you to crack it open much more quickly than they can."

"I did actually have the foresight to bring a copy," said Jim, "because I was hoping you might make an offer of that sort."

"Ah, you're a cautious man Mr. Brooks, I see, bringing a copy. I like that. In my business we trust no one until they have earned that trust. I hope to earn a little of your trust in a few moments when I share with you what I know so far. But please, do go on. I have reason to believe you have not reached the end of your little tale yet."

So they went on to tell Mr. Holmes of the burglary at Frank's house, the disappearance of his dog, and then the shocking story of what they suspected was the attempted murder of Detective Chief Inspector Mary Fowler and the murder of her wife Claire.

"So, now that we have told you everything we know," said Jim, "it's your turn. You promised you would share with us what you have found out."

"And indeed I will," said Mr. Holmes. "So, let's start back in the 1960s. You will remember that this was the height of the Cold

War between the Soviet Union and the West. Europe was divided by the so called Iron Curtain. The Government greatly increased the budget of the Security Services, especially MI6 who were engaged in espionage on the Russians. One of the things the Soviets accused the West of was being soft, corrupted by wealth, and effete, without the backbone to withstand their empire. So from what I can gather from the files a group of intelligence officers came to agree with this view, not because they shared the Communist ideology of the Soviets. Just the opposite in fact. They were very right wing. They believed that strong leadership was needed if the West was to survive and not succumb to Communism, and this would not be provided by a democracy. They were what we would now call neo-Facists or neo-Nazis. We didn't have a label for them back then but a few far sighted people realised that they were very dangerous and started to keep an eye on them.

This group called themselves the Black Fists. It's a bit of a childish name, I know, but it stuck. It was a kind of up yours gesture to the Black Power movement of the 1960s which used a Black Hand as its symbol. Anyway, they were quite successful at recruiting people to their cause. It was all very secret of course. They targeted people in law enforcement, the criminal justice system, the military, and of course the government and the Civil Service. And so they had friends in high places.

One of the people who we believe was pretty high up in this group was one Commander Charles Hardcastle of Naval Intelligence, the same Commander Hardcastle who was based in Hull and was charged with spying on the Russians using the trawler fleet there. This group of intelligence officers was extremely worried by the Soviet threat, and very distrusting of our own intelligence community, which admittedly at the time leaked like a sieve having been infiltrated by Soviet double agents. So they decided to recruit their own spy ring in the Soviet Union. This was all very hush hush and they obviously could not use official channels of communication. That meant that they had to set up an alternative means of communicating with those agents.

It was a very clever plan. They diverted money from MI6's budget to purchase three trawlers which they fitted out as what we in the Intelligence Community call numbers stations. They had three so that they could always have at least one at sea at any time, a bit like the nuclear deterrence submarine fleet. And they dispersed them around different fishing ports so as not to draw attention to them. These trawlers did actually fish but they required extra electricity generating facilities to power the short wave radio transmitters with which they were fitted. Hence the small fish hold capacity on the Catscope and her sister ships.

Some of this was known to the authorities at the time and this group were being watched. However MI5 did not want to shut them down in case their spy ring produced some useful intelligence. So they let them carry on. Now obviously your Mr. Bielby discovered some of this and had to be silenced before he could blow the gaffe on the whole thing. Unfortunately for them our sharp eyed detective here, Mr. Fogg, didn't believe the story they were putting about that Mr. Bielby died of natural causes and persisted in investigating Bielby's death as a murder. They got their tame pathologist Jamieson, who was a member of their group by the way, to come up with the right conclusion in his report, but you, Frank Fogg, just would not leave this alone. Then you went and found a witness who they tried to discredit and then tried to bump off but you managed to hide him away somewhere. Where was that, by the way, I couldn't find that information in the file? Never mind, you can tell me later. So then they had to get Superintendent Walker to get heavy handed with you and suspend you in order to get you off the case. Superintendent Walker was also a member of the group. We knew that. There was even a suspicion that your then Chief Constable might have been a part of it, but there was never any proof of that.

And then all of a sudden, at the end of 1973, the whole thing went away. They shut down their Soviet spy network and scrapped the three trawlers and the group went totally quiet. We assumed that either they had been rumbled by the Soviets and things had become too hot for them; or they got wind of the fact that we were watching them and became worried about arrests for treason and such like. But either way they called the dogs off. Commander Hardcastle disappeared off the radar altogether and we never have found out what happened to him. Walker suddenly decided to take early retirement and you were reinstated and the whole thing was hushed up. Let me just explain why that was, Frank, because I know it has bugged you all these years that you were never able to get justice for Billy Bielby."

"You're damn right there," Frank interjected.

"Well, the thing is Frank, it was not in anybody's interest for the truth to come out, which it would have if anyone was ever arrested and tried for murder. Obviously the Black Fists did not want that because they did not want the world to know they existed. And as far as they knew nobody did know apart from the members of the group. But MI6 had as much interest in covering up the truth. Can you imagine how embarrassing it would have been for them if it ever came out that a group of rogue officers were conducting their own spying mission in the Soviet Union? They could have inadvertently started World War Three. Besides which there was the small matter of officers syphoning money out of MI6 budgets to conduct their own operations and run a secret group. They could not have the world knowing about that. So obviously it was best that the whole thing was hushed up at the time.

I am only telling you this now because of all the good work you have done on this case. But if you tell another soul outside this room, the government will deny that I exist and there will never be any proof of any of what I am telling you. Do you understand, both of you?"

Frank and Jim both nodded their assent.

As it looked like their meeting was going to go on for some time yet they decided to have a break and get something to eat. And Frank by this time was more than ready for a smoke.

CHAPTER 41

Monday 13th April 2009

T aking himself off outside to enjoy his cigar Frank reflected on what he had just been told. He wasn't sure how he felt about the state covering up murder and allowing the perpetrators to go scot free simply because the truth coming out would have been embarrassing. He assumed that somebody in the security services must have known who was responsible. He thought maybe when they resumed he would sound out Mr. Holmes and see if he would divulge any names. There was still a chance the perpetrators might be alive and could still be brought to justice.

Once they had refreshed themselves Holmes continued with his revelations.

"So, where was I? Ah yes. After 1973 everything seemed to have gone quiet and we thought maybe we had seen the last of the so-called Black Fists. However, it turned out that was not the case. You've probably worked out by now that Commander Hardcastle had a son. His name is David Hardcastle, who is now listed as a director of BFC. This is where they got a bit careless, or maybe overconfident, thinking we would never link BFC to their earlier activities. Anyhow, David Hardcastle followed in his father's illustrious footsteps, becoming an officer in the Royal Navy and reaching the rank of Captain. There was no reason to believe that he shared his father's political views however, otherwise he would not have had such a successful career.

In the early 1990s he became the Naval Attache at the British Embassy in Moscow. The Soviet Union was by this time dead and gone and a new Russia was emerging. But it wasn't clear what kind of state it would become. In 1991 the KGB staged a coup against then President Gorbachev, which failed, and led to the end of the KGB and the end of the USSR. Another attempted coup in 1993 by hardline communists against President Yeltsin also failed. Yeltsin attempted to reform the economy into a more western style capitalist economy. But his reforms led to shrinking GDP throughout the 1990s and declining living standards. As a result they were deeply unpopular. Meanwhile various neo-nazi popular movements flourished in Russia.

Around about 1995, we think, Captain Hardcastle was recruited by the SVR, Russia's successor to the KGB First Directorate which conducted foreign intelligence operations. He was coming to the end of his tour of duty at the Embassy and was due to come back to the UK. From what we now know, we think he was lured by the prospect of Russia going in the direction of becoming a fascist state with a strong leader. We think he was sent back here with a mission to promote neo-fascism here and recruit people to the cause to foment social unrest here.

You see, although we took our eyes off the ball in the wake of the collapse of the Soviet Union, the Russians still regarded America and Britain as their primary enemies who were set on their destruction. So Captain Hardcastle eventually retired from the Navy in 1999 and must have decided to revive his father's old company and use it as a front to promote his activities. He met up with a kindred spirit in Major Farquharson.

Now there is a piece of work, Major Farquharson. He had a career in the military, a somewhat chequered one. He is a proper hard nut – was in the SAS. He was dishonourably discharged in the end because he seems to have been a little too fond of killing people. Nothing was ever proven against him, not enough to bring charges at a Court Martial. But there were suspicions that he had been involved in the slaughter of innocent civilians during the first Gulf war. He was later sent to Afghanistan in the wake of 9/11. When similar suspicions emerged there the Army had had enough of him and decided to get rid of him. Of course he was not too happy about that and bears a huge grudge against the British state. So he was ripe for recruitment by Hardcastle into his little criminal enterprise.

They adopted a similar strategy to the one Hardcastle's father had used back in the 1960s of recruiting people within the armed forces, the Police and government who were sympathetic to their aims. No prizes for originality there. So they in effect revived the Black Fists. We think they have at least one mole within the security services, although we have not identified who it is yet. So when Mr. Bielby Junior started asking questions and researching the history of BFC it started to set off red flags and they were alerted, in the same way that your ACC was when you asked the same questions. I think that is what led to his death, and yes I am sure it was murder. I think Hardcastle wanted to protect his father's legacy and good name. He doesn't know that we know what his father was up to. And so he wanted to silence Bielby Junior before he got any closer to the truth and also to find out how much he did actually know. Because if Bielby went public with what he knew that could blow their new operation and they could not tolerate that. So either he or Farquharson, or probably both of them, conspired to run him down, get rid of the offending vehicle and search his property.

Two things got in the way of that. The first was that Hardcastle did not know that we were onto them and had actually put trackers on all their company vehicles."

"So it was you," said Frank. "That's where the tracking device came from. That's why Farquharson was so surprised when Mary turned up at his office and even more surprised when she told him that they had identified the vehicle used in the hit and run through a tracking device."

"Correct, Mr. Fogg. Now if I may continue. The second thing that let them down was their search technique. Neither of them is as professional at this game as my team are, or the Police for that matter as it turned out. You found Tommy Bielby's records hidden away. And with any luck they will have even more incriminating evidence on them."

"So what do we do now?" asked Jim Brooks.

"Well the first thing I want to do," jumped in Trevin, "is to pull all the communications records of this ACC of yours – work emails, private emails, phone records, the lot – to see if we can find evidence of her communicating with either Farquharson or Hardcastle. Because I strongly suspect, from what you have told me, that she is involved in this Black Fists mob somehow. Then if we do find any credible evidence we pull her in for questioning and see what she will tell us about the rest of them."

"I agree, Chief Superintendent," said Holmes. "Meanwhile we will maintain our surveillance on Hardcastle and Farquharson and see what other information we can pick up, and see if they give us any clues as to other members of their organisation. We will also prioritise decrypting that memory stick to see what else Mr. Bielby Junior knew. Rest assured gentlemen we shall not let this matter rest. These people are a threat to national security, as well as being serious criminals who have attempted to murder a senior Police officer and succeeded in the murders of others."

"So what, we just wait to hear from you now, is that it?" asked Frank.

"Mr. Fogg, please be assured this is not another attempt to cover up by the state. I can understand your cynicism, but believe me I have no interest in covering up the activities of these animals. If we can find enough evidence to arrest and try them, we will. And we will make sure that their trial and sentencing obtains the maximum publicity possible. We need to make sure they are punished for their crimes and to deter others from going down the same path of being enemies of the state. That is why both I and Chief Superintendent Jones are here. We have the intelligence and the Police have the powers to arrest and bring to trial."

"I'll give you the benefit of the doubt for now," said Frank grudgingly. "Just tell me one thing, if you can. Who was actually responsible for the murder of Billy Bielby?"

"From the descriptions your witness gave you, and the ones you and your friend Tim gave of the men who came after your witness, I would say almost certainly that the murderers were Commander Hardcastle, the tall lanky fair haired one, and his sidekick, an ex-Warrant Officer in the Marines, the shorter bulky dark haired one, who went by the name of Dave Martin, I think. And before you ask, Mr. Fogg, no, I don't know where either of them are. They both disappeared at the same time in late 1973 and we have not heard anything of either of them since. So either they did a very good disappearing act abroad somewhere, or they are dead by now. That is all I know. I promised you total transparency and that is what you have had."

"Alright, alright," said Frank. "I thought I'd just ask since that's a question that has been bothering me for 35 years and more."

"OK. Well gentlemen," said Trevin, "I think that concludes our meeting for now. We will keep in touch with you and let you know what we find out from our further investigations. I promise you, you will be the first to know."

"Thanks Trevin," said Jim. "We really appreciate this."

"Alright, we shall speak soon," said Trevin. "Bye for now."

With that they were on their way home, digesting Mr. Holmes' revelations as they went.

CHAPTER 42

Monday 20th April 2009

O
f course they had to wait several days, which tried the patience of both Jim and Frank. Frank had been in to see Mary and kept her updated on what was happening. She was making a slow but sure recovery. Her head injury did not seem to have caused any lasting damage. All the tests and scans appeared to show that her brain was functioning normally, which gave Mary cause for a wry smile, and Frank thought that must be a good sign. Her broken legs would take much longer to mend; the doctors had told her that she might always walk with a limp and that she would have to learn to walk again which would involve lots of physio. It was the emotional scars that worried Frank. She was understandably grieving the loss of Claire, but Frank could tell she also felt an enormous amount of guilt about the fact that Claire had died because of her work. She was even talking of quitting the Police and doing something else with the rest of her life. Frank tried to reassure her that those kind of feelings would pass, and also encouraged her not to make any decisions until she was in a better place physically and emotionally. He asked Jim to pop in and see her to reassure her that whatever support she needed from the Police to return to work would be provided, including counselling to help her deal with her guilt.

On the Friday Jim received a phone call from Trevin to say that Holmes' people had cracked the encryption on the memory stick and they would both like to meet with him and Frank again. But he emphasised that on no account was ACC Forbes to know they were meeting. Jim wondered what that meant but knew better than to ask about the progress of an investigation into his own senior officer. So Monday saw them heading once again to Nottingham to meet up for further revelations.

Once they were settled with coffee Trevin began: "So it would seem that your Mr. Tommy Bielby was a very busy man in his retirement. He managed to unearth lots of information which none of us here knew before. His notes on the memory stick are like gold dust. No wonder Hardcastle and Farquharson wanted him out of the way. I'll let Mr. Holmes begin."

"So you already know that Tommy had his father's notes, and you know what was in them. It seems that as a result Tommy started doing some detective work of his own. First of all he looked into the Catscope and discovered the information about British Fishing Company and the other trawlers they owned, as you did. One of the things he worked out, which none of the rest of us did, is what the names mean. It just goes to show how arrogant these people were. They thought they would never be found out. But Tommy worked out that Catscope comes from the Greek word *katascopeo* which means to spy out. I'm surprised your priest friend didn't work that one out Frank, it's used in the Bible. Custos in Latin means watchman, lookout, a kind of spy. And even more cheekily "espion" means spy in Russian. So they were kind of hiding in plain sight.

Anyhow, as a result of his father's interest in Catscope Tommy started asking around and looking for people who knew anything about her. So he had worked out what we already knew about the extra generating capacity being used to power radio equipment for short wave radio transmissions. And he had come to the conclusion that these ships must have been used as numbers stations for brief encrypted shortwave radio messages.

He must have inherited his father's nosy nature because he was very dogged in ferreting out information. He found someone who saw the Catscope being loaded up for her last voyage, the last time she was seen in Hull, and guess who was seen boarding her? Commander Hardcastle and his sidekick Dave Martin. Tommy said in his notes that his witness, who he didn't name, was very definite about both of them being on board when she left Hull.

But now this gets even better because Tommy managed to track down another witness (again anonymous. I'm guessing he didn't want to commit their names to any record in case it put them in any danger) who saw what happened to the Catscope. This person was on board another Hull trawler that was off the North Cape on 18th December 1973. It was getting towards dusk and the light was bad. He was on deck on his own and he saw another trawler in the distance. He couldn't be sure it was the Catscope but he said it was definitely registered in Hull. He saw the H on the side but couldn't make out the number but it looked like the Catscope. Suddenly there was a big explosion amidships and the ship broke its back and sank within minutes. There were obviously no survivors, she had gone down so quickly, so he didn't raise the alarm. The witness said that for all the world it looked like she had been hit by a torpedo. He had seen similar things in the convoys during the war.

So now I'm putting two and two together and thinking that explains why everything went quiet just before Christmas 1973. Commander Hardcastle and his sidekick went down with the Catscope. Whoever else was left in the operation must have panicked that the Russians were on to them and decided to close the whole thing down to protect everybody.

And here's the best bit that Tommy discovered. The witness said that the Catscope went down in the same area in which the Gaul later disappeared in mysterious circumstances in which there has been so much public interest. So all of this sheds light on why the "authorities" were so anxious for the wreck of the Gaul not to be found. It wasn't the Gaul they were concerned about being found at all. It was the wreck of the Catscope, because then all of this would have come out. And that could have caused a major international incident. If the Russians had proof that we were spying on them, and it became public that the Russians had torpedoed a British fishing vessel, the embarrassment for both governments would have been severe. But believe me when I say that I am going to look into this matter and do my best to find out who was trying to stop the Gaul being found. Because that will most certainly lead me to more members of the Black Fists and we need to root out as many of them as we can. Some of them will be long gone by now but there may be others still in the employ of the government."

"And speaking of members of the Black Fists," Trevin continued, "your Mr. Tommy Bielby had Farquharson and Hardcastle under observation. Can you believe that? He found out where their office is and rented a property opposite the entrance to the industrial estate from which he could see the comings and goings at their office. Talk about dogged and persistent. As a result we have car registration numbers, photographs and descriptions of a number of visitors to their office. We are working at the moment on identifying who these people are, but I can tell you for starters that there are some very senior people in the military and the Police, as well as politicians and civil servants. It would appear that they have some friends in very high places and were plotting something. We are in the process of also tracing their communications, all emails and phone calls. We now have a tap on their phone so we can listen in.

Oh, and I can tell you that your ACC Forbes was among their visitors. Now that we have some proof that she was definitely in communication with Hardcastle and Farquharson she is going to be arrested on suspicion of Misconduct in a Public Office. In fact that should be happening as we speak. She will be interviewed by an officer of equivalent rank, as is her right.

That officer will be my Commander from the Met, who is an even tougher female cookie than Forbes thinks of herself as. My prediction is that she will crumble and spill the beans on the whole lot of them.

So the plan is, once we have on record whatever it is Ms. Melanie Forbes has to tell us, we will move in on Hardcastle and Farquharson. We will arrange to raid their homes and their office at the same time, with a warrant, and seize everything, computers, paper files, everything, and see what incriminating evidence we can find to corroborate whatever it is they have been up to. I have a suspicion about what it is, but we need the evidence to prove it. I think they are plotting a coup to take over the British Government and replace it with a fascist government. If that is the case then Forbes will be offered a choice. She can either face a charge of misconduct in a public office to which she will plead guilty, if she agrees to give evidence against them; or she can face trial on the much more serious charge of treason and most likely spend the rest of her life in prison, and you know what happens to coppers in jail."

"And I suspect," chipped in Holmes, "that they are being aided and abetted in this by the Russians. They have a track record of interfering in the domestic politics of other sovereign states. And Putin is becoming increasingly autocratic. And before you say that he is not President any longer, he might as well be. We all know who is pulling the strings."

"My goodness," said Frank, "they don't believe in doing things by halves, these people, do they? But do they seriously think they could pull off a coup and get rid of the democratically elected government in the UK. Surely people would not stand for it. There would be mass civil unrest."

"Yes, but don't underestimate how ruthless these people are," said Trevin. "They would impose martial law in that case and say that it was a national emergency and they could use emergency powers. Then they would send in the Army to quell any unrest. They wouldn't bother with unarmed Police. They would use the Army without a doubt. That's why they have some senior military people on board.

Anyhow this is all speculation at the moment until we have some proof. And it may be that their plan is unrealistic, but we still have to take it seriously. We have to be aware that these people are very dangerous, far more dangerous than the Islamist terrorists I am dealing with on a daily basis. They will most certainly be armed and prepared to use their weapons. So we will be going in mob handed with as many Firearms Teams as we need. We're going to arrest them under anti-terror laws so that means we will have up to 28 days to question them. Hopefully that should be long enough to get at least one of them to crack. And if we can find enough proof of what they have been plotting then we will be arresting all their known associates. They'll be facing charges of Treason which carry a whole life sentence."

"And all of this," added Holmes, "is thanks to you gentlemen and your DCI Fowler. You have all been very persistent with your investigation in spite of being thwarted at several turns."

"I don't know about that," said Frank. "We only found out a half of what Tommy already knew."

"Ah, but you found his precious USB stick with all this valuable information on it. Without that we would not be where we are today."

"So, does that mean," asked Jim, "that we get to be in on the end of it all, when you go and make the arrests and raid their premises? This is after all my case. I am the Senior Investigating Officer. I admit that I called you Trevin, for assistance, but I have not handed the whole thing over to you."

"Of course, my friend, of course," said Trevin. "I wouldn't have it any other way. And I will be needing the assistance of some of your Firearms Officers anyway. We will use the North Yorkshire Police, but we're going to need some extra assistance from elsewhere. I will be ringing you to co-ordinate that operation, when we are almost ready to go. We just need a little more time to see what comes out of the interview with Ms. Forbes and to comb through all the data from their communications. I will let you know."

CHAPTER 43

Thursday 30th April 2009

Organising the raid on the Black Fists HQ in Scotton was a complicated logistical exercise. Trevin's boss, Commander Julia James was to be Gold Command, in overall charge of the operation since this was being deemed a Counter-Terror operation and therefore within the remit of the Metropolitan Police. A Superintendent from North Yorkshire Police, along with Jim Brooks representing Humberside Police, would be present. The team involved officers from North Yorkshire's Firearms Support unit, the Humberside Police Special Operations Unit, and dog units. A Police helicopter would provide air support at a discreet distance so as not to alert the suspects. In addition the MoD Police had been alerted and were on standby as this raid was taking place just outside the boundary of MoD property. Consequently this had taken a few days to organise.

In the meantime their surveillance of the property had continued. They had taken over Tommy Bielby's rented property and installed a surveillance team and had continued to monitor the communications. All of this, together with the interview with ACC Forbes, had led them to believe that something big was afoot, and it was planned for Friday 1st May. In the months since the financial crash of 2008 the economy had tanked and many people were worse off. As a result major public demonstrations were planned in a number of countries for May Day, the traditional Labour Day. It appeared that the Black Fists were going to try to incite the demonstrations into major acts of violence so that they could use this as a pretext for claiming that the government had lost control of the country and they could take over and impose martial law.

This gave an urgency to getting the raid set up in order to decapitate the organisation before it could gain control of the country. So it had been decided at the very highest level that

it should go ahead on the morning of Thursday 30th April. The plan was to put teams in place under cover of darkness and then wait until the major players arrived at their office and go in mob handed and hopefully sweep all of them up at the same time. Meanwhile, other teams, armed with search warrants, would raid their homes and hopefully find more incriminating evidence.

The raids had been carefully planned, especially that on the Black Fists HQ in Scotton. The raid teams had obtained, and carefully studied, plans of the building. A mock up of the building layout had been constructed so that the teams could practice and would be familiar with the layout when they entered. Every avenue of escape had been identified and hopefully would be secured. This had to be done in the utmost secrecy since no one could be entirely sure who was in on this plot to undertake a coup. Information had been given out on a strictly need to know basis. It would be imperative, when they went in, to move as quickly as possible to stop the occupants of the building destroying vital evidence which could be crucial in securing their convictions.

Jim Brooks had kept Frank updated on this situation as it unfolded. Frank, being the man of action that he was, was desperate to be in on this particular piece of action which would bring to a close such a long chapter in his life. When Trevin had put this to Julia James and pleaded his cause the answer had been a flat out "no". She did not want a civilian involved in a police operation which could potentially turn very nasty. Eventually they had compromised and Frank had been given permission to travel to the scene with Jim Brooks in Brooks' car. As Jim had explained to him: "Since you are no longer a serving Police officer you cannot carry a firearm. Therefore you will not be allowed anywhere near the scene of the action. Your orders are to stay in my car which will be parked out of the way around the corner from the Black Fists HQ. You will stay in the car until you are given further instructions. You can listen in to the action on a Police radio. That is the deal Frank, take it or leave it. You either agree to that, or you will not be there at all." So Frank had reluctantly agreed to those conditions.

Jim had picked Frank up at 3.00am, wanting to be in place before sunrise at 5.30am. Janice had had some misgivings about Frank going on the raid but he had reassured her that he would not be in any danger. He only wanted to be there to see Hardcastle and Farquharson arrested. When they arrived at Scotton they made contact by radio with the other Police units. Jim was instructed to park his Black Vauxhall insignia in a quiet cul-de-sac just around the corner from the office block which housed the Black Fists and join the others for a final briefing, leaving Frank in the car. He drove to the bottom of the cul-de-sac, turned around and parked at the top end next to an abandoned Second World War concrete pill box. "You're going to have a long wait, I'm afraid, Frank," he said as he prepared to leave the car. "There's a Police radio there so you can listen in to the action. But do not, on any account, leave the vehicle."

"Yes, sir. Understood," said Frank. "Am I allowed to stand outside and have a smoke if the coast is clear?"

"Of course. Just don't do anything silly, OK?"

"Go on then. And the best of luck Jim. I hope you nail these bastards."

"Oh, don't worry Frank, we will. This is one of the best planned raids I have ever been involved in. I'll see you later."

Jim disappeared down the road and Frank settled in for his long wait. "It's been a long time since I did this," he thought to himself thinking back to his days as a Detective Constable doing observations on suspects, sometimes for a whole night. At least he didn't have to keep alert on this occasion as others were doing the watching. He rifled through Jim's CDs in the car and found a couple of compilations of 60s and 70s rock music that contained some half decent tracks which would help to pass the time. He listened to one of these right through and then decided to get out of the car for some air and to have a smoke. As he wandered around the car he noticed something that he had not seen in the dark when they parked up. The pill box next to which they had parked was slightly odd. Most structures of this sort were abandoned and open to the elements. This one had a wooden door in the concrete doorway with no visible handle or keyhole on the outside and a notice on the door saying: "MoD Danger Keep Out." Frank shrugged and thought it must be there to stop people getting in and using it as a public toilet which was what happened with most disused air raid shelters and pill boxes.

He climbed back in the car, poured himself a cup of coffee from his flask, and listened to some more music.

9.00am arrived and with military precision and punctuality reports came over the Police Radio that both their main suspects had arrived at the office. Trevin had been given the role of commander on the ground for this raid, his boss Julia being in overall control of the simultaneous raids which would be taking place in various places at this moment. He decided to wait five minutes for their suspects to take off their coats and make themselves coffee and then they would go in.

A team of armed officers had been stationed since before dawn in the undergrowth surrounding the small stream which ran behind the hedge down the back of the offices. They were there to prevent any escape over the field at the back. Frank heard Trevin over the radio checking with this team that they were all in place and ready to go, and then with the entry teams who were hidden in unmarked vans around the corner from the office. When they had all checked in that they were ready he gave the command to "go, go, go."

Three unmarked vans came around the corner at high speed and disgorged Police officers in full combat gear with flak jackets, helmets and Heckler and Koch semi-automatic weapons at the ready. They proceeded to surround the building on three sides and then the entry team unceremoniously battered in the front door with their enforcer and made entry. Frank could hear the lead officer over the radio giving commands to his team. They must have proceeded upstairs to the top floor of the two-storey building and gained access to the BFC office. He heard shouts of "Armed Police, stay where you are," and then more worryingly "Armed Police, drop your weapon" and then "Shots fired, officer down." Then he heard the Team Leader report to Trevin, "one main suspect disarmed and in custody. Second one has gone down Fire Escape. Intercept at the bottom, repeat intercept at bottom of fire escape."

Frank remembered from studying the plans of the building that the fire escape from the first floor was an internal stairway which led down to a set of fire doors which opened at the rear of the building. A further flight of stairs also led down to the basement which was used for storage and which only had one entrance/exit. He knew that the armed officers were covering the external fire doors and would be ready to arrest anybody trying to escape that way. If their fugitive went into the basement there was no way out. So either way they would get him.

He listened as the search team officers reported in to their leader. There was no sign of anyone coming out of the ground floor fire escape reported the officers outside. A couple of officers were despatched down the fire escape stairs to see if there was anyone lurking on the stairs which produced a nil result. The leader then tasked six officers with going down to the basement to do a thorough search of the basement, exercising extreme caution as they did so, since the suspect was believed to be armed and extremely dangerous.

The basement walls were lined with built-in storage cupboards and in the centre of the room were two lines of tall filing cabinets placed back to back. They opened and searched through all the cupboards and the filing cabinets and found.......absolutely nothing. It was as if their suspect had vanished into thin air. The Team Leader sounded increasingly anxious as the officers in his search team had nothing to report. The anger in Trevin's voice was palpable when he came on the airwaves: "Damn it. We can't have lost him. On no account can we let this guy get away. Where the hell is he? He has to be there somewhere."

CHAPTER 44

Thursday 30th April 2009

Frank had listened to these exchanges on the radio and was wishing that he was there, in on the action, searching for the fugitive. As he was thinking this there was a loud tap on the car window. He turned in surprise to find himself staring down the barrel of a gun. He noticed out of the corner of his eye that the door to the pillbox which had been closed was now swinging open. So that was your escape route he thought to himself. The figure brandishing the gun shouted through the closed window: "Open the door and move over." Frank did as he was told and opened the passenger door and then moved over into the driver's seat. "Now drive," said the figure who Frank now knew to be David Hardcastle. He could tell because he looked so like his father, whose image was burned in Frank's brain from all those years ago when he had fought him off outside the Vicarage.

Fortunately Jim had left the car keys with him in case he needed to leave the vehicle or move it for any reason, so he was able to comply with the command to drive. Also, fortunately for Frank, Hardcastle had not spotted the Police radio which Frank had immediately turned to silent when he heard the rap on the window. As soon as he realised what was happening he had surreptitiously slipped the radio in the pocket of his jacket. Frank knew a bit about the technical specifications of Police radios, having been responsible for purchasing them in his time as Assistant Chief Constable. The one Jim had given him was a top of the range model with a Panic Button which Frank immediately pressed, and a facility to do continuous transmission, which Frank turned on. He knew that whilst this was switched on the radio would remain silent but others would be able to hear what was going on. He also knew that the radio had a GPS device in it so that someone would know where he was as long as the radio remained with him.

"So where am I driving to?" asked Frank.

"The Army base," responded Hardcastle. "Get me to the gates and I will get us in."

"OK," said Frank. "You're in charge. But you'll have to give me directions."

"Turn left at the top of the road and then drive for about half a mile and you'll see the main gate on your left. Drive in. I'll deal with the sentry on guard duty. And step on it. I'm in a hurry."

"So what's your plan then, Hardcastle? As far as I can see you're never going to get away." Frank didn't want to antagonise the man since he was now a hostage. But on the other hand he did want to let the listeners on the radio know where Hardcastle was.

"What? How the hell do you know who I am? You're too old to be a cop. Wait a minute. You must be that nosy interfering ex-cop that was involved in investigating Billy Bielby's death. Well, for your information copper, I'm leaving the country."

"Don't be a fool Hardcastle, there's no way they are going to let you do that."

"Oh no? Well I've got my escape route planned and in motion and now you have fortuitously fallen into my hands as a hostage. So I think I just might get away with it."

"So what is this escape route?" asked Frank trying to elicit more information for the listeners.

"You'll find out soon enough, Mr. Nosy Copper. Now shut up and drive. Faster," he said tightening his grip on the gun pointing at Frank's temple.

Meanwhile back in the Police Mobile Command Post, from which Trevin was directing operations, the officer who was monitoring the comms beckoned him over. "I think you need to listen to this Sir," he said. "A Panic Button has gone off on a Police radio on our network and its on permanent transmit. It sounds like Hardcastle is there but he's taken a hostage."

"Play it back to me, as quick as you can," said Trevin. "Who is that?"

"It's one of the radios that were issued to Superintendent Brooks, sir," said the officer.

"Dammit, that's bloody Frank Fogg. What's he doing with a Police radio? I didn't authorise that. And how the hell has he got himself taken hostage? This is all going to shit."

"Yes, but wait a minute Sir. Now we know where Hardcastle is, and he said something about heading for the Army base so we have an idea where he's going. And that radio has GPS on it, so as long as Fogg still has it we know exactly where he is."

"Good lad. Yes we do. Can you get a comms link with that radio?"

"I can't transmit a message to it while it's in permanent transmit mode, Sir."

"OK. So I need to work out where they are going. They're heading for the Army base so Hardcastle must think he has a way out of there. We've got MoD Police on alert and surrounding the place so there's no way he's getting out on foot or in a vehicle. It's got to be by air. It must be a chopper. Can you get me the MoD Police on the phone?"

"Yes Sir. Right away."

Moments later a voice came on the phone: "Chief Inspector

Mackie, MoD Police. How can I help you?"

"Chief Inspector, it's Chief Superintendent Trevin Jones of the Met Counter Terrorism task force. You were put on standby because of this raid we were doing next door. One of the suspects has escaped. We have reason to believe he has taken a hostage and is heading your way, to the base. Do you have air transport on the base? Helicopters specifically?"

"Yes, we do Sir. But none of them are flying today. We grounded all flights because of the alert next door and the presence of your Police helicopter in the vicinity."

"Can you check and make sure none of them are being readied to fly. I have a strong suspicion that is our suspect's planned escape route, given his military connections."

"I will check and get back to you Sir."

"Oh, and Mackie, do you have armed officers on the base?"

"Of course Sir."

"Can you deploy them straight away to cut off any access to any choppers that might be being prepared for take off?"

"I'll see what I can do Sir. I'll get back to you shortly."

Meanwhile Frank was doing as instructed, driving towards the Army base. When they reached the main entrance Hardcastle said to him: "Now not a word out of you. I'm going to show my ID and get us in and then you are going to drive where I tell you. Understood?" Frank nodded his understanding. He drove up to the sentry on duty and Hardcastle leaned over and showed what looked like a MoD Pass of some kind. The sentry looked at it and then raised the barrier and nodded the car through. Frank was tempted to say something but did not want to antagonise the situation. However he did want to keep up some sort of running commentary in case the radio was being listened to. So he said to Hardcastle: "So Hardcastle, now we're into Catterick Garrison what are you going to do? They'll have the place surrounded in no time. In here will be swarming with MoD Police and outside will be my colleagues. So where are you going to go?"

"We, my nosy friend, are going over the wire. We will be flying out of here in the next few minutes. Now shut up and drive."

"It's confirmed, Sir," said the Comms Operator to Trevin. "He just said they are flying out of there."

"Good work. Well done Frank. Just keep him talking. Now young man, is there any way we can get a communications link established with an Army helicopter?"

"I don't know, Sir. That's a new one on me but I'll see what I can do."

"Get me that Chief Inspector Mackie back on the phone will you?"

Moments later Mackie was back. "Mackie, I've just had it confirmed that Hardcastle is planning to leave by air. Have you found any stray helicopters gone missing?"

"We have identified a Whistling Chicken Leg Sir, sorry a Gazelle helicopter. They're all supposed to be grounded today but one is out of its hangar with the engine running looking as if it's waiting for something. We haven't approached it yet. We're waiting to see if your suspect appears."

"Well do not on any account approach. This man is armed and very dangerous and has a hostage with him. I don't want him doing anything rash. Can you patch my comms through to the helicopter pilot by any chance?"

"I think that should be possible Sir. Let me just contact our control tower and see what we can do."

By this time Frank and Hardcastle were approaching the stationary helicopter and Frank was ordered to pull up close to it. Hardcastle said to him: "Now get out."

"What?" asked Frank.

"Get out. You're coming with me. You don't think I'm leaving my security here do you? They'll just shoot us down out of the sky unless you're on board."

Trevin meanwhile was consulting with Julia James, the operation Gold Command, about their next steps. "Trevin, I cannot allow that aircraft off the ground. I have orders from the very highest level not to let Hardcastle escape. Ideally we want to capture him and take him in for questioning. But if necessary I have been given authority to shoot to kill. The Army is now on standby with ground to air missiles to stop them taking off, and just in case that fails the RAF has launched two Quick Reaction Force Typhoons armed with air to air missiles."

"But Ma'am, what about the hostage? We can't kill a hostage in cold blood. Besides he's one of ours. Retired or not he's still one of ours. At least let me try and negotiate with Hardcastle and see if I can get him to give himself up."

"Alright, but don't take all day about it. I'll give you 30 minutes and then we're going in with the heavy hitters."

"Have I got that comms link yet?" Trevin shouted to the Comms Officer.

"Coming up Sir, and you're through."

"This is Detective Chief Superintendent Trevin Jones of the Metropolitan Police. Who am I speaking to?"

"Lieutenant James Watson. I can't speak to you right now. I'm in the middle of my pre-flight checks and about to take off."

By this time Trevin knew that Hardcastle had exited the car with Frank in tow and boarded the helicopter.

"I need to speak with Captain Hardcastle. Give him a headset and let him talk to me," said Trevin.

"Hardcastle," came a voice over the radio. "What do you want?"

"Hardcastle, you're going to have to give it up. You're totally surrounded by Police and the Army. You've got nowhere to go."

"I am leaving here and I'm taking your bloody nosy ex-copper with me and you're not going to stop me."

"David, see sense now. The government is not going to let you get away now. We know too much about what you have been up to. But give up your hostage now and that will be seen as a gesture of goodwill. It will go down well with a judge at trial. And give yourself up now and I will personally see to it that you get a fair trial."

"Fair trial?" snorted Hardcastle. "What, you're going to have me tried for treason when all I am doing is trying to protect this country from itself? And then I'll get sent to prison for life. I don't think so. How is that fair? When did we become so soft in this country anyway? Life in prison….we used to have some balls and execute traitors."

"Is that what you want David? To die for your cause? To become a martyr? Is that what this is all about?"

"It's better to die for a cause than to live knowing that you could have done something to make this country better and didn't."

"Look David, you may want to die. But what about your pilot, Lieutenant Watson? I bet he's got a wife and family. Did he sign up to your cause so he could become a martyr too and leave them without a husband and father? And your hostage, Frank Fogg, he doesn't deserve to die. He's been a loyal and faithful servant of his Queen and country."

"Enough of this talk, talk, talk," said Hardcastle. "I'm leaving now. Goodbye Mr. Copper."

"Wait. Before you decide to do that David, you should know that at this moment there are several ground to air missiles trained on your helicopter and the Army has orders to shoot the moment you leave the ground. And if you should by some miracle survive that, there are two Typhoon jets circling overhead with orders to shoot you down. There's nowhere to go David."

"They won't do that. Even if they had the balls to give the

order to kill me our lily livered politicians won't kill an innocent civilian hostage. Now enough of this," roared Hardcastle. "Go James, go, go, go."

With that several things happened at once. The pilot opened the throttle and the revs began to build on the helicopter's rotor. Frank had been listening to Hardcastle's side of this conversation and could see it was getting nowhere. Hardcastle had sat in the rear seat of the helicopter so that he could keep his gun trained on Frank's head. There was no headset in the rear seat so he was leaning forward between the two front seats to use the pilot's headset. Frank lifted the radio out of his right hand jacket pocket and brought it backwards as hard as he could on Hardcastle's head. It was not enough to knock him out, but it was enough to move his gun hand out of the way and send him reeling backwards in his seat. At the same time, with his left hand, Frank opened the door of the helicopter just as it was beginning to lift off the ground. He dived through the door and hit the ground and rolled away from the helicopter. He got up as quickly as he could and broke into a run, afraid that Hardcastle would try to fire on him.

He need not have worried about that, but as the helicopter was lifting off the ground, a soldier had fired a Stinger missile at it. That was the order that had been given by Commander Julia James and confirmed by his Colonel. Any movement of the helicopter and it was to be shot down. As Frank was diving through the door the missile was unleashed and on its way. It hit the helicopter seconds after Frank had left it with a huge explosion which knocked Frank off his feet and the Gazelle immediately burst into flames. This was followed by a further explosion as the helicopter's fuel ignited.

Frank lay unconscious on the ground, stunned by the blast of the explosion, and bleeding from a shrapnel wound to his scalp and various others on his arms and back. Trevin, who had been watching all this via a video link in the Police Mobile Command Post, was livid. As the Commander on the ground it should have been his decision when to fire on the helicopter. However the military were not under his direct command on this operation. As a result one of his men lay bleeding and possibly dying on the tarmac. He knew the firecrews would be on their way. He screamed down the radio to Chief Inspector Mackie, "Get a bloody ambulance there right now. You must have one on the base somewhere." And then he turned to the Constable helping out in the Command Post and yelled: "Get me my car right now and drive me to the Army base." Then he said into the radio: "Jim, if you're out there and listening get yourself to the command post right away. You're coming with me."

Jim, who had been dealing with the arrested prisoners and sorting out where they were to be sent since they were all being held in different Police Stations, was unaware of the goings on at the base. One of his officers alerted him to the message on the radio and he hurried off to join Trevin. On the way Trevin updated him on the situation with Frank. Jim was shocked because as far as he knew he had left Frank safe and sound in his car. "Well, somehow bloody Hardcastle managed to escape from that building under our noses and reach Frank in your car and hijack him and the car."

"One of the prisoners said something about tunnels. I didn't have a clue what he was talking about but maybe that was it. Maybe there is a tunnel under the building that Hardcastle somehow knew about."

"If that's something the MoD knows about and hasn't told us I'll have their bloody guts for garters Jim. They of all people should know how important it is to have all the information at your disposal when you're planning an operation like this."

Trevin's driver was driving like a maniac to get them to the Army base. When they arrived at the gate they were stopped by the sentry and asked for ID. Trevin quickly produced his warrant card. When the soldier asked them what their business was there Trevin went ballistic. "I'm fucking anti-terror Police from the fucking Met. One of my officers is lying in there unconscious, possibly dying because of you lot. Now let us in or we'll drive straight through your barrier. Drive on Constable," he said to the driver. The shocked squaddie rushed to move the barrier and let them in, wondering what sort of bother he would get in for doing so. "Put the blues and twos on and drive like the wind constable, down that way," said Trevin.

They arrived just as Frank's almost lifeless form was being loaded into the back of an Army ambulance, being tended to by an Army paramedic. "How is he?" asked Trevin rushing up.

"He's lucky. I think he'll live if you get out of my way and let me do my job sir," replied the paramedic.

"Alright," replied Trevin "that's put me in my place. Jim, you go with him in the ambulance. We'll go in front in the Police car and clear the way. Where's the nearest hospital?" he asked the paramedic.

"Darlington," was the reply. And with that they were off, lights flashing and sirens wailing.

CHAPTER 45

Monday 4th May 2009

It was Bank Holiday Monday, and the weather was proper Bank Holiday weather. Outside the hospital in Darlington the wind was blowing and the rain was falling. Inside Frank was well enough to sit up in bed. He had had a minor concussion from hitting his head on the tarmac when the force of the explosion blew him over. His other injuries were all superficial cuts and bruises. He was very lucky, as the Doctor had told him. Janice had got there as soon as possible after getting a call from Jim saying that he was in hospital. Jim had laid on a Police car to transport her. As soon as Frank woke up she had laid into him about putting himself in danger and what did he think he was playing at, especially at his age. Frank had taken her tirade on the chin, at least until she got to the bit about his age. He carefully explained to her how none of this was his fault, he just happened to have been in the wrong place at the wrong time. But she was having none of it, insisting that he should never have been anywhere near the action whilst it was going down. He should have been safely at home with her.

Whilst this domestic tiff was going on Jim appeared at the door of Frank's hospital room, knocked and came in. "Glad to see you're well enough to have a domestic, Frank. I'm not going to need to call the Police am I?" he asked with a grin. "Now, if I can just add my two penn'orth, for what it's worth I can tell you that our friend Mr. Hardcastle escaped from their HQ via a tunnel which connected to the pillbox. I suspect it was no accident that their HQ was located above this tunnel. It will have been planned years in advance as an emergency escape route. Apparently the tunnels date from World War 2 and were used as a secure supply route for ammunition to the outer defences of the base in case of attack. Of course the MoD knew of their existence, but did not tell us because they thought they were all sealed off and unusable. Little did they know, eh?"

"So now if you two would like to just put your argument on hold for a few minutes, I have two very important visitors here to see you. That's if you're up to receiving guests?"

"Sure, wheel them in," said Frank with unconscious irony, who then caught sight of Mary coming through the door in a wheelchair.

"So, Detective Chief Inspector Fowler you already know. I'm pleased to say that she and I have been talking and she will be resuming her rank of DCI when she is well enough, and who knows what awaits her in the future."

"Hi Frank, good to see you looking so well," smiled Mary.

"Back at you, Mary," laughed Frank.

"And your second visitor, may I introduce The Right Honourable Maisie Caldwell, the Home Secretary." A large beaming Afro-Carribean face appeared around the door, a face Frank recognised from numerous appearances on TV news programmes.

"Mr. Fogg! Frank. May I call you Frank?"

Frank was, for once, struck dumb by his visitor and struggled for words. After a moment he managed to blurt out: "Yes. Yes of course, Home Secretary."

"Now," she beamed, "I am here on behalf of the government. I was going to bring the Prime Minister but the hospital staff said

I shouldn't overwhelm you with visitors at the moment. But I want to say a massive thank you, on behalf of the government, and of the people of this country, to you Frank for foiling this plot to overthrow democracy, which came pretty close to achieving its aims. And Mary," she said, turning to Mary, "you are included just as much in those thanks for the part you played."

"But I didn't do anything ma'am," said Mary who had not lost her voice. "All I did was lie in a hospital bed and miss out on all the action."

"No Mary. From what I hear it was your persistence and tenacity in pursuing this investigation, even when your Assistant Chief Constable pressured you to drop it, that achieved the outcome we celebrate today. And I am very sorry for the loss you suffered in the process, an irreplaceable loss. I'm just very glad to hear that we have not lost your services to the future of policing in this country in the process. And the said Assistant Chief Constable, together with her co-conspirators, will now feel the full force of the law.

And you, Chief Superintendent Brooks, you also deserve a lot of credit for encouraging Mary, and for finding a way around the roadblocks placed in your way.

Nothing can ever adequately express our gratitude to all of you for your work on this. But as a small token of our appreciation I shall be recommending to Her Majesty that you Jim, and you Mary, are awarded the Queen's Police Medal for your distinguished service to your Queen and country.

And you Frank, for your courage and bravery in the face of extreme danger, and your quick thinking which stopped a fugitive escaping and doing who knows what kind of damage to the country, you have been recommended for the George Cross.

Now I know we are not allowed to consume alcohol on our wonderful NHS premises, but we have to drink a toast to all of you – so come on James" she said turning to her aide, "break out the alcohol free sparkles and let's have a toast."

COMING SOON

If you enjoyed this book watch out for the exciting new crime thriller Dead Bod, coming soon. Frank and Mary team up again to investigate a decades old disappearance of a young woman. Following the surviving evidence is difficult but eventually leads them to a site where they believe a body may be buried. They find not one, but seven bodies, and none of them the one they are looking for. Read the full story at Amazon.co.uk.

Watch out for further announcements.

ABOUT THE AUTHOR

Dave Rogers

Dave Rogers grew up in, and lived and worked for much of his life in, the city of Hull, or Kingston upon Hull to give it its official title.

He now lives in the rural East Riding of Yorkshire, with his wife Lydia and two dogs. Dave enjoys reading, walking, playing guitar, listening to a wide variety of music, and writing. He also loves steam trains and cricket (though watching rather than playing these days). This is his first venture into fiction. His stories are woven around places which he knows. This first tale in the Frank Fogg series was sparked off by his experience of working on Hull's Fish Dock in the early 1970s which engendered a lifelong interest in the fishing industry and its history.

Frank will return in another story soon.

Printed in Great Britain
by Amazon